*He desperately wants the
one woman he can never have…*

"You went to the club because you wanted to live for yourself. Have your own experiences. Correct?"

She nodded jerkily, her eyes unblinking and so wide in her face that they actually ached.

"Then let's continue."

She couldn't react. Not with him looking at her that way. Not with him this close. Her gaze unerringly went to his mouth, and she knew. She already knew how good it could be. But this time was different than before.

There were no masks. No disguises. It was simply her. And him.

His hand curled around the back of her neck, hauling her mouth to his. She moaned, her hands coming up to cling to his shoulders. Everything changed then. Became fast and desperate.

"God, you taste so sweet," he growled against her lips, crouching for the barest moment to lift her, his big hands cupping her bottom through her nightgown. "Bloody clothes."

"Take them off," she gasped.

By Sophie Jordan

A GOOD DEBUTANTE'S GUIDE TO RUIN
HOW TO LOSE A BRIDE IN ONE NIGHT
LESSONS FROM A SCANDALOUS BRIDE
WICKED IN YOUR ARMS
WICKED NIGHTS WITH A LOVER
IN SCANDAL THEY WED
SINS OF A WICKED DUKE
SURRENDER TO ME
ONE NIGHT WITH YOU
TOO WICKED TO TAME
ONCE UPON A WEDDING NIGHT

Available from Avon Impulse

THE EARL IN MY BED

Sophie Jordan

A Good Debutante's Guide to Ruin

The Debutante Files

AVON

An Imprint of HarperCollinsPublishers

AVON BOOKS
An Imprint of HarperCollins*Publishers*
195 Broadway
New York, New York 10007

Copyright © 2014 by Sharie Kohler
ISBN 978-0-06-222250-3
www.avonromance.com

First Avon Books mass market printing: August 2014

10 9 8 7 6 5 4 3 2 1

For Mary Lindsey,
whose friendship has added so much to my life

A
Good Debutante's
Guide to Ruin

Chapter 1

Rain hung thick in the air, the threat of which turned the early evening gray and mist-shrouded. Mrs. Heathstone knocked smartly on the immense double doors of the Duke of Banbury's Mayfair residence.

Rosalie slid an anxious glance down her body and winced, smoothing a hand over the well-worn wool of her cloak. *Serviceable.* That's the word that came to mind. *Shabby.* That was another word.

It wasn't how Rosalie envisioned her return to London. She dreamt of bright skies and heralding trumpets. Ridiculous, but what fantasy didn't possess a touch of the absurd? At least for her. She was an expert at dreaming up the absurd. She had imagined returning a debutante of the first order, outfitted in a wardrobe that royalty would envy. With swains lining up to pay court on her. With parties and galas that kept her out all hours. An invitation to court from the queen herself. She had imagined all this and more.

She had imagined him.

The words whispered through her mind and made her wince. Perhaps not precisely *him*. Only someone as handsome as her stepbrother. Whenever she imagined a suitor for herself, he always bore a striking resemblance to Declan. She supposed it was a testament to her lack of exposure to suitable gentlemen during her time at the Harwich School for Young Ladies. Certainly some time about Town would dash such daydreams.

She sighed. Daydreams had long kept her company as she rusticated in Yorkshire, waiting for her mother to claim her. Waiting for a Season. Waiting for her life to begin. She had perfected waiting to an art form.

Now, standing on Declan's stoop, the cold evening vapor folding over her, those fantasies were a very distant thing. But at least the wait was finally over. She stood two steps below Mrs. Heathstone's formidable personage. The headmistress was taller than any man of Rosalie's limited acquaintance even without the advantage of said steps.

She huddled deeper into her cloak as Mrs. Heathstone rapped yet again. The sound reverberated out onto the street, and Rosalie shifted nervously on her feet, casting uneasy glances over her shoulder, certain that eyes were already upon them from every neighboring window, wondering at the bedraggled pair calling upon the Duke of Banbury.

The mist suddenly gave way to rain as though it could be denied no longer.

"Drat!" Mrs. Heathstone growled, throwing a gloved hand over her head as if that would offer some protection.

Rosalie shrank back inside the voluminous hood of her cloak. She knew from experience that the slightest moisture turned her hair into a wild, frizzy mess. She pushed a coppery curl behind her ear. There was no help for it. She would not be making a sterling impression this eve. Of course, until this moment she had not realized how very important it was to her that she do so. She had told herself through the entire journey here that he would likely not even remember her.

"Perhaps we should call again later?" The ring of hope in her suggestion was unmistakable even over the drum of rain.

"Nonsense. Someone is at home."

Of course, *someone* was at home. The duke maintained a staff of dozens at his Town residence, but the gentleman himself? The gentleman they needed to see? He was unlikely to be home. A matter of circumstance that appeared to only bear consequence to Rosalie. Mrs. Heathstone was quite prepared to deposit her on the duke's threshold and then bolt. The headmistress had made up her mind weeks ago when she arranged this trip, and she was not to be dissuaded. As she had regretfully explained again and again, the duke was family. If her mother would not step up to claim her, then responsibility fell to him.

At last the door opened.

It was the only invitation Mrs. Heathstone required. She charged inside, shoving past a sputtering butler. Rosalie ascended, hesitating on the top step, peering inside the grand foyer that was at once familiar and alien. She knew it shouldn't look so large and formidable now that she was a woman grown and no longer a child, but it actually looked bigger.

Mrs. Heathstone shook her cloak, spraying

water onto the marble floor as she flung back her hood, revealing her lush silvery gray hair. Her sharp eyes narrowed on Rosalie. "Miss Hughes, come inside at once before you catch ague." Her long, elegant fingers flicked impatiently on the air.

Rosalie obediently stepped inside, looking in awe up at the high-domed frescoed ceiling. Lowering her gaze, she sent the butler a small smile. She did not recognize him, but then she wouldn't. She had been very young the last time she visited here. She had been relegated to the duke's country estate most of the time. Her mother preferred it that way. Preferred to have her in the country while she entertained in Town. Out of sight. Out of mind.

The butler's face puffed like a bloated fish. "Madame, you cannot barge in here—"

"Oh, no worry, I'm not staying." She dropped Rosalie's valise to the floor, her manner brisk and efficient as she closed her hands around Rosalie's shoulders. "Remember all you've been taught. You're a lady, Miss Hughes, no matter . . ." Her voice faded, but Rosalie knew what she was going to say.

No matter who or what your mother was.

"Yes, ma'am." She nodded.

Mrs. Heathstone squeezed her shoulders gently

a final time. "You're a good girl, Rosalie. Smart, too. I wish we could have kept you on, but your future was never at Harwich's. Your future is in this world." She glanced around the opulent foyer.

Rosalie swallowed back her protest. This didn't feel like her world at all. For the last ten years she had shared a drafty room with Rachel, a former pupil like herself who now taught French at the school. Rachel had been top in their class and spoke French like she was born to it. When Mademoiselle Leflore decided to return home to tend to an ailing aunt, Rachel had been offered the position.

Unfortunately, there was no position to be had for Rosalie. She had remained the last two years merely due to the goodwill of Mrs. Heathstone. She'd tried to make herself useful in that time. However, her situation was always awkward. Not a pupil and not an instructor. She merely took up space.

And yet her meager room back at Harwich felt more familiar—more like home—than these lavish surroundings.

She wasn't certain the Duke of Banbury would welcome her any more than her mother would, but Mrs. Heathstone was confident this was the right course of action, and Rosalie acknowledged that something had to change. She could not live on the charity of others. She should have left two years ago.

"Thank you, Mrs. Heathstone." She nodded jerkily, emotion clogging her throat. In many ways, this woman was the closest thing she ever had to a mother. "For everything."

Smiling, the headmistress brushed her cheek with gloved fingertips. "Dear girl. Take care of yourself."

And then she was gone. Rosalie watched as she swept out the door, her chest tight and achy. She rubbed gloved fingers against her breastbone, willing herself to be brave. To embrace this next phase of her life.

The butler sputtered anew, and Rosalie sent him a halfhearted smile as she smoothed her hands down the front of her damp cloak.

"Good evening," she greeted him, her voice a fraction too squeaky.

"You cannot be here." The butler looked her up and down with the faintest curl of his lip. "His Grace is not at home at the moment to receive—"

"I shall wait for him." She lifted her chin, attempting to emulate Mrs. Heathstone's haughtiness.

"That is not possible, Miss . . ."

"Hughes," she supplied. "Rosalie Hughes."

At the butler's blank stare, she elaborated. "The duke's stepsister."

Her announcement was met with a moment of stunned silence. Deciding not to give him too long to consider this revelation—and why the duke's stepsister had been relatively absent for the last ten years—she brushed past him and moved toward what she hoped was the drawing room. Her memory could not recall.

She walked up the stairs, her gloved hand skimming the ornate stone balustrade as though she knew where she was going. "I'll wait in the drawing room," she called over her shoulder as she reached the second floor. Hoping she chose the correct room, she pushed open the double doors to the first room on her right. She breathed in relief. Her guess was accurate.

The butler followed her inside, hovering close but saying nothing even though he looked mightily tempted. It was a masculine room, full of rich colors and dark wood furniture. A fire crackled in the massive hearth, drawing her forward, her boots sinking deep into the plush Aubusson rug. Rosalie sank down on a blue oversized settee on the far side of the room that was angled toward the fireplace. She dropped her valise at her feet and held out her hands, greedy for the warmth.

She stared solemnly at the butler, hoping to convey an air of . . . belonging. "I'll wait His Grace's audience in here." Somehow, miraculously, her words rang with confidence.

His shoulders slumped slightly and she knew, in that moment, he had capitulated.

"Very well. Can I fetch you any refreshments as you wait, Miss Hughes?"

Her stomach rumbled at the offer. She had not eaten since their last stop several hours ago. "Yes, that would be lovely." She was grateful her voice did not quiver with her eagerness.

With a nod, he departed, slow to take his gaze off her, slow to turn and present her with his very ramrod back. As though he could not quite reconcile a female of her humble appearance in the duke's vaunted drawing room. She could understand that. She could scarcely reconcile it herself.

As soon as the door clicked behind him, she relaxed and fell back on the settee. It felt as though she had just succeeded in some grand deception.

She winced and tried to remind herself that she had every right to call on the Duke of Banbury. Especially considering the unavailability of her own mother. What else was she to do? She was a gentlewoman. A lady. She nodded to herself as

Mrs. Heathstone's arguments played silently in her mind.

Her stepbrother would not turn her away. True, he had not responded to Mrs. Heathstone's letter, but Mrs. Heathstone insisted he would do his duty. Rosalie hoped she was correct.

She bit into her bottom lip, gnawing it until she forced herself to stop. She didn't need a bloodied lip when she came face-to-face with Declan. She blinked hard and long, reprimanding herself. He was no longer Declan to her. She must not think of him so informally. He was a duke now and as far removed from her as the moon. A man full grown. She must forget the boy she remembered with such fondness. Oh, very well. With such adoration. Natural, she supposed. So often relegated to the country together, he had accepted her. Five years her senior, he had not minded when she traipsed after him. He even rescued her from a tree a time or two. She was always climbing trees. And always managing to get herself stuck. *Come, Carrots*, he would beckon her with waving hands and wide, encouraging eyes. *Come down. I'll catch you.*

A maid entered the room pushing a cart. She smiled at Rosalie shyly and bobbed a tiny curtsy.

"Thank you. I'll serve myself."

"Yes, miss."

With another bob of her head, she left Rosalie alone.

She fell upon the tray, making short work of the tea and delicious frosted cakes and tiny sandwiches. She ate everything and then regretted it, eyeing the crumbs. She would appear a graceless sloth when they come to claim the cart.

She collapsed back on the settee with little refinement, one hand rubbing her full belly, the other idly stroking the elegant brocade pillow beside her. She blew out a repleted sigh and glanced around the well-appointed room. An enormous painting depicting Persephone's abduction hung along a wall, taking nearly the entire space. It was riveting. Bold and dramatic. The dark Hades clasped the fair Persephone about the waist, one large hand splayed just below the swell of a breast that threatened to spill from her white tunic as he pulled her into the murky cavern of hell lined with demons and skeletons. Rosalie swallowed, her stare fixing on Hades's feral expression, clearly intent on possession. Something curled in her belly at the idea of a man *wanting*, *needing* a woman that much.

The clock on the mantel ticked in the silence of the room. Only the occasional pop from the fire interrupted the still. She yawned widely into her hand. The journey had taken its toll. She had not left Harwich in ten years. No visits anywhere. She was unaccustomed to the rigors of travel.

Her head lolled against the back of the sofa, grateful that she was turned partially from the door, not in full sight of anyone upon first entering the room. She'd hear them before they spotted her. It would give her time to compose herself.

The warmth of the fire licked over her and her limbs grew boneless. This was the most comfortable she had felt since leaving Yorkshire.

Her eyes drifted shut. Just for a moment she would rest them. She snuggled drowsily into the sofa. No doubt the duke would arrive soon. She'd hear his approach. Better yet, she'd hear the approach of the maid when she returned to reclaim the cart.

For just a moment she would rest her eyes.

Chapter 2

*D*eclan, the eighth Duke of Banbury, entered his home, accompanied by his usual companions: William, his cousin, the Earl of Merlton; and Maximus, Viscount Camden. He'd known them since Eton. His cousin, Will, of course, even longer. Veritable scoundrels, the both of them. Especially Max, who lacked the burden of family to frown over his exploits.

But then Dec was a scoundrel himself.

Of course, they weren't unaccompanied this night. There were women. There were always women. One for each of them. Lovely, buxom armfuls attired in gowns that revealed more than they covered.

A footman bolted awake from where he slept in a chair along the wall. "Y-Your Grace," he stammered, hastily running a hand down his rumpled waistcoat and wiping the drool from his chin.

Declan waved him off. "To bed with you, Link."

"Yes, Your Grace." The footman bowed, a grateful smile playing about his lips as he disappeared from the foyer.

Declan assumed his old butler was lost in a deep sleep somewhere in the bowels of the house. Pendle had served Declan's father faithfully since before Declan's birth. Although the servant had never said anything, Declan sensed he had not approved of the way his father treated him. He'd seen warmth glowing in Pendle's rheumy eyes the day he took occupancy of the house, shortly after his father's death.

Pendle's hearing was not quite what it used to be, the only reason Declan could credit for him not rousing at the sound of their return. That and the fact that his friends were busy using their mouths in a manner that did not involve speech.

He led the group into the drawing room, his

arm wrapped loosely around his companion for the evening.

The fire still flickered and danced in the hearth. The room was warm and cozy, inviting them in.

"Gor, is this place all yours?" Janie or Janet or some such name asked, her head tilted back to take in the high-domed ceiling. She snuggled against his side, all round curves and pliant flesh. Her Gypsy dark eyes settled back on him, appraising him with fresh admiration. It seemed he had grown in her estimation since stepping into his home.

Home. The word rang hollowly. Ever since his father cast him out all those years ago, this place had not felt like a home. His father would roll over in his grave to know that he brought these women here. He would consider them beneath his ilk. Fallen doves fit for a tumble at a bawdy house, but never to cross the threshold of his house. A slow, satisfied smile curled Declan's lips at the happy thought.

"You like it, poppet?" He dipped a finger inside her bodice and dragged it against the swell of a generous breast.

A breathy gasp escaped her and she pushed deeper into his touch. "Oh, aye, I like it, milord," she replied, a little too dramatically for his taste, but then she was an actress. She and her companions had performed in the bawdy production of *The Education of Miss Annabel Hammersham* at the Weymouth Playhouse just this evening. A titillating performance, to be certain.

Dimly, he was aware of his friends moving throughout the room to the assorted furniture, taking their companions with them.

Declan's partner for the evening was the woman who had portrayed the much lauded Miss Annabel Hammersham. She looped her arms around his neck and lifted on her tiptoes to nibble at his throat. She tugged his cravat loose and tossed it to the floor. "That's better," she murmured, her cockney accent fighting its way forward. He closed his eyes, appreciating the play of her mouth on his neck.

"Oh, look what we have here? A present. For us, Dec? How thoughtful."

Declan opened his eyes to follow his cousin's gaze——landing on a sleeping female curled up on the settee near the fireplace. He frowned.

Who in the bloody hell was that?

He processed the shock of copper hair spilling over the blue upholstery.

Loosening his arms from Janie/Janet and approaching the settee, he gave voice to his thoughts. "Who is she?"

Will and Max crowded around him. "You don't know her?"

He shook his head slowly, eyeing the slim length of her. He could discern little of her shape beneath the shapeless cloak, but he didn't think her very ample. Not in the manner he preferred. He enjoyed sinking into curves . . . filling his hands full of them.

"Well, then." His cousin sank on the couch beside her. "Shall I wake her with a kiss and find out how precisely she came to be in your drawing room at this hour of the night?" Will brushed a fiery strand of hair back from her forehead. She sighed and rolled onto her back, giving them all a better view of her features. A vague cord of recognition stirred in him. He grasped for the thread but it eluded him.

"I can only imagine what she came here for at this hour," Max murmured, which only made the woman at his side titter stupidly. "She's likely a former bedmate interested in a repeat performance from our Dec here."

Janie/Janet pressed herself close against him, reminding him of her presence. "I thought this was a private tête-à-tête." Her bottom lip pushed out in a pout. "I'm not as adventurous as you may think, milord. I prefer my men to myself."

"No surprise there. You're not the sharing kind," one of the other females taunted.

"Shut up, Hettie," she snapped and then turned to face Declan, sliding her hands up the front of his waistcoat in an effort to reclaim his attention. "I thought you and I were going to get acquainted better." Her voice lowered to a husky whisper. "Just the two of us."

"Indeed," he tossed out carelessly as his gaze drifted over her head to the girl on the couch. The female stirred restlessly, no doubt the sound of their voices disturbing her sleep.

He frowned as Will skimmed a hand around her waist in an overly familiar manner, gliding up her rib cage. "She's a little thing, but fetching, no? Like some woodland nymph."

Unease skittered down his nape. The situation did not sit well with him, and just as he opened his mouth to command his cousin to remove his hands from her person, her eyes flew wide open and he was treated to the sight of her face in full animation.

Confusion followed by horror crossed the smooth features. She scrambled into a sitting position, shoving Will's hand off her and treating him to a resounding slap across the face.

The *crack* reverberated on the air like cannon fire.

No one moved. No one breathed.

They all stared. At her.

She stared back, her cat eyes darting to each face in the room, her chest heaving as though she had just run a great distance.

Then one of the females laughed thinly, shattering the silence. It was a tinny, nervous sound. "You realize you struck an earl? You'll likely hang for that."

Dec snorted, swallowing the noise as he watched all color bleed from the strange girl's face.

Will, still clutching his cheek, found his voice. "What was that for?"

Instead of answering him, her gaze darted around the room, assessing, taking their measure. When her gaze landed on him, she stopped there. "Declan," she murmured, her lips barely moving.

He cocked his head to the side. "Do I know you?"

Her chin came up. She lowered her legs so that her boots brushed the floor. A scuffed, well-worn pair of boots. His housemaids owned better boots.

"It's me." As though remembering herself, she held his gaze with disarming directness and added, "Rosalie. Rosalie Hughes."

He stared, his throat tightening as memories he did not know he even possessed flooded him. Rosalie following him about the countryside. Rosalie spying on him flirting with the vicar's daughter. Rosalie stuck in a tree. Now he knew why she was so familiar to him. Bloody hell.

Carrots.

As if her mere name were not enough explanation, she added, "Your stepsister."

Her hair had deepened. It was not quite the orange-red of her childhood, but it was still as bright as a sunset, especially cast in the fire's glow. The wide eyes set in the elfin face were familiar, too. They glowed like cat's eyes, fringed in long lashes and as watchful as ever.

"Rosalie?" he said, his voice hoarse.

She nodded once, tossing that wild hair of hers around her slight shoulders.

All eyes swung to him, awaiting his reaction with rapt fascination.

"Out," he managed. No one stirred, and it occurred to him that they might not have heard his low utterance. "Leave us!"

Everyone scurried to action at his bark.

A tug on his sleeve drew his attention to the woman pressed up against him. He had forgotten all about her. Clearly his bark had not sent her running.

"Banbury," she whined in a singsong voice. "I thought we were going to have fun this evening."

Without a word, he reached inside his waistcoat. He extended several notes to her. "Here you are. For your troubles."

With a huff, she looked from him to the money. She tossed a baleful look to the woman on the settee and then leveled a glare back on him. "Enjoy the rest of your evening with your 'sister.'" From the way she emphasized *sister*, she clearly did not believe they were related.

Snatching the notes from his hand, the actress swished past him in a flurry of skirts. Everyone else followed, casting him speculative looks. His cousin and Max no exception.

Will was the last to step from the room. Arching one dark eyebrow at Dec, he closed the door after them with a sharp click.

And then it was just them.

Dec all alone with a girl he had not seen since the night his father cast him out. He could still recall his final glimpse of her. Carroty hair wild around her head and shoulders, clutching an old doll as she spied on them from the top of the stairs. She had witnessed his shame. A boy of fifteen years weeping like an infant.

A sour taste coated his mouth. He could think of no one he would rather see less. Well, apart from her mother, of course. Both females belonged to an era of his life he wished to forget.

"What are you doing here?" he demanded.

She scooted to the edge of the sofa, folding her hands primly in her lap. "Mrs. Heathstone, the headmistress of Harwich, deposited me here." She paused at his blank look, apparently hoping he might say something. He held silent and she plunged ahead, "Harwich is the school I've been attending for the last ten years."

He continued to stare, still waiting for further explanation. Those slim, pale fingers of hers fidgeted and shifted restlessly.

"She sent you a missive."

"Yes," he acknowledged stiffly. He vaguely recalled receiving it. Once he realized it had to do with his stepmother's daughter he'd stopped reading.

She processed this reaction with a blink before continuing. "I completed my studies two years ago." Her fingers flexed in her lap. They were slim. Like her. She could use a meal or two. Did they not feed her at this school? He assessed her critically. She might have grown taller, her hair may have somewhat darkened and her features may have sharpened and lost some of their baby roundness, but the rest of her hardly gave a nod toward womanhood.

"Two years ago," she repeated, as though this should mean something to him. "When I was eighteen."

"Congratulations," he managed to get out, still lost as to why she was here.

She twisted her fingers until they looked bloodless. "And now I am twenty." She spoke slowly, as though he was dense or she was trying to reach a child.

He shook his head, certain she was trying to explain something but simply not following her. "Are you in some kind of trouble, Miss Hughes? Is that why you're here? You want something from me?"

Even in the murky glow of the room he could discern the bright splash of color in her cheeks——they seemed to darken the smattering of freckles over her nose and cheeks. "Forgive me, but this is terribly awkward, Your Grace."

"Just arrive at the point, then."

"I've been at Harwich for two years. Not as a

pupil and not as a member of the staff. It has been Mrs. Heathstone's sheer goodwill that has kept me on there. Mama has not sent a penny for my care. Not since I completed my studies. She has ignored all of Mrs. Heathstone's letters."

He blinked at the mention of her mother. His stepmother. *Melisande.* He had mostly banished the memory of her. Except in the darkest dream, but there was little he could do to prevent that.

Seeing no way around it, he asked, "Where is your mother?"

"That is it precisely, Your Grace. I do not know."

I do not know. A simple enough declaration, but it held a wealth of implication. If she didn't know where her mother was, and she had essentially been dumped here by her schoolmistress, then she was his problem now.

Bloody hell.

Oh, he supposed he could cast her out. There was no one to force him to take her in, house her, feed her, but he could not abandon her to the streets. A lone female with no other relations. It was unconscionable, even for him.

Just to be certain of that point, he asked, "And have you no other relations? Your father's people? What of them?"

She shook her head, her gaze dropping. She

made a perfect study of those hands in her lap again as she answered him. "No. My father's parents are gone. I believe he had a brother . . . but he never married. The last I heard, he settled somewhere in America."

With a muttered epithet, he strode across the room and lifted the snifter of brandy from its tray. He poured himself a healthy swig and downed it. This evening had taken a decidedly foul turn. "I suppose that leaves me then, doesn't it?"

At her silence, he turned to look back at her, sitting so small and quietly. "No reply? You used to be full of chatter." That's what he remembered of her. A little magpie. When she followed him about, she would pelt him with questions mercilessly.

She shook her head and then nodded and then shook her head again as though she could not make up her mind. "I was hoping with your . . . resources . . . you could help me locate my mother. I have no wish to be a burden to you."

He poured himself another drink, feeling too damnably sober all of a sudden. "I imagine I could locate her." She was likely underneath some man. A poor sod like his father who believed every poisonous word she spouted. "And until then, what am I to do with you?"

He strolled back across the room, stopping in front of her, holding his glass loosely with his fingers.

Her gaze lifted, crawling up him slowly. Cat's eyes. Topaz gold. He frowned, again struck with how almost otherworldly she appeared. Feylike. Had she always looked thusly? He remembered her with more meat on her bones. And all wild hair, obscuring much of her face. "I shall endeavor to stay out of your way . . . if you would allow me to stay beneath your roof."

If? There was no choice in the matter. He would feed and house her until he located her mother and forced her to take responsibility for her daughter.

He moved for the door. "I'll show you to a room. The staff is already retired for the night."

"Thank you, Your Grace." The sound of rustling fabric signaled she was following him. He didn't look over his shoulder. "I promise not to bother—"

He stopped suddenly and turned. "Let us be clear. Your presence here bothers me. Greatly."

She stopped and backed away so as not to stand too near. "I'm s-sorry, Your Grace."

Inhaling, he continued as though he had not heard her. "There is nothing to be done for it tonight, but on the morrow, I shall send for my cousin and aunt to come stay. For propriety's sake."

"I don't think that is necessary—"

"And what do you know of Society, Miss Hughes?" Bitterness leaked from his voice. "You've been rusticating for the last ten years at some school." He scanned her up and down. "I'll not have tongues wagging that you're here unchaperoned. Unless you prefer the dames of the *ton* to whisper loud enough for you to hear that you're my latest conquest?"

Her slender form stiffened. "Of course not. I merely had no wish to inconvenience you. After all, propriety does not seem to be very high on your list of priorities."

He blinked, wondering if he had heard her correctly. The veiled insult was there. The corner of his mouth quirked. She was no mild-mannered miss after all, it appeared. The kitten had claws.

"No doubt you reference what happened earlier in the drawing room. My guests for the evening invading upon you?"

"Forgive me," she hastily offered, shaking her head. "I meant no judgment—"

"Of course you did. That's what people do. Judge and condemn." He sliced a hand through the air, indicating it made no difference. "It won't happen again. I'll not entertain while you're in residence."

"Be that as it may, we are kin," she insisted. "Of a sort. I doubt anyone would question me under your roof—"

"With my reputation, I guarantee they would. I grow weary of this discussion. My cousin and aunt will join us. The matter is closed."

She pressed her mouth into a hard line and gave a single nod of acceptance. But she looked miserable and ready to burst from relenting to him. She abhorred the situation. He saw it gleaming in her golden eyes.

Well, that made two of them.

"Come." He turned and led her up the set of stairs to the bedroom. He knew several of the bedchambers would have been prepared for his guests. The staff was accustomed to one or several of his friends staying the night on any given occasion.

He led her to the room two doors down from his. It was mostly pink and yellow. He assumed it fitting for a young lady. Whatever else she was, she was that.

He cast a glance over his shoulder at her, noting her small steps, her slim shoulders pulled back in very correct posture. Definitely a lady. Ironic, considering the little hoyden she used to be. And the identity of her mother. But then Melisande had fooled his father. Perhaps Rosalie was all pretense, too. His eyes narrowed, sweeping over her slight form in her shabby attire. Was she another social climber in the making?

"Here you are." At the door to her room he pushed it open and waved her within.

She peered inside and gave a brisk nod. "Thank you."

"I'll begin the search for your mother on the morrow. With luck, she is in Town." His lip curled. "She always did prefer it to the country."

She swallowed, the delicate muscles in her throat working as she no doubt recalled the truth of that statement. "We can only hope."

Despite her words, her voice lacked a ring of anticipation. Surely she wanted to find her mother. She couldn't want to remain here. Here, in the lavish town house of a duke. Bitterness welled up inside him. *Perhaps that's exactly what she wanted.*

"Don't make yourself too comfortable, Miss Hughes," he warned, unable to stop himself.

She blinked and then her cheeks flushed darker. Clearly she read his suspicions. "I'm certain that won't happen, Your Grace."

"Might I also suggest we stay out of each other's way? I don't see the need for us to reacquaint ourselves. We are not truly family, after all."

She nodded, her eyes unnaturally wide and bright in her face—as though she was forcing herself not to blink. She made him think of a kicked puppy right then and he shoved back the sensation that he was a veritable bastard. She looked down at her boots for a moment before meeting his stare again. "Indeed. We are not."

With a lift of her chin, she slipped inside the room and closed the door.

He lingered in front of her door, staring unseeingly at where she had stood moments before, wondering how soon he might be able to locate her mother.

Chapter 3

The chamber was cavernous. The bed swallowed her. She felt like a child at its center, engulfed in the fine linen sheets, her head lost deep in the plump pillows that smelled faintly of lavender.

It was nothing like the room she shared with Rachel back at Harwich's, and despite its opulence, she longed for that room right now. She longed for her friend. For the familiar. For smiles and eyes that did not stare coldly down at her.

He hated her.

She could see that at once. Perhaps this was just what he had become. Arrogant and pompous. A haughty nobleman immersed in his sparkling world of privilege. She was simply an unwanted relation to be tolerated.

He was a duke now. Not a boy to abide her with grudging affection and fetch her down from trees. Something inside her chest softened at that memory. He had more than tolerated her back then. He had answered her questions, endured her following him all about the countryside with good humor. Where had that boy gone?

She laced her fingers across her stomach and stared into the dark of the canopy above her as if she could see something there. Some truth, some bit of strength she so desperately needed right now. It did not matter how he felt about her. He would do his duty. He would shelter her until he located her mother, and then . . .

Well, she wasn't certain what came next. With her mother, one could never be certain. That much she had learned. One thing she did know, however, was that she could not count upon her. She would have to forge her own future. Rosalie rolled onto her side and tucked her hands beneath her cheek as the image of Declan filled her mind.

He had changed. At age fifteen he had been

a mere shadow of the man he was now. He was more fleshed out now. Muscular, his chest and shoulders broad, filling out his jacket to an impressive degree. She'd seen very few gentlemen in Yorkshire. Just local villagers and neighboring farmers. If she wasn't careful, she would let the old infatuation return. And nothing good could come of that.

Declan would not—

She stopped the thought, crushing it with a wince. She must cease to think of him thusly. She was practical. He was a duke. She was a nobody. Daughter of a barrister and a woman he had never accepted as his father's wife. She should simply consider herself fortunate he had agreed to let her stay on . . . and begin planning for the future.

She blinked in the darkness and closed her eyes only to a deeper dark, wondering why that thought did not provide her with any real comfort. It was well and good to decide she needed a plan, but until she had that plan, she doubted she would sleep well.

With a sigh, she opened her eyes again and stared sightlessly ahead for long hours into the night, her mind churning. Only as dawn tinged the sky, peeking through the partially opened drapes, did she succumb to sleep.

Chapter 4

Aunt Peregrine and Aurelia arrived soon after breakfast—a feat that duly impressed Declan. Especially since they came armed with their maids, too many trunks and valises to count, and a slit-eyed cat that looked thoroughly displeased to be carted about.

He had sent a missive explaining the situation and requesting that they stay with him until the matter with Rosalie could be resolved. He could not imagine he would require their presence longer than a week. He'd already sent several of his footmen about Town. He was confident he would know the location of Melisande by the end of the day. She was hardly inconspicuous. She thrived on attention.

Although he didn't expect her to be in Town. That would be too easy. And he would have likely heard if she was. He always heard. Rumors he ignored. People dropped tidbits of his stepmother's activities in his ear as though he might actually care. They watched his face closely as though they might witness his outrage at the exploits of his father's widow. They were disappointed every time.

She was the type of female that caused ripples wherever she went. She'd taken many a lover since his father's death, and doubtlessly during his father's life—only then with more discretion. He'd heard no gossip of late, so she must be out of Town. Perhaps in Bath. Or the Lake District. Over the years, whenever his mind brushed on the memory of Rosalie, it was with the thought that she was better off away at her rustic school. He supposed it should have occurred to him that she would eventually leave the schoolroom.

He joined his aunt and cousin in the drawing room. The same room where he had found his stepsister the night before, sleeping like some child who had fallen to slumber with no care or thought for her surroundings. He had directed the massive amount of luggage to be carried upstairs, with Aurelia's belongings being placed in the bedchamber beside Rosalie. They were of like age, and he rather liked Aurelia, even if she was one of those creatures he dreaded—a young lady of the *ton*. She would be a good influence.

Rosalie with her candid stare and drab garments flashed before his eyes. She dressed atrociously. Clearly, a proper lady's wardrobe was not of any importance at the school she had attended. Or was it simply because her mother had neglected to send the necessary funds? In any case, he was certain his aunt and cousin would see that she was properly attired. They could also polish any rough edges off her.

He frowned at the direction of his musings. How she dressed or comported herself was not his concern.

Aunt Peregrine looked up from her tea as he entered the room. "Ah, there you are, Declan-dearest. I began to fret that you had forgotten us."

"Hello, Aunt Peregrine." He bent and fondly kissed the cheek of his father's sister.

The enormous cat in her lap hissed at him, not caring for his proximity. Dec bared his teeth at the beast and the cat growled. His cousin giggled and his aunt sent him a cross look. "Be kind, Declan-dearest."

She only ever addressed him as Declan-dearest. As if that was his full name. She was kind if not a little vacant-minded at times, but he could not fault her for that. When his father cast him out, she had always welcomed him into her home. Every holiday from school, he always had a place beneath her roof and at her table. She was the closest thing to a mother he had ever known. Will and Aurelia were more like siblings than cousins.

He bent and kissed his cousin on the cheek as well. "You're looking well, Aurelia," he greeted.

Aurelia patted the space between her and her mother as though she expected him to squeeze between them. That infernal cat growled low and deep again as if to warn him not to even consider it.

"Come, seat yourself and tell us of this . . ." Aurelia paused, watching him carefully. Unlike her mother, she was ever astute. Her doe eyes were watchful and took everything in at a swift glance. She finally arrived at her words. "Tell us of this new development, cousin."

Development. Trust Aurelia to use such a vague term with such meaningfulness.

Aurelia was not like other females, given

toward emotion and histrionics. At two and twenty, she was a bookish girl with a stinging wit. She missed her first Season when her father passed away, casting the family into deep mourning. A setback she never seemed to recover from. Now with one Season fully behind her and well into her second, Aunt Peregrine never hesitated to bemoan her only daughter's unwed status. Aurelia teased that she would reside with Will once he married and produced the requisite heir.

I'll play doting aunt, she always declared. Will always looked terrified at that announcement. Whether it was the prospect of him marrying and becoming a father or his sister living with him permanently, Dec could only hazard a guess. His cousin grumbled enough at having his mother and sister spend the Season with him. Will would probably thank him the next time he saw him for taking them off his hands and out from beneath his roof for the Season.

Dec seated himself across from them on an overstuffed sofa chair. "It is no more than I said in my letter. Rosalie . . ." He paused and looked at each of them. "Do you recall the girl?"

His aunt's eyes brightened and she sat straighter. "Was she not Melisande's child with that dreadful orange hair?"

"Er. Yes." He didn't bother adding he thought the color rather pretty. Unique. Then and now.

She sniffed and her shoulders slumped back. "Tell me her hair has faded to a more palatable auburn."

"Not quite."

"Well, unfortunate that. Red hair is not the most fashionable. So many fabrics and colors don't suit."

Aurelia rolled her eyes and took a sip from her teacup.

He stifled a smile. He was familiar with his aunt's inane comments and his cousin's thinly veiled forbearance.

"Yes, well it seems that Rosalie has completed her studies and her mother . . . forgot to collect her." He didn't bother adding that she forgot to collect her two years ago.

Aunt Peregrine tsked. "She doubtlessly doesn't want her. Shame on Melisande. It's time the girl was ushered into Society properly."

He shrugged. "That is not my responsibility."

"Is it not?" his cousin asked, her brown eyes wide over the rim of her cup. "She is your step-sister."

He glared at Aurelia. "I'm not her father. Or even her brother."

"But you are the head of her family . . . as far as Society is concerned," Aurelia replied, unruffled. "That does make you responsible for her, does it not?"

His aunt nodded, her gray-blond curls bobbing. "True. That is true, Declan-dearest. This does cast light upon you."

He ground his teeth and sent Aurelia a look that clearly did not convey gratitude to her for pointing this nuance out to Aunt Peregrine. "No. I am only responsible for her *if* I take responsibility."

Aurelia and Aunt Peregrine stared at him, looking unconvinced.

He stared back, astounded that they should give him such looks. His father had cast him out in favor of Melisande. They could not expect him to go to such lengths for her daughter as though all was well and right between them. "I intend to leave her in the care of her mother once she—"

Aurelia lowered her teacup to its saucer with alacrity. "Well, that might be difficult to do considering she is in Italy with her latest paramour."

His aunt swatted her daughter's arm. "Aurelia, where did you hear such a thing? That is far too risqué to fall from your lips."

Aurelia lifted her chin, looking exasperated.

"Mother, you would be surprised how much one hears when they are invisible."

"You're not invisible," Aunt Peregrine objected. "And who said such things in your hearing, I'd like to know?"

"Mother, I'm not a child . . . and to answer you precisely . . . everyone."

Dec would have smiled over their banter. It usually amused him, however, his cousin's proclamation was the only thing he could think upon—the only thing he could *feel*. Like rocks sinking to his stomach. "Melisande is in Italy?"

"Yes," his aunt admitted, sliding her much aggrieved gaze from her daughter with a sigh. "She departed a week ago with her latest . . . friend. It has caused quite a stir, you see, because the viscount is a good deal younger than she is."

He grimaced. She always did like them young.

His aunt continued, "Everyone had thought he was shopping for a bride this season, as he is quite destitute, but then your stepmother—"

"I understand," he broke in, tempering his tone with a smile. He really did not wish to hear of his stepmother's exploits. "So that leaves me with Rosalie." He rubbed his forehead. "What am I supposed to do with her?" He lifted his gaze to his aunt and cousin almost pleadingly.

"Oh, we can't take her. We live with William. That wouldn't be suitable. And I already have one unwed daughter to contend with."

Aurelia flinched. It was imperceptible, but Dec noticed it. Aurelia lowered her gaze and took another long sip from her tea.

"No, I should not wish to impose on you," he murmured, his mind racing, working . . . wondering a little desperately if he could not simply dump a settlement on her and never have to see her again. Much like the arrangement he had with his stepmother.

Melisande received a town house and a settlement upon the death of his father—a settlement that she had obliterated in under a year's time. She had come to him then, full of tears and pleas. She was penniless, money lenders hunting her down all hours of the day.

She had wept in his drawing room like there was nothing between him. No ugliness. No past. No night ten years ago where his world had died. Jumped off its axis and placed him on the path that led him to where—and who—he was today.

She was going to have to sell the house. She had nowhere to go. She would have to plead with friends to keep her . . . and oh, how ill that would paint him, she pointed out. Her own stepson did not care to support her. Tongues would wag.

He no longer cared what others thought of him. Everyone knew his father died despising him. The speculation over that did him no favors. He was accustomed to others thinking the worst of him.

He could have cast her out . . . much like his father had done to him. And perhaps that was why he did not. Instead he had agreed to give her an allowance every fortnight, and paid off her debts while spreading word that the Duke of Banbury would not honor her debts again.

He had not seen her since. He assumed she had grown some sense of economy. He snorted. Apparently she had not wasted a penny to look after her own daughter these last few years.

"Might I make a suggestion, Declan-dearest?"

His attention snapped back to his aunt. She shot a quick glance to Aurelia and then looked back at him, her eyes bright with whatever plan she was hatching.

He nodded.

"Why not usher her into Society this Season alongside your cousin." She smiled almost ruefully. "Perhaps the attention of two might draw more bees to the honey pot."

Aurelia's face reddened. "Indeed, what's another sow to market?"

"Aurelia!" his aunt cried in outrage. "Must you be so vulgar?"

"*I* did not just use an offensive bee metaphor, Mama."

Declan casually covered his mouth to stifle his laughter.

"Assuming this girl does not bear some hideous deformity and you bestow a respectable dowry on her *and* she can smile like any well-trained monkey, you should be able to marry her off, cousin," Aurelia offered in her most sober tones, nodding her head with over-exaggeration, her brown curls bobbing. "Only I can't seem to manage it."

Aunt Peregrine nodded agreeably, missing her daughter's sarcasm. His aunt fairly bounced in her seat. It was the final straw. Her cat meowed its protest and bounded from her lap, waddling its fat arse somewhere behind the settee. "Indeed, indeed! Place a dowry on her, if you truly want to be rid of all responsibility for her. Who knows when her mother will return?"

Dec considered their words. His aunt was serious. His cousin looked like she couldn't care one way or another. This would involve more than a week. And yet he might be rid of her faster and permanently if he helped her secure a match for herself.

As much as he didn't relish ushering Rosalie through a Season, he recognized the merit behind the plan. It was a short investment of time, but then he'd be finished with her once she married. He wouldn't have to worry about her turning up on his doorstep again when her mother shirked her responsibility.

"Very well," he agreed. "I'll give her a dowry." He'd give her an obscenely fat dowry. "And I give you leave to do whatever you need in order to prepare her."

Aunt Peregrine rubbed her hands together with satisfaction. "We'll stay here with you through the Season, but the world needs to see firsthand that the Duke of Banbury has taken her under his wing. The *ton* needs to laud her as much for her connection to you as for her dowry."

"Meaning?"

"We request your presence at several of the Season's functions."

He sighed, nodding. "Very well. Let's do it properly and then be done with it."

Aunt Peregrine grinned. "The Colton ball is next week. We can introduce Rosalie then. That should give us enough time to ready her. Oh! We have much to do."

He nodded, not really caring, just grateful that he could pass the chore of shepherding Rosalie through the marriage mart to his aunt and cousin. He'd endure a few balls for that.

"Make certain your calendar is cleared."

He winced, not liking the sound of that.

She continued, "Everyone needs to see you there like a proud papa—"

"I'm not her father."

Aunt Peregrine shrugged her thin shoulders. "Very well, then, a doting brother."

"Nor am I her brother," he said tightly, his jaw aching with sudden tension.

"It might help if you behave as though you can abide the girl," Aurelia pointed out.

He forced his jaw to relax. "Of course I can abide her." It was her mother he despised. He simply wanted no contact with either one of them, but he wouldn't dwell on that. This was the situation he found himself in and he would suffer it. "You have carte blanche to do what you must to see her wed as soon as possible."

Then he would have his life back.

"Carte blanche?" Aurelia tsked. "Two little

words you should think about carefully before saying them to Mama."

Aunt Peregrine's eyes fairly glazed. Will kept his mother on a fairly strict allowance, claiming it necessary. Dec knew his uncle had left them with little other than the entailed properties. Will had mentioned on more than one occasion that he would have to wed an heiress sooner rather than later. Aurelia's dowry was woefully insubstantial, doubtlessly explaining why she remained on the shelf. That and her sharp tongue.

"Ladies." He rose. "I think everything is well in hand. I've an errand." He was meeting with his solicitor today over another matter, but now it was just as well, considering he would have to make arrangements for a dowry for Rosalie.

"I trust you will reintroduce us to Rosalie before you scurry off," his aunt said. "It's been years since we last clapped eyes on the girl."

"You're family, Aunt. You don't need me here to become better acquainted."

She started to protest, but he said his farewells and made a hasty retreat.

Chapter 5

Rosalie woke slowly, stretching languidly. She felt delicious . . . the bedding was positively the most luxurious thing to ever touch her skin. She had been too weary the night before to even dig through her valise for her nightgown. She had merely stripped down to her shift and climbed into the vast bed.

She must have slept late. Sunlight poured into the room through the parted damask drapes. She blinked up at the canopy overhead as she replayed the events of the night before.

She had seen Dec. He had been cold and harsh and uncompromising.

And even more beautiful than memory served.

She sighed and dropped her hands to her stomach. It was such a disappointment to see that he had grown into such a beast. Clearly, he loathed his connection to her. He was probably embarrassed. She was without rank or standing in Society. She didn't possess money or even clothes that qualified her to rub elbows with him.

His words echoed through her head. *Stay out of each other's way.* Indeed. She would quite gladly stay out of his way.

"Well, you're not so hopeless. Not hopeless at all. I see we have much to work with despite that shocking hair."

Rosalie squeaked at the sound of the voice and yanked the counterpane to her chest, popping upright in bed.

Her gaze landed on a well-dressed lady holding an absurdly fat cat in her arms. The stranger approached the bed, scrutinizing her carefully as she stroked the animal in her arms.

"Who are you?" Rosalie demanded, her fingers tightening around the bedding, quite certain good manners weren't necessary when one was confronted in a state of dishabille in her bedchamber.

"You don't remember me? I'm Lady Merlton. Declan's aunt. He sent for me."

Staring at Lady Merlton, she vaguely recalled her now. Mostly Rosalie recalled that her mother had not liked her. Lady Merlton was far too pretty. Even now with her ashy blond hair and past the first blush of youth, she was an attractive woman. And Mama didn't like pretty ladies. It drew too much attention away from herself.

Lady Merlton's words slowly registered, sinking into her spinning thoughts. "He sent for you? The duke? *Declan?*"

"Yes. It seems we're to find you a match this Season." She cocked her head, continuing to evaluate Rosalie. "Not such an impossible task, I think. Especially not with the dowry that Declan has placed upon your head. And oh my, your shoulders and arms are quite lovely . . . we shall have to show those to full advantage."

Everything inside her seized. "I'm to . . . *marry?* Who?"

"Well, that remains to be seen, dear girl."

So they had not at least presumed to choose a husband for her? Small blessing.

Lady Merlton dropped down on the bed beside her. The cat rolled out of her arms and made itself comfortable, pawing and scratching at the coun-

terpane before circling several times and dropping onto the bed with a plaintive meow.

Lady Merlton's face lit with animation. "You
shall be the toast of the Season." Her keen eyes
scanned her, still assessing, evaluating as though
Rosalie were some fatted calf to deliver to market.
"Fortunately the pastels so expected among the
debutantes will look quite lovely on you. Don't
you agree, Aurelia?"

It was only then that Rosalie noticed there was
a second woman in the room. She lurked near the
door, watching in silence, her arms crossed. An
air of wariness clung to her, as though she did
not fully trust Rosalie. Which was strange. Why
should she view her suspiciously?

The young woman—Aurelia—was elegantly
dressed, in the pastels Lady Merlton had just mentioned. Only they did not look quite flattering on
her. She was dark-haired and olive-complexioned.
Perhaps there was the bit of the Mediterranean in
her ancestry. The pale green she wore made her
look rather sickly.

"Indeed, Mama."

Mama? So this was Dec's cousin. She searched
her memory, vaguely recalling a dark-haired girl
a little older than herself with her nose perpetu-
ally buried in a book.

Aurelia stopped at the foot of the bed. One corner of her mouth curled upward. Almost as though she were smirking. "She will be a diamond of the *ton*."

Something snapped inside Rosalie. A fine thread she had not even known existed simply broke loose from within her. She hopped up from the bed and marched toward the chair where she had laid out her clothes from the day before. She struggled into them, pulling them on over her shift, indifferent to her audience. Her fingers worked furiously up the row of tiny buttons lining the front of her dress.

"Rosalie?" Her name hung on the air, an unspoken question attached to it.

Her gaze snapped up to meet Declan's aunt directly. "Yes, my lady?"

"Are you going somewhere? Shall we ring for a maid to help you—"

"I've been dressing myself for quite some time, thank you very much." Her gaze flicked to Dec's cousin. Her expression had altered. She did not quite smirk anymore. Instead, she looked . . . intrigued as she studied her.

Lady Merlton's lips thinned into a line of displeasure. She looked to her daughter as though seeking assistance. "That is a matter that should be rectified, my dear. We must have Declan assign a maid—"

"Is your nephew at home?" Rosalie asked, cutting her off. Rather rudely, she supposed, but there was no help for it. Matters were dire as far as she was concerned and must be attended to at once.

Lady Merlton blinked. "He was on his way out. We just left him moments ago in the—"

Her voice died as Rosalie swung on her bare heels and began marching toward the door of her bedchamber, heedless of her bare feet and untended hair. She was past caring what kind of impression she made on her stepbrother.

She grabbed the door latch, freezing at the strangled shriek behind her.

Startled, Rosalie tossed a look over her shoulder.

Lady Merlton stretched out a hand as though she meant to grab hold of her. "You cannot mean to step out of this room looking like *that*?"

"Mama, it's not as though she's stepping out of doors," Aurelia offered dryly.

Lady Merlton shot her daughter a quelling look. "The staff shall see—they shall know." Her voice dropped to a harsh whisper. "And heavens knows how they gossip with the staff of other households! It would not serve to have her gossiped about before she even makes her first appearance in Society."

Rosalie shook her head. It wasn't to be borne. This discussion about her—about her life, her very *fate*!—she had not been consulted on any of it.

Lady Merlton waved a hand wildly in her direction. "You c-cannot go about thusly," she sputtered.

Rosalie didn't even bother looking down at herself. She knew she looked a fright in her travel-worn garments that had not been the height of fashion even when they were new and her hair a tangled nest. She simply did not care. She could not stand by as Dec—*argh!*—the Duke of Banbury decided her fate as though it were his right. He was not her father. He wasn't even her brother.

The sound of laughter suddenly drew her attention to Lady Merlton's daughter. She had dropped to sit on the edge of the bed. The cat took objection to sharing the bed with her and swiped a paw at the girl.

Still laughing, she slapped back at the cat, the gesture automatic, as if it were normal byplay between them.

She held her side as if her laughter actually hurt. "Oh, oh!" Aurelia gasped. "This is going to be brilliant." She pointed to the door Rosalie was on the verge of escaping through. "If he's still here, you'll likely find my cousin down the hall. Take a right at the turn. His private study is near the top of the stairs. Hurry if you wish to catch him."

"Aurelia!" Lady Merlton scolded. "You're not helping."

Shaking her head at the odd girl, Rosalie charged from the room and down the corridor, following her directions.

She didn't bother knocking. She was too angry. Emotion ruled her. She'd never been quite this in-furiated. Well, her mother managed to annoy her, but then, her mother was never around to face the brunt of her ire. Perhaps for the first time she would vent her spleen on the subject of her wrath.

Wretched man! He'd said nothing of marrying her off last evening. Plan her future, would he? Marriage! Un-bloody likely.

She barged into his study to very nearly collide with him. His hands settled on her shoulders, steadying her. She stepped back quickly, severing the contact, relief coursing through her that he had not yet departed.

"Miss Hughes," he greeted evenly. "Forget to knock?"

"I needed to speak with you," she said breathlessly.

His gaze scanned her, skipping down to her bare feet and back to her face, eyeing the mess of her hair. "It appears you forgot more than how to knock." He arched a dark eyebrow at her, and that supercilious gesture only provoked her further.

"I have forgotten nothing," she snapped, propping one hand on her hip and fighting back her nervousness. Perhaps she should have composed herself before this confrontation. He looked unflappable. Tall and beautiful and . . .

Perfect.

She moistened her lips and reminded herself that no one was perfect. "It seems *you*, however, have forgotten something, Your Grace."

"Indeed?" The eyebrow winged even higher.

"Indeed," she echoed, mimicking his haughty tone, and that chased away the mild amusement lurking in his eyes. Now he just looked annoyed. His square jaw locked tight. Good, she thought with some satisfaction. Because that is precisely how she felt. Let him be annoyed. "*You* have forgotten yourself. At least when it comes to your role in relation to me. You're not my guardian, but it seems you have taken it upon yourself to act as such."

He crossed his arms. "I take it you heard the news."

"That I'm to be married." She nodded once.

Hard. "Not that I was consulted, but that's the news I woke to this morning."

"And you're not happy about this?" He snorted. "Well, that's foolish."

She released a breath in a hiss. "How's that?"

"I'm offering you a Season, a future free from the unreliability of your mother. Unless you prefer to live with uncertainty, one step from the gutter. Begging for favors from people you hold only loose connections to."

Meaning him. He was right. The truth stung.

They studied each other for a moment. Her initial anger began to fade as she considered that what he was offering her was so much more than anything she had hoped for. So much more than many women ever received. A Season as a debutante. The thrill of parties and balls. Excitement, adventure. *Suitors.* The possibility of finding someone. A chance at love. To put a life of loneliness behind her.

"I see," she finally said, lacing her fingers together in front of her and now feeling a little foolish for barging in here after all.

He angled his head. "Do you now?"

She did. "I suppose I owe you my gratitude."

He let loose a bark of laughter. "Doesn't sound too heartfelt."

Heat scored her cheeks. "My apologies," she mumbled, flexing her toes in the carpet. "You're very generous. You don't have to do this."

He smiled thinly. "I'll tell you what I told your mother the last time I saw her. My generosity has its limits. Don't squander this opportunity."

She nodded once. "Understood. Now understand this. I'm not my mother."

He looked her up and down and his smile turned faintly smirking, as if amused. As if he didn't believe that. Indeed, he didn't believe that at all.

"Noted. Now. If you'll excuse me. I'm late for an appointment." He stepped past her and exited the room, leaving her alone and staring after him.

Chapter 6

*T*he modiste arrived promptly the next morning after breakfast with four assistants in tow. Rosalie felt her eyes widen as they entered her chamber carrying fabrics and boxes that soon outnumbered the number of articles she had ever possessed. Ever. In her entire life ever.

"Oh, very nice, very nice!" The modiste, Mrs. Ashby, clapped approvingly as she surveyed Rosalie's body. "We have much to work with here."

Rosalie smiled uncertainly as she eyed the modiste and four assistants. It was difficult to process that they were working class. They were all attired better than she was in elegant dresses and perfectly coiffed hair.

"Did I not say so?" Lady Peregrine nodded eagerly, her turbaned head bobbing.

And still the boxes and baskets continued to arrive, more maids arriving now to help carry them into the room.

Rosalie leaned down to where Aurelia sat on the chaise, tormenting Lady Snuggles with a scrap of ribbon. The cat appeared in no mood to play, but that did not stop Aurelia from repeatedly flipping the blue ribbon at the growling animal.

"Would it not have been easier to go to their shop?" Rosalie whispered. "Rather than forcing them to come here?"

Smiling, Aurelia shook her head. "Mama does *not* visit Mrs. Ashby's shop. Madame Ashby brings the shop to her. To any other highborn lady, for that matter." Aurelia's lips twisted wryly. "It's always so." Her voice dipped low to add, "No matter that Will's pockets don't run deep enough for such lavish treatment, one must keep appearances. She can't have any of her friends see *her* calling on the dressmaker."

Rosalie nodded as though she understood the habits of the aristocracy.

Evidently having enough of Aurelia, the fat tabby lurched at her, swatting her several times with a paw before plopping down to the floor and waddling away.

"Aurelia!" Lady Peregrine snapped. "Leave Lady Snuggles alone!"

Aurelia shrugged and dropped the ribbon and sighed, looking bored.

Mrs. Ashby was a large woman, elegantly dressed, with plump, swollen hands that moved and fluttered like overfed pigeons as she directed her staff with sharp commands.

Rosalie sank down on the chaise, taking Lady Snuggles's spot. "So . . . much . . . much," she murmured as three of the assistants departed to fetch yet more.

"Oh, this shall be no small undertaking," Aurelia remarked. "You require a full wardrobe. Brace yourself for day-long misery."

"This is going to cost a fortune," she grumbled, feeling guilty. She did not like the idea of spending Dec's money so recklessly. And all of this in addition to her dowry? It was far too much. When she thought back to her years at Harwich, and the many girls there who had so little—Mrs. Heathstone herself wore the same frocks year after year after year—it made her chest pinch with discomfort.

She turned and caught Aurelia looking at her oddly. "What?"

"You're quite the anomaly."

She frowned. "Why does that sound like an insult?"

"I meant no offense. Any other female would gladly step into your shoes at this moment with no thought whatsoever to the expense. They would greedily take all that my cousin is giving without the slightest hesitation. Goodness knows Mama would accept such generosity if Will would allow it. My brother is too proud to take anything from Declan, and trust me, he has offered. Clearly you are more like my brother, for here you sit. Looking uncomfortable and faintly pale about the gills."

Rosalie watched with ever-widening eyes as yards of glittering fabrics continued to pile upon the bed for Lady Peregrine's examination. Dec's aunt dove into the bolts of fabric with a feral glint to her eyes, sorting through them with expert care, already deep in conversation with the modiste over the various types of gowns Rosalie would need. Morning dresses. Walking dresses. Day dresses. Traveling dresses. Ball gowns.

Nightgowns. Riding habits. Corsets. Stockings. Petticoats. Chemises . . .

It made her dizzy. "This is quite out of my depth."

"You are the daughter of a duchess," Aurelia reminded her.

A duchess who never had much use for her. Rosalie had been away at school for the last ten years, living a modest existence without even the smallest dose of extravagance. The greatest luxury she ever had at Harwich was, occasionally, mint jam with her toast.

The last of the shop girls returned then. Her arms full of ermine-trimmed cloaks of every conceivable shade.

"Close your mouth," Aurelia gently suggested.

Blinking, she shut her mouth with a snap, but not before she silently vowed to send a trunk of clothing to Harwich at her first opportunity.

The morning passed in a blur. She was pinched and prodded and pinned. She stood still for their ministrations until her feet ached. Several gowns were pulled over her head, measurements noted, and then two assistants went to work with needle and thread so that she would have something to wear when they left today. It would be several days before the bulk of her wardrobe was ready.

"Mama." Aurelia fell back on the chaise, clutching her stomach. "We're hungry. Can we not take a respite for lunch?"

Lady Peregrine looked up from the swatches that she held up for comparison against Rosalie's face. "We've much to do and a short amount of time. Really, Aurelia, think of Rosalie and don't be so selfish."

"I am thinking of Rosalie, Mama. She looks on the verge of expiring, too!"

Lady Peregrine shot her an exasperated look before fixing her attention once again on two swatches of blue that looked very much alike in Rosalie's opinion. "Which one for the Colton ball?"

Aurelia flopped back on the chaise with a moan. "Mama, they are identical. We're tired and famished."

"Very well, you little monster." Lady Peregrine flung a scrap of silk at her with a decided lack of heat. A smile played about her lips. "I'll ring for some refreshments."

"No need." Aurelia popped back up, suddenly revived. "Rosalie and I will go. I want to make certain Cook gives us plenty of those little lemon biscuits with the raspberry icing." When her mother looked ready to object, she added, "And those sandwiches you love, Mama. Enough for all. I'm certain that Mrs. Ashby and her staff could use some fortification, too."

The modiste's head jerked around from where she was surveying an assistant's work on one of Rosalie's day dresses. "That would be lovely. I am feeling rather peckish," Mrs. Ashby agreed. The assistants nodded avidly.

"Oh, very well," Lady Peregrine relented.

Aurelia grabbed Rosalie's hand and tugged her down from where she stood on a small dais.

"Tell Cook to prepare enough for everyone. But really, must you both—"

The door closing behind them muffled Lady Peregrine's final words.

"There now. You're free. Go. You can thank me later. I'll fetch enough food that Mrs. Ashby and her assistants shall be occupied for a good hour."

"Go?" Rosalie shook her head. "Where?"

"Use your imagination. It's a large house." She batted her hands at Rosalie before turning for the stairs that led to the kitchens.

Rosalie stood there for a moment, weighing her options. Her room was in use. The library seemed a rather obvious place, as Lady Peregrine had already noted her fondness for books. She would know to look for her there.

Deciding a little fresh air might do her some good, she slipped out the back of the house into the small garden. The sun fought through the clouds, and she lifted her face to its feeble rays. She was accustomed to colder weather in Yorkshire. This felt as good as the warmest day she was ever treated to there.

She descended the steps and strode across the brick courtyard, past the bench and out onto the lawn. Bending, she removed her slippers and enjoyed the cool grass beneath her toes. Leaving them behind, she walked deeper into the garden, turning between two thick hedges of heather, stopping when she came to a large oak. She sank down before the base of it, the bark at her back. Stretching her legs out in front of her, she wiggled her exposed toes in the air, inching her skirts up to her knees.

Arching her neck, she looked up at the thick canopy of leaves, rustling softly in the wind. This almost felt normal. Out here she could almost forget what waited for her in that enormous house just beyond the courtyard. A luxurious life that suddenly felt too big. Frightening in its strangeness.

"You still have a fondness for the outdoors, I see."

Her gaze dropped and she straightened, pushing her skirts back down to her ankles as she focused on Banbury standing before her.

"Your Grace." She pulled back her head to look up at him, following the lean lines of his frame. "What are you doing here?"

"This is my house." He waved a hand. "My garden."

She flushed and started to rise. "Yes, of course. Of course, it is."

"No, remain as you are. I did not mean to disturb you."

"You didn't disturb me." She watched with some alarm as he lowered himself to the grass and stretched out his long legs. He kept several feet between them.

His boot flat on the ground, he bent one knee and propped an arm casually upon it. "I understand the dressmaker is here."

She nodded with a wincing smile.

"And yet you are out here?"

She nodded yet again.

He gazed at her curiously before looking down and plucking a blade of grass between his fingers. "Most girls would love an afternoon spent with a dressmaker, planning a grand new wardrobe."

She held her tongue, uncertain what to say that did not make her appear ungrateful.

"You're not most girls." Not a question, but a statement. And one she did not know how to respond to. Indeed, he likely thought her mute.

He angled his head, his expression growing rather perplexed. "You were once a garrulous creature."

She finally found her voice. "You remember me so well, then?"

It was his turn to stare at her in silence, as though she had caught him off guard with the question.

"Do you remember," she began, clearing her throat and smiling slightly, "the time when I did not want to get wet so you carried me across the pond?"

She stared at him hopefully, waiting for his answer. She recalled that day often over the years. They had laughed so uproariously when he lost his balance and they splashed together into the pond.

He studied her slowly, looking her over, missing nothing. Not even the bare toes peeping out from her hem. He must think her terribly provincial, whilst he was so sophisticated in his rich dark jacket and silk cravat.

"No. I don't."

Her foolish heart sank.

Then he looked away again, flicking that bit of grass out into the yard with a sharp move. "Although I confess more memories have resurfaced since your arrival here."

So he truly hadn't thought of her over the years. Not as she had thought of him. Only now did his mind search back.

She nodded wordlessly. It was a sobering thought and stung more than it should. Clearly he had served a bigger part of her childhood than she had for him. A necessary realization, however. It put things in proper perspective.

He lied.

He remembered that day they fell in the pond with utter clarity. Aside from the hilarity of that afternoon, he remembered because when they returned home, dripping wet, it had been to the surprise of his father and Melisande's arrival.

It was that visit when everything had changed. When his father had ceased to look at him fondly, proudly, as fathers looked at their sons.

It was the end of one life and the beginning of another.

"I remember you liked climbing trees," he announced, compelled to give her something. She looked so crestfallen when he claimed that he didn't remember that afternoon.

Her gaze snapped to his face, a smile tugging on her lips. "You do?"

He lifted one shoulder in a begrudging shrug, resenting that her smile should somehow satisfy him. "Only you could never quite manage to get down on your own."

She laughed then, and strangely enough, the sound curled warmly around his heart. "I don't know why I continued to try. I remember always thinking: I can climb this tree. This one will be different! Only once up there I could never successfully get down."

He chuckled, nodding. "It was rather comical."

"Your father never seemed to be amused. My antics drove him mad with worry. He said I would break my neck someday."

Dec fell silent. Yes, he remembered that, too. His father had cared for her. More than her own mother had. He'd called her strawberry-top. Ultimately, his father had cared for her more than even his own son. Not too difficult, he supposed. Not when his sire grew to despise him.

She studied him warily, evidently aware the subject of his father was an unwelcome one. She would remember that night, after all. She had been there, watching from the top of the stairs, her child's eyes wide with incomprehension as his father cursed him, struck him, and cast him from his house.

"Good thing my father was only around some of the time then," he managed to say in an even voice. "He was not fully aware of how deeply your penchant for getting stuck in trees ran."

"I suppose the *good* thing was you." Her eyes softened, mirth returning to her mouth as she gazed at him, clearly relaxed and at ease in this moment. "Being around so often to get me down."

His chest tightened uncomfortably. He looked from her, to the garden, and then back to her again. He could not recall being alone with a woman in such a companionable way as this when they were not both naked. And she was a woman now. No giggling little girl.

His gaze skimmed her slight form, considering her from the top of her head to the small feet peeking out from her hem. Her toes looked delicate, her ankles as shapely as any woman's he had ever tasted. His gaze shifted back to her face and noted that her cheeks were flushed. She had not missed his inspection. His thorough study of her. He'd looked his fill. And he liked what he saw.

Suddenly, it seemed wise to put some distance between them. He'd given over her care to his aunt. There was no reason for this. For him to be out here talking with her, reminiscing like they were old friends. He did not have women who were friends. He had women he shagged. It only made sense that the more time he spent around her, the itch to get beneath her skirts would overtake him. That's what he did. How he existed through life. She was clueless as to what manner of man he was.

"Aunt Peregrine is probably looking for you."

She nodded hastily and rose to her feet, appearing almost anxious to be rid of him, too. He shoved off that sting to his ego. Perhaps she wasn't as clueless as he assumed.

At any rate, he moved then, not bothering to wait for her as she reclaimed her shoes. He left the garden with swift strides lest she come to expect such moments as this. Moments of them together where he would drop his guard and soften, forgetting who he was—forgetting who *she* was.

He would be careful never to let that happen again.

Chapter 7

*I*n a week's time, Rosalie arrived at her first ball dressed in a gown she would never have imagined for herself. She had never worn anything so fine in her life. This fact only filled her with acute embarrassment. As though at any moment someone might look up, point at her and cry, *Fraud! Imposter!* Of course that didn't occur.

She was dressed no more elegantly than any of the other ladies in attendance. In fact, her gown was simpler than some. The modiste had insisted that her slight frame needed no embellishments. None of the lace and ribbons and bows that adorned so many of the Season's other debutantes. Her blue gown fit snugly at the bodice before flaring out in a full skirt, the hem of which was intricately threaded with black embroidery and pearls. The tiny cap sleeves were no more than thin scraps of black lace. The small, transparent sleeves, coupled with the heart-shaped neckline, made her feel decidedly exposed. She'd never revealed so much skin in her life, but Lady Peregrine insisted it was respectable.

As she stepped into the ballroom, she was awash in sensation. The lights, the sounds, the colors of gowns swishing past.

This was all she had dreamed. So why did it feel as though snakes writhed in her belly?

"Let the games begin," Aurelia murmured at her side.

Lady Peregrine was quickly swallowed up by a bevy of chattering ladies—but not before looking over the head of one lady and narrowing a pointed look on both Rosalie and Aurelia.

Aurelia laughed lightly with a shake of her head. "We've been given our task. Let's get to it then, shall we?"

Rosalie turned blinking eyes on the girl. "I beg your pardon?"

"Chin up. The wolves are already eyeing you." Aurelia hid her mouth with her fan, leaning closer. "Mama has already seen to it that word of your dowry has spread throughout the *ton*, so you have blessed little to do. Simply smile and make yourself amenable."

Rosalie faced the ballroom again, unsure how she felt about this information. She saw that several ladies and gentlemen were indeed looking her way, eyeing her avidly. She couldn't help thinking that the look in several of the gentlemen's eyes was more than simply speculative . . . but rather measuring. Like she was a sow at market to be judged and considered.

She lifted her chin as Aurelia advised and fought back a tide of nausea.

"Come. Let's brave the den. I hope your slippers are comfortable. I expect you shall dance more than any other lady in attendance tonight."

Rosalie glanced down at her slippers.

Aurelia chuckled, leading the way. "Try not to look so wide-eyed. It's like waving a red flag for all these fine young bucks to come and devour you."

She nodded jerkily, ignoring the whispers that erupted in their wake. Snatches of words drifted to her ears. *Banbury . . . rich as Croesus . . . biggest dowry of the Season . . . fifty thousand . . .*

She reminded herself that she had wanted this. Desperately. She had craved adventure. A chance to find love. The kind she read about in novels. The kind that the poets wrote of . . . she knew it was out there. Why else would the idea of it exist? She simply needed to be lucky enough—and persistent enough—to find it.

"And here comes the first."

Rosalie looked up, her heart pounding in her chest as a man a good two decades older than herself approached. His chin disappeared amid the folds of his cravat.

He bowed to Aurelia, wiping a hand over his balding head.

"Lord Strickland," Aurelia greeted. "How fine to see you again."

He nodded and mumbled something so low that Rosalie could scarcely hear him.

"Yes, this is my cousin, Miss Rosalie Hughes."

Lord Strickland clicked his heels together and bowed smartly over Rosalie's hand, pressing a sloppy kiss to the back of her glove. His lips moved like slugs crawling over the thin fabric.

Upon rising, he motioned to the dance floor with another inaudible mumble. She glanced at Aurelia, who gave a nod of confirmation that he was indeed requesting a dance.

"Yes, I should like to dance, my lord," Rosalie murmured very correctly, and allowed herself to be escorted onto the dance floor. Even not very tall, she stood a good half foot taller than Lord Strickland. She had no trouble looking over his head, which gave her a decided advantage in observing those who watched her. She frowned. All gentlemen twice her age, much like Lord Strickland. Where were all the young, handsome men of her fantasies?

In your fantasies.

She sighed and wondered if perhaps she had been naive when thinking about the manner of suitor she would find. Her gaze connected with Aurelia across the ballroom. She, too, danced, caught up close in the embrace of a man as wide as he was tall. Aurelia wiggled her fingers in a halfhearted wave over the swell of his shoulder. Rosalie grimaced, realizing in that moment that the lot of a debutante was not the most desirable fate after all. That the dream of adventure and excitement . . . *love*. It was just that. A dream.

"Must we be here?"

Dec glared at Max. "Yes. We must. And I've already explained why."

Max leaned against the wall with a scowl. "I

haven't been to a ball since . . ." His eyes lifted as he considered. "Well. Since never."

"No one said you had to come."

His friend shrugged. "You said it wouldn't take long." He tugged at his cravat. "Can you make haste? The way some of these ladies are eyeing me is making me decidedly nervous."

Dec laughed. "The elusive Viscount Camden is in their midst. Dance with a few of them. You'll be all over the scandal sheets tomorrow."

"Bloody hell," Max growled. "I'll resist the temptation."

"Breathe easy. My aunt requested I make an appearance, dance with the chit once, and then we can be off."

"Then be done with it." Max gestured to the crowded room. "Before I'm set upon."

"If I can locate her, I shall." Dec's narrowed gaze swept the room, searching for Rosalie among the mad crush of brightly colored gowns. He should have inquired the color of dress.

"There's your cousin." Max nodded toward Aurelia. "Termagent. She's actually dancing with some poor sod."

Dec's lips lifted in amusement. "She's only nasty to you, you know. She can be quite civil to other people. Pleasant, even."

Max snorted. "A facade merely. I've known her since she was all of eight years old. The female is a barbed-tongued little witch."

He chuckled and shook his head, but his laughter quickly faded as he spotted Rosalie on the dance floor. "There she is," he murmured, assessing her in her finery. She looked right at home amid the glittering *ton*. Her hair was stunning. A fiery sunset that drew the eye.

"Ah. She does polish up rather well, although I must confess I preferred how she appeared the other eve," Max mused beside him.

He shot his friend a quick glare. "How's that?"

"She was rather beddable looking . . . all soft and sleep-tousled. Bodes well that a female can look appealing when so little effort has been made with her appearance."

"I suppose," he allowed, wondering at the tight pull of his skin and the clench of his fists. He didn't like his friend looking at Rosalie that way . . . or talking about her in such a way. She was not some chit at Sodom for them to appraise.

" 'Tis true. Look around you. A good amount of sparkling doves in attendance . . . but they all required hours to accomplish such a feat. It's all illusion."

The orchestra slowed and he knew the song

was coming to an end. He inhaled and squared his shoulders. "Best see this done."

Max clapped him on the shoulder. "Try not to look so miserable. You might send her cowering into one of the ferns."

Somehow he found that unlikely. She'd already shown a fair amount of courage barging into his office in a fit of temper last week. Her fury had diminished. He'd watched it fade from her eyes as she reached the conclusion that a dowry—a season—wouldn't be so bad. She forgave his presumption. She was no fool. She recognized it was a boon.

He arrived at her side just as the final notes came to a close. He recognized her partner as Lord Strickland. The man was older but not infirm or decrepit. Of good family, he had nothing sordid or illicit associated with his name. Unlike himself, Declan thought. Aunt Peregrine would deem Strickland the perfect candidate and entirely eligible.

Lord Strickland's small, squinty eyes landed on him. "Your Grace, so good to see you. I've just had the pleasure of dancing with your sister—"

"Stepsister," he corrected, his gaze dropping to Rosalie. Color painted her cheeks at his quick declaration, making her freckles almost more pronounced, dark brown flecks in her usually porcelain complexion.

"Yes, quite," he uttered in that mumbling voice of his. "Well, she dances like an angel."

He nodded, his gaze riveted to Rosalie. She wouldn't meet his stare, instead training her attention somewhere just beyond his shoulder. Her disregard of him was blatant . . . and not a little annoying.

"Indeed, my lord. I shall have to see that for myself, then."

Her gaze snapped to his face as if shocked by his words, treating him to the full blast of her topaz eyes. If possible, those twin red flags on her cheeks burned brighter.

"Oh, quite right. You must, you must," Lord Strickland agreed effusively, stepping back with a wave.

Dec squared off in front of her and reached for her gloved hand, so small and slender. His bigger hand swallowed it. Her fingertips curled over the edge of his hand, and the corners of his mouth tugged upward as he gripped her waist. He tugged her closer. She came forward grudgingly. "I would almost think you didn't want to dance with me, Carrots."

"Don't call me that," she snapped.

He grinned then. Couldn't help himself. They danced for several moments. Strickland was right. She danced very well. It was more like she floated, skimming the floor, the only thing keeping her anchored was his hands.

"You might not want to appear so averse when someone calls me your sister."

His smile slipped. "You're not my sister."

Her gaze clashed with his. "And must you appear so vehement on that point? You're acting as my guardian and ushering me through the Season. You might not want your distaste to appear so obvious."

He stared down at her but said nothing. To be fair, he was not sure how he felt about her other than that he wanted her gone from his life. All his thoughts of her were tied too closely with his ill opinion of her mother. It was a tangled knot and he didn't see any way to separate the strands.

The music came to an end and she dropped his hand, stepping back hastily. "I think that served to adequately give me your endorsement. In case the dowry was not sufficient enough. My thanks, Your Grace." At those stiff words, she gave a hasty curtsy before weaving her way through the crowd, disappearing in the crush of bodies.

He slowly turned, glancing over his shoulder several times as if he would catch a glimpse of her.

"There now. Ready to go?" Max asked.

He nodded absently, trying to shake her from his thoughts and how she was nothing like he had imagined. Nothing like her cloying mother. Rosalie appeared almost as eager to be rid of him as he was of her.

"Yes. I'm finished here."

Chapter 8

*R*osalie flopped back on the bed with a heavy sigh. Her feet ached from another night of dancing. It had been much the same for close to a week now with no reprieve. Tonight was especially unpleasant, as she'd danced with a portly baronet with very little grace who trod all over her slippers.

She kicked off both slippers and rubbed her aching, stocking-clad toes. "Can we not have one night where we are not rushing off to some ball or party?" Releasing her foot, she speared her fingers through her hair, tugging the thick mass back from her head.

"You mean you're weary of it already?" Aurelia clucked. "Oh, dear. You are in trouble, then, for there is no foreseeable end to it. At least not this Season."

Rosalie propped herself up on her elbows and scowled down at her friend, reclining at the bottom of the bed. "You needn't sound so satisfied. You don't appear to be enjoying yourself either."

Aurelia grinned and shrugged. "I'm accustomed to it. You are not." She shook her head. She'd already unpinned her head, and the dark, rich waves tumbled around her shoulders. "I simply didn't think you would be quite so . . ."

"What?"

"Well . . . quite so much like me, honestly."

Rosalie cocked her head and started to pull the pins from her own hair, not bothering to wait for her maid. "And why does me being like you not sound like a compliment?"

Aurelia made a face. "There's a reason I'm still unwed."

"I thought you lost a year while you were in mourning and then another for half-mourning—"

"Yes, but I've had one Season. Last year. Mama was hoping for a match then."

"So how are we alike? Tell me." Rosalie pulled the last pin and shook her hair free with a soft moan of relief.

"I loathe the balls and parties. Perhaps not at first, but they soon became tedious. One is much like another. All the girls our age wax on and on of fashion and gossip. And the gentlemen . . ." She sighed, falling back on the settee edging Rosalie's bed to gaze forlornly up at the ceiling. "Have you met a single one to stir your blood?"

Rosalie stared at Aurelia for a moment, caught off guard from her candid speech. But that was only part of her hesitation. She was a little surprised to find that this elegant young lady, brought up with all the polish and advantages afforded one of high birth, wanted something else. Something more.

Aurelia glanced her way. "Come now. Be truthful."

Rosalie gave a nod, agreeing. "No. No, I have not. Not that I've spent much time with anyone besides Lord Strickland in the last week."

Aurelia grimaced. "Indeed. He did close in rather quickly on you, didn't he? You're simply too nice."

"Should I be impolite?" Rosalie demanded

helplessly. "I can't be caustic and sharp-tongued like—"

"Me?" Aurelia rolled to her side and pulled her knees to her chest, her pastel green skirts a pool around her as she faced Rosalie. The color did nothing for her friend's olive-toned complexion. Sadly, it made her look mildly ill.

They fell into silence, each lost in their thoughts.

Aurelia bit her lip until she finally said with a heavy exhale, "I don't suppose I can continue to behave that way either. Mama is at her end with me. She's complained to my brother . . . he's threatening to send me to live with my elderly Aunt Daphne in Scotland. Once there, I might as well give up all hope of ever . . ."

Her voice faded and Rosalie prodded, "Ever what?"

"Of ever experiencing adventure, love . . . a kiss that doesn't make me want to wipe my mouth off afterward."

Rosalie sat up anxiously. "Someone kissed you?"

"It happened last season. Archibald Lewis, the vicar's son, isn't that ironic? He snuck a kiss on me." She wrinkled her nose. "It tasted of fish and soured milk. Wretched experience. But that's beside the point." She fluttered a hand. Rosalie nodded, feeling a bit dizzy in her attempt to follow. "Wouldn't you want to know what a kiss felt like from someone who knew *how* to kiss? And isn't old enough to be our father? And doesn't look like the back end of a mule?

"Er, well. Yes."

"Me, too." Aurelia punched a fist into her palm. "It's simply not fair that my brother and Dec and that boor Camden can sow their oats to their hearts' content while we must wither on the vine, waiting to be plucked up by an eligible gentleman."

Rosalie shook her head. "But what can we do about it?"

Aurelia gestured wildly. "Something. Anything!" Her arms flopped at her sides. "If I'm to be sent to rusticate with Aunt Daphne until I'm old and dead, then I should blasted well live a *little* first." Her voice dropped to a conspiratorial pitch. "We should go to Sodom."

"Sodom? As in Sodom and Gomorrah? From the Bible?" Rosalie frowned, not sure if this was some *tonnish* expression she had yet to learn.

"It's a private club host to all manner of illicit activity."

Illicit activity? Her cheeks warmed even though she was not entirely certain what that meant.

Aurelia continued, "I've overheard Dec speak of it with Camden." She sat up on the settee, apparently warming to the subject. "You must be a member. Or get an invitation from a member." Her lips twisted wryly. "I'm sure no such invitation would be forthcoming from Dec."

Rosalie snorted, imagining her stepbrother's face if Aurelia approached him with such a request. "No. I imagine not."

"So we would have to secure memberships for ourselves. I've enough pin money set aside. I don't know the cost, but I'm sure we could manage some manner of temporary membership that—"

"Aurelia," Rosalie broke in. "Slow down a moment. You cannot be serious. Ladies of repute cannot attend such a—"

"I'm certain they *do*!" Aurelia nodded doggedly. "Wearing dominos, with no threat of discovery, why ever not?"

Rosalie stared at her, trying to process what she was suggesting and come up with a reason why this was the worst idea in the history of terrible ideas. She only arrived at: "You are serious."

Aurelia nodded. "I am quite serious." She scooted closer on the great big bed, her brown eyes luminous. "Will you not join me?"

"I—I—"

"Do you not crave a taste of adventure before you marry the likes of Lord Strickland?"

"I'm not marrying Lord Strickland," Rosalie was quick to object.

Aurelia sank back on the settee with an arch of her dark eyebrow, flopping her arm onto the bed where Rosalie's skirts pooled. She toyed with the pink fabric. "Indeed," she said mildly. "You're not? You're certain of this?" A decided glint entered her brown eyes.

Rosalie sat up a little straighter, crossing her legs beneath her voluminous skirts. "I think I would know who I will and won't marry."

Aurelia made a humming sound and crossed her arms over her chest. "I heard Strickland mention to Mama that he wished to call on Dec."

Rosalie said nothing for several moments as she processed this. "I'm sure it has nothing to do with me—"

Now Aurelia snorted. "It has *everything* to do with you. Did you think Mama and Dec were merely planning your social calendar for you? Oh, Rosalie," she tsked, and shook her head. "They're planning your life . . . right down to the groom."

Rosalie inhaled sharply through her nose. "You're mistaken."

Aurelia gave her a pitying look that seemed to say, *We shall see.*

Rosalie shook her head, a sick feeling starting in her stomach as she watched her companion rise from the bed and smooth down her skirts. "If you say so. Meanwhile, if you change your mind . . . I'm sure I can get us inside Sodom."

"Thank you, but I don't think so."

Aurelia groaned. "Oh, very well. I shall die a dusty old spinster with only the memory of Archibald Lewis's kiss to comfort me."

Rosalie fought down a grin. Aurelia was nothing if not entertaining. "Dusty and old are not words that come to mind in association with you. I doubt you'll behave old even when you are."

"Very well." Turning, she held up her hand and fluttered her fingers. "Good night."

"Good night," Rosalie murmured, rising to her feet as her maid entered the room, bypassing Aurelia.

She moved to stand before the mirror, gazing at her reflection as Sally moved behind her and began unhooking the tiny buttons on her gown.

"Good evening, miss," the maid said. "Have a nice time tonight?"

"Yes, Sally, thank you."

"You look lovely in this pink gown . . . so brilliant with your hair."

"Thank you, Sally."

"I'm sure all the gentlemen were tripping over themselves for you."

Rosalie winced and ran a hand down the brocade of her bodice. "Indeed. With my dowry how could they not?"

Sally cast her gaze down and fell silent at this and Rosalie regretted her words, regretted making the poor girl feel uncomfortable. Of course she knew of her outrageous dowry. All of Britain knew by now. That didn't give her cause to make the poor girl uneasy. She wasn't any of the countless gentlemen attempting to woo her.

Lord Strickland's chinless face floated before her mind. It was bad enough that he mildly repulsed her, but to know that he didn't even really want *her*, that he wouldn't be giving her the barest notice if not for the obscene dowry Dec had placed upon her . . .

It was galling. And yet a fact she would have to accept, dismal as it was. Any man she married would be marrying her for that reason and that reason alone.

In that moment, she understood Aurelia's motives for wanting to break free and do something bold and reckless. Such an act would be purely selfish. It would be about pleasure and fun. It wouldn't be about the wealth she brought to her husband. It wouldn't be about marrying for position or title. It would be an adventure.

Rosalie could understand the desire for that. She understood.

But she could never risk it.

"Ah, Your Grace, good morning. I was just coming to call on you."

Dec froze on the bottom step of his town house. His gaze collided with Lord Strickland as he descended from his carriage and stopped before him. He nodded warily. "Strickland. What brings you here?

"Your sister," Lord Strickland began, removing his gloves and twisting them nervously.

Bloody hell. What had the chit done now?

He reluctantly waved in the general direction of his front door, not bothering to correct Strickland again. The man seemed determined to view Rosalie as his sister rather than stepsister. "Shall we discuss this inside?"

The man nodded swiftly and followed Dec inside. He waved off the butler who stepped forward to take Strickland's coat and offer refreshments. Hopefully, this would not take long and he could still keep his appointment at Jackson's Saloon.

He closed the door to his office and took position near the great hearth, waiting with a knot of dread in his chest, quite convinced he was about to hear some tirade regarding Rosalie. And what could he expect? Stuck in that school for so many years, she was not precisely trained in the nuances of Society.

He nodded grimly at Strickland as the man flipped back the tails of his jacket and sat rather stiffly on the edge of the chaise. He tugged on his collar and began in his mumbling voice, "This is quite . . . awkward. I've never done anything like this before—"

"Strickland." The earl's eyes shot to Dec's face. "Just spit it out."

"Quite. Quite so." He nodded doggedly and cleared his throat. "I would like to request the honor of your daughter—er, I mean sister's hand in marriage."

Dec stared.

Strickland flushed and continued, his words a nearly unintelligible ramble. "I realize I have only made her acquaintance, but I've found her to be very amenable. I think she is absolutely the sweetest creature on earth—"

"Rosalie?" he bit out before he could consider his tone.

"Indeed. She is the kindest—"

"Rosalie?"

The earl nodded, his chin lost somewhere in his neck. "I'm not the only one paying particular attention to her—"

"You're not?" Other than the night he'd danced with her at the Coltons' ball, Dec had left her in his aunt's hands, ignoring his aunt's requests for him to join them again. He'd deemed it unnecessary, assuming Aunt Peregrine was quite capable of ushering the girl about Town. Apparently he had been correct. His aunt had proven herself *very* adept. Perhaps *too* much. The girl had already garnered a proposal.

He quickly squashed his annoyance with his aunt. She had accomplished for Rosalie what she had not yet accomplished with her own daughter. She was to be commended. He was free of her.

He realized that Strickland was still talking. " . . . so I wanted to be the first to declare myself." His smile wobbled and he looked a little sheepish. "I imagine she will attract other offers, but—"

"I accept."

"Wh-What?"

"Rosalie will be honored, I am certain."

Strickland blinked. "Truly?"

Dec nodded, ignoring the small niggle of discomfort at the back of his throat. This was what he wanted. The fact that it happened sooner than expected was a boon he should not examine too closely. Strickland was a good man. He came from good family. He was reputed to be a gentleman. Certainly, Dec had never seen him at Sodom or any of the other less than reputable places he had frequented over the years. She could do much worse. *She could have ended up with someone like you.*

The thought came unbidden, and he shoved it aside. He'd never agree for her to marry a man of his ilk. It would be unconscionable. She might be Melisande's daughter, but he would do his duty by her and make certain she only joined with an honorable man.

He focused on Strickland again. Once again the man was babbling, his hands moving rapidly with his enthusiasm as he discussed a spring wedding.

Dear God. Did Strickland actually think he gave a damn over the wedding particulars? He pushed off from where he leaned against the mantel.

"You've my blessing. I leave you to discuss plans with my aunt."

"Very good, Your Grace." The much shorter man seized his hand and pumped it in a handshake several times, simultaneously clapping Dec on the back. For one terrible moment it actually looked as though the man would hug him.

"Congratulations, Strickland." He extricated himself and made his way to the door. "I believe you can locate my aunt in the salon. Rosalie will likely be with her. You're family now. You're welcome to find your way there and tell them the happy news."

Strickland ran a hand over his bald, perspiring scalp. "Indeed. I shall go find them directly."

"Good day." Turning on his heels, he strode from the room, from the house, not considering the clipped pace of his stride. Or that he found himself looking over his shoulder several times, watching as the earl practically skipped toward the salon. Or that his stomach churned like he had just consumed a bad bit of fish.

She would be a countess. He had done his duty by her. And some.

Any female would be thrilled from such an arrangement. *He* should be thrilled.

A vigorous bout at Jackson's Saloon would do him some good. Suddenly, he felt the need to unleash himself.

"I beg your pardon, my lord?" Rosalie's hands curled into fists in her lap. "Could you repeat yourself?"

Certainly she had misheard. Or misunderstood.

In fact, nothing Strickland had said since he entered the salon made a dash of sense to her. Nor did she even quite understand his unexpected presence here at all. He had not mentioned calling upon her last night, and on the heels of her conversation with Aurelia, she was not feeling kindly disposed to his sudden appearance.

"We're to be married!" Strickland dropped beside her on the sofa where she sat before the fireplace, a book forgotten in her lap. For once, his speech rang clear and loud.

She looked from his eager countenance to Aunt Peregrine and Aurelia, who stared back at her with a cocked eyebrow that seemed to say: *See there, I told you so.*

"Are you mad?" The words escaped without deliberation. It was simply the only thought in her head.

Aunt Peregrine gasped. An irreverent laugh escaped Aurelia, which she quickly silenced by slapping a hand over her mouth.

Strickland blinked, his smile slipping ever so slightly. "Er, what . . . Uh, no. I spoke with your brother—"

"Stepbrother," she snapped.

He inclined his head at the error. "I only just spoke with him moments ago and he accepted—"

"He told you I would marry you?"

Strickland stared at her as if unsure how to proceed, his mouth parted like a gaping fish.

She demanded again, the point very important to her, "*He* told you I would marry you?

At last, he nodded and found his voice. "Indeed. Quite happily so, he gave us his blessing."

The wretch! She pounded a fist into her lap, indifferent to the book sliding from her lap to the carpet.

"Rosalie," Aunt Peregrine scolded.

She vaulted to her feet, ignoring the warning. "Without even asking me?" She flattened a hand to her chest. It was inconceivable that he would accept an offer without consulting her.

She began pacing the room, heedless of anything in that moment save for Dec's utter gall . . . his arrogance. She should have known this would come about. He was the one who decided to give her a Season and a dowry without consulting her, after all. All with the express purpose of winning her a husband. It stood to reason that he would accept the offer on her behalf.

"My lord," Lady Peregrine began in a placating tone. "Miss Hughes is simply surprised . . . delighted . . . but surprised. I am certain you understand."

Aurelia snorted and muttered indiscreetly into her hand, "More like *disgusted*."

Fuming, Rosalie reached for her composure and sucked in a calming breath. Before she did anything else, she must dispel the notion that she would be marrying Lord Strickland, and she needed to do that as graciously as possible. Stopping, she faced him and forced a brittle smile. "I am truly honored. You humble me with your offer, but I'm afraid I cannot accept, my lord."

Aunt Peregrine cleared her throat in the sudden silence. "Rosalie, dear—"

She held up a hand, cutting off Lady Peregrine. She held the earl's gaze, waiting for him to say something.

Strickland blustered, his face flushed varying shades of red. "But your brother—"

"My *stepbrother* was working under the misapprehension that he has the authority to accept marriage proposals on my behalf. I apologize for any embarrassment this has caused you."

"Apologize! Apologize!" Strickland lurched to his feet. "I should say so!" He wagged a finger at her. "I was under the impression you welcomed my suit . . . your brother—"

"Stepbrother," she interjected, not that he paused for breath to acknowledge his mistake.

"—made a fool of me by accepting my offer of marriage before the words had even left my lips. He was that eager to be rid of you!"

The words shouldn't have stung. They shouldn't have.

She shook her head. "I am very sorry . . . I just do not feel we suit, my lord."

He stormed toward the door and yanked it open, rattling the wood on its hinges. "Indeed! We do not! I should have known better to consider anyone connected with Banbury! He's a morally repugnant scoundrel unfit for good company! Duke or no duke! Any sister of his is equally tarnished, I'm quite certain. And there is the matter of your mother." His lip curled. "If half the rumors of her misdeeds are true, I was quite cracked in the head to consider you for a bride." With that parting shot, he stormed out of the room.

They held silent for some moments, staring at the empty door.

"Well," Aurelia began—no surprise she should find her voice first. "I suppose that tirade nursed his wounded ego."

"Let us hope." Lady Peregrine sighed. "Oh, Rosalie, what have you done? He shall not have kind words to say of you! He's probably on the way to his club to share with everyone how— "

"He'll do no such thing. He's a proud little peacock and will not wish to advertise his shame," Aurelia interjected. "And her dowry will not slow the flow of suitors pursuing her."

Rosalie settled her gaze on them both. "What I have done is establish that I alone shall choose my husband."

Lady Peregrine shot accusing eyes to her daughter. "Is this your doing?"

Aurelia held up both hands, palms facing out. "Do not look at me. I didn't tell her to reject him."

Rosalie dragged in a deep breath, expanding her lungs. Anger simmered in her blood, ready to burst free, looking for release. There was only one person who deserved it. "Where is he?"

Lady Peregrine shifted on her chair, looking uneasy. She began petting her fat tabby cat faster. The animal meowed plaintively and stared unblinking at Rosalie. Almost accusingly. As though the beast knew Rosalie was responsible for the rough treatment.

"I heard him mention to the housekeeper that he was going to be gone all day and not to wait dinner for him," Aurelia volunteered. "You shall have to wait to vent your spleen, although I hope I can stand witness. Please?" She turned to her mother. "I'm so glad we came here. This is the most entertainment I've had in . . . well, ever." She frowned, her shoulders slumping a little. "Oh, that's a depressing thought. I really do lead a dull existence."

Rosalie resumed her pacing. This was really beyond the pale. If Dec thought he could plan her life, her future, right down to her husband, then she would dissuade him of that notion posthaste.

"Rosalie, you're giving me a neck ache." Aunt Peregrine motioned to her neck. "Seat yourself. Let us talk this through."

Shaking her head, she sank back down on the settee. "There is nothing to discuss. I will have a say in who I marry—no, *I* will *choose*." She patted her chest.

Lady Peregrine looked at her rather sadly, slowing her death pet on Lady Snuggles. "What were you expecting, my dear? A knight on a white horse? Strickland would have been a brilliant match . . . do you hope for better, then?"

Yes.

Why did she feel so wrong admitting that? Why was it wrong to want more? She had hoped for better. If not love, then something close. Affection at least.

She met Aunt Peregrine's suddenly grim stare and read her thoughts perfectly. Just for good measure, she added, "Not better precisely." She was such a coward. She couldn't even state the truth of her desires. "Simply different. I want something more."

"More?" Lady Peregrine shook her head. "You sound like Aurelia here." She tsked. "Don't let her fill your head with foolish ideas."

A marriage of her choosing? That was so foolish, then.

Realization dawned. She finally understood. This jaunt down the marriage mart—she was never expected to voice an opinion through any of it. Her fate was to be decided by Dec all along. That was the price to be paid for the gift of a dowry.

This was her fate, then. Spinsterhood or a loveless marriage to the likes of Strickland.

Only she did not even have the luxury of

spinsterhood to fall back on. Her fate was less secure than Aurelia's. She did not have an elderly aunt in need of a companion. Or Will for a brother who would always see to her care. She had her mother. And Dec. Neither of whom wanted her around. Her mother neglected her for years and Dec had tossed her to the first suitor to come calling.

She looked with singular focus at Aurelia, trying to convey what she was thinking, *feeling*, in one look—what she dared not declare in front of Lady Peregrine.

Aurelia's eyes widened and her lips parted in a surprised little O.

Rosalie nodded once. Swift and emphatic, sending her friend a silent message.

She wanted more. And she was willing to take a risk to get it.

Chapter 9

The house was silent when Dec returned later that night. He'd stayed away all day, through dinner and after, having no desire to return home to a house full of women chattering on about wedding plans.

His tread fell silently over the runner, his movements slightly stiff. He'd taken a beating today at Jackson's and his knuckles were tender along with the side of his torso, but he didn't regret it. It had helped. For a time at least. It always did—always helped chase the numbness that seemed to encase him every day of his life. He felt in those moments. Even if it was painful. Pounding his fists into another man's flesh and taking another's blows into his body always made him feel alive.

He was almost to his bedchamber door when the door to the chamber two down from his was flung open. "Finally. I've been waiting for you all day, Your Grace."

He turned, watching in bewilderment as Rosalie advanced on him, her arms folded across her chest like some sort of militant headmistress.

"You've been waiting for me?" He arched a dark eyebrow. "Whatever for?"

Her topaz eyes flashed gold fire. "How dare you accept a marriage proposal on my behalf?"

She stopped before him and he looked down at her, his bewilderment no less abated. As if realizing how close she stood—and how much larger and taller he was, she stepped hastily back one pace.

He leaned against his door, crossing his arms in much the same manner as her pose. "Was marriage not the idea? I thought we were in agreement on that. Why else would I have bestowed a dowry on your head? Sent for my aunt to usher you through the Season."

"Marriage, fine. Yes. I understood that was the

goal, but that does not give you the right to choose who I will or will not marry. You are not my father. I make that decision. Me." She pressed a hand to her chest, drawing his attention to the slight swell of her breasts beneath the modest nightgown.

He slowly lifted his gaze back to her face. "And I take it you do not approve of Strickland?"

"He is not my choice, no," she bit out. "A fact that you might have discovered if you had only but asked me."

"Fine," he bit out. "Far be it from me to force you to wed anyone against your will. This is not the dark ages."

She blinked. "Y-You will not attempt to coerce—"

"As you said, I'm not your father."

She nodded, eyeing him uncertainly. Did she think him such a monster that he would force her to the altar against her will?

He unclenched his jaw to add, "No, not your father—merely the man whose pockets you prevail upon whilst you go about on your merry quest to find a husband to your specifications. Tell me, have you any notion how long it will take you to find this paragon of manhood good enough to tempt your lofty personage to the altar?"

She pulled back, clearly affronted. The color

rode high in her cheeks and her eyes sparked. "You mock me?"

He feigned an innocent look. "Never."

"I was not aware there was a time limit. Perhaps you should alert me how long I have, Your Grace?"

She spat his title like it was an epithet. She was maddening.

A humorless smile tugged at the corner of his mouth. Had she always been so insufferable? "I simply hope you do not intend to drag this out into next Season." He motioned around him. "This is a bachelor residence. Precisely how I like it and hope to soon reclaim it."

"Indeed." That nose went up a notch and the motion sent her hair tumbling back over her shoulders. He eyed the fiery banner falling over her shoulder, undulating in waves to the middle of her back. His hands curled at his sides, itching to touch, to feel the mass, to see if it felt as soft as it looked. A sudden image of him wrapping a fist around it and tugging her head back for—

He shook his head once, hard, knocking the thought out of his head.

She kept talking, looking so indignant, that impertinent mouth of hers moving like she was the aggrieved party and not he. "My apologies for being such an imposition . . . perhaps my mother will return—"

He huffed a breath. "Do not rely upon your mother." The very suggestion sent a flash of annoyance through him. "I think you would have learned that lesson by now."

"But I'm to rely on you?" she rejoined, her expression skeptical.

"Your odds are better relying upon me, yes. Your headmistress knew that. That's why she left you here."

She held his gaze for a long moment, her lips parted slightly. Her breath, he noticed, seemed to fall a little faster. As if this entire encounter agitated her . . . affected her. Was it just that he had angered her by accepting Strickland's offer? Or was it more than that? He seriously doubted the same manner of inappropriate thoughts tripping through his head even crossed her mind.

She clearly lacked the experience to entertain such lascivious ideas. She probably wouldn't even know what to do with that impertinent mouth of hers. His gaze fixed on the plump bottom lip. Her top lip was equally appealing . . . dipping deeply at the center, sharply delineating her lips. He was tempted to lean forward and lick that mouth, trace their fascinating shape with his tongue.

The sudden impulse made his cock stir and strain against his breeches. He shifted where he stood, willing his arousal down. *Bloody hell*. This was inopportune. Especially with her looking at him as though he was something to be scraped off the bottom of her boot. Perhaps he should have stopped off at Sodom and eased himself in some willing female. He was overdue a visit there.

He slid his gaze down the long length of corridor before returning his eyes to her. They were alone, but anyone could hear them and emerge. He really should end this conversation. Restraint wasn't his strong suit. Especially concerning females. His body was having a hard time acknowledging his mind's instructions that this one was off-limits.

She moistened her lips, her eyes gleaming brightly with bitter emotion. "Sad testament to my life, is it not? That you are the only one I can rely on." Instead of looking sad or pitiable, she actually appeared furious over the circumstances of her life. He drank in the sight of her—unbound hair, cheeks afire, eyes bright with emotion, and, the thought slipped in, unbidden, treacherous, *unpardonable* . . .

Was this how she would look beneath him, moving and arching as he buried himself deep?

He sucked in a breath. The sudden thought startled him. Felt more jarring than a fist to his ribs—and he knew precisely how that felt. He'd taken several such blows today.

"We all have our burdens to bear," he replied, his hand moving to the latch on his door, suddenly anxious to flee her and the image that was now branded on his brain.

He did not *like* her. Any more than she liked him. He did not want her here, in his life.

And he most especially did not want *her*.

Very well. That last part was a lie. He wanted her. But no more than any other sweet-smelling female of passing good looks.

He enjoyed women. All manner of women. He liked them short. Tall. Brunettes. Fair-haired. His gaze skimmed her hair again. *Carrot-haired.*

As long as they were willing and enthusiastic, they served to chase the numbness, for however long the tryst lasted, at least. Which was perhaps why he never went long without a tryst.

His mind backtracked and it suddenly dawned

on him that he hadn't slaked his lusts on a woman in a fortnight. That explained his over-active libido in her presence. A matter he should correct. Perhaps then he would cease to wonder what Rosalie would feel like beneath him.

He shifted his feet and the action pulled at something tender in his side. He winced at the ache, a hand moving to his ribs.

Her gaze shot from his face to his hand. "Are you injured?"

"'Tis nothing." He forced his hand down to his side.

Frowning, she reached out as though to touch him. He stepped back a pace, dodging her hand, and the sudden move had him wincing again.

"You *are* hurt," she insisted. "Shall I ring for a physician?"

"'Tis nothing."

She eyed him skeptically, half turning with the clear intention to hunt down a servant on his behalf.

He sighed. "I visited Jackson's Saloon today."

Her blank stare conveyed that this meant nothing to her.

"Gentlemen visit there when they wish to box."

"Box?" she echoed. "As in pugilism?"

He nodded.

"You mean you let someone strike you with his fists?"

He squared back his shoulders. "I manage a few blows of my own."

"That's savage and—and idiotic."

He stiffened, quite certain no one had ever called him that before. Scoundrel, yes. Rake, yes. His father had a few choice words for him, but never idiotic. "I don't recall asking for your opinion."

"Inviting bodily injury can be called nothing else. Why on earth would you desire such a thing? Would you care to stick your hand in this door?" She waved a hand toward his chamber door. "I can slam it on you several times."

He looked heavenward before leveling his gaze on her again. "There would be no sport in that, now would there?"

With a growl of disgust, she reached for him again. "Let me see."

"What? No!" He sidestepped her hands. "It's not that bad."

"How do you know you haven't broken a rib?"

He snatched hold of her wrists, trapping them between their bodies. Bodies, he realized, that were suddenly much too close. His nostrils flared, catching the scent of her. Clean, sweet female. No cloying perfumes. She watched him mildly, clearly unaffected at their proximity, immune, unaware of how close he was to shedding restraint and doing what he did best when he had a woman this close to him.

"I know," he managed to get out between his clenched teeth, "because I've suffered a broken rib before. 'Tis nothing."

Her eyes flitted over his face before lowering to where his fingers locked around her wrists, easily spanning them. He flexed his grip. Her bones felt so slight and small, as though the barest pressure could snap them. He quickly released her, adding distance between them once again.

"I think you've said all there is to be said," he declared after an awkward silence.

She rubbed her wrists as though trying to rid herself of the memory of his touch, and the gesture pricked at his pride. "That's it. You're dismissing me, then?"

"You've made your point. I shall never presume to accept a marriage proposal on your behalf again."

"Indeed." Nodding jerkily, she pressed her lips into a defiant line and marched into her room, shutting the door not too gently behind her. If his aunt and cousin were asleep, then they no longer were.

He began to turn for his room, but then stopped. His cock still felt uncomfortably hard in his breeches. There would be no sleep for him. With a curse, he turned and strode back down the stairs, intent on rectifying the matter.

Perhaps, then, the next time he found himself alone with his stepsister he wouldn't fantasize about burying his nose in all that soft-looking hair as he sank into her body.

"Rosalie! Are you asleep?"

The query came loud, for all that it was whispered through her door.

"If I was, then I am no longer," she groused, sitting up from where she had flung herself across the bed not so long ago, still troubled over her encounter with Dec.

What was wrong with the man, that he sought out physical pain? A sensible man would avoid such abuse. There was nothing sensible about him. She did not understand him. Not at all. Nor did she understand the undeniable pull she felt toward him. True, he was offering her a roof over her head . . . a Season, a dowry, but he was not a kind man for all of that. He was hard. Rude and curt and high-handed. And yet when she was near him, she wanted to stand closer. Those big hands on her wrists . . .

She wanted to feel them again. There and elsewhere . . .

The door opened. Aurelia hurried across the room, an abundance of white fabric in her arms.

"What have you there?" She nodded at the profusion of white.

"A gown." Her friend dropped it on the bed, and it was then that Rosalie was given the full impact of Aurelia's attire.

She was not garbed in her nightgown . . . although a nightgown might have been more modest than the black ensemble she wore. The dark fabric complimented her olive-hued skin much better than the pastels she usually wore. It was scandalously low-cut and lacked the fullness of a skirt, as was current fashion. It was very Grecian in style, and form-hugging. Which for Aurelia, with her ample bosom and curves, was almost criminal. Typically, her clothes made her look plump, but in this gown, the truth of her narrow waist and lush, womanly curves was on full display.

"What are you wearing?"

"A gown. Do you like it?" She smoothed a hand over her rounded hip. "This one is for you. Hopefully it fits." Aurelia pointed at the lump of white fabric on the bed.

Rosalie reached for the garment and held it up between her fingertips to see that it, too, was in the same style. The fabric very fine and diaphanous. "Where did you get these? They're scandalous."

"I did it."

Rosalie stared at her uncomprehendingly. "What?"

She continued. "I went to Sodom. This afternoon. I called on the proprietress, Mrs. Bancroft, all by myself."

Rosalie lurched up on the bed on her knees. "You did what?"

Aurelia nodded, her brown curls looking almost as black as her dress. "She met with me in her private office. Oh, Rosalie, she was ever so sophisticated. She promised us discretion."

"You are serious?"

Aurelia frowned. "Were you not? Earlier today. I did not mistake your meaning, did I?"

Rosalie shook her head. "No . . . I am . . . I am ready for . . ."

What precisely? Was she ready for Sodom?

"Oh, excellent! I do not know if I could have gone it alone." Aurelia exhaled and then snatched Rosalie's dress back from her. "Come. I'll help you into your gown. My maid, Cecily, will fetch us a hack around back. And look. Mrs. Bancroft gave us these. To protect our identities on this adventure."

Aurelia nodded to the two dominos she had dropped on the bed. Rosalie lifted the masks. One was black and the other red.

"I think I should wear the red . . . offer some contrast with my black gown. And the same purpose should serve for you with the black. Don't you think?"

Rosalie lifted the midnight-dark mask to her face, fingering the satin that stretched over the stiffer brocade.

"Oh, that looks splendid." Aurelia hopped where she stood for a moment, jiggling her breasts so much that they looked dangerously close to spilling free of her scandalously tight bodice. "And let us not forget these." She waved two wigs in the air.

"Wha—"

"Mrs. Bancroft said it will help protect your identity. And with your very recognizable hair, it's really a must. I'll take this lovely golden wig. You wear the black one. It's very Cleopatra, no? With your white gown . . . perfect!"

Rosalie fingered the sleek black strands, excitement humming low in her belly. *She was really doing this.*

Aurelia clapped her hands. "Let's get you in the dress first, shall we? No corset, mind you. It won't look right."

Rosalie's gaze snapped up to her face. "No corset?"

Aurelia stretched out the scrap of bodice between her hands as though that served as explanation enough. "Come. Let's simply see, shall we?"

She permitted Aurelia to help her undress and slip into the gown. Turning, she could scarcely breathe as her friend buttoned the tiny rows of buttons at her back. It had nothing to do with the fit of the dress, either. It was all nerves. The riot of butterflies in her belly.

What am I doing?

"Oh, and these stockings! We mustn't forget these."

Rosalie put them on, blanching at the decadent pair of sheer stockings—nothing like the serviceable, modest ones she always wore. These were thin as cobwebs with a thin strip of lace running up the outside of her thighs. She shifted, stunned at the decadent sensation of the material on her bare legs. Aurelia helped her tie them off with lacy garters.

"There. Now . . . the wig." She struggled for some moments, knotting Rosalie's hair close to the base of her scalp before securing the wig in place. The dark strands swished sleekly just past Rosalie's shoulders.

Aurelia stood back and waved her arms with a flourish. "Oh! You look like some princess from an ancient era, ready for seduction. See for yourself."

On shaking legs, Rosalie moved to stand before the mirror. Her mouth parted on a gasp.

A stranger stared back at her. The white material clung indecently, appearing soft, beckoning the hand. The bodice dipped so low it revealed not only the top swells of her breasts but the pale, smooth expanse of skin between the small mounds. She even imagined she could make out the dusky outline of her nipples beading against the white fabric. The black mask was startling a stark contrast against the creamy canvas of skin and gown.

The dark wig framing her face altered what was visible of her features, creating the illusion of bigger eyes, coal-dark and faintly exotic within the domino.

Denial surged on her lips. She couldn't go out like this. But then the realization sank in that she enjoyed it . . . the way she looked excited her. Filled her with courage and emboldened her.

And no one had to know it was her.

Smiling, she faced Aurelia. "Now let's finish you off and be gone from here."

Chapter 10

The town house loomed three stories high. It was located in a good neighborhood. Modest. Nothing lavish. A middle-class home of white-washed brick, well-maintained.

It certainly did not appear to be a place where illicit activities took place night after night.

They stepped down from the hack to a quiet street. Lights blazed from windows and outside front door sconces, but there was no line of people beating a path to the door.

She glanced at Aurelia. "Are you certain this is the place?"

"Yes. I paid a call to Mrs. Bancroft here this very afternoon. Come along." With an encouraging smile, she clasped Rosalie's hand and led her up the steps to the front door.

It was promptly answered at their knock.

"Ladies?" A butler greeted them with a very correct nod of his head.

Aurelia offered the card Mrs. Bancroft had given her to present at the door.

He accepted the card and stepped aside, waving them in. A footman stepped forward to take their cloaks. She resisted the impulse to cover herself with her hands. Her skin had never felt so much air before. "This way."

They followed him down a narrow corridor that opened up onto a larger room. A crowded room. At their arrival, heads turned to assess them. Avid, hungry eyes. She shifted her weight. As uneasy as she felt to find herself under such scrutiny, she was not the only female dressed so scandalously.

In fact, heat crawled up her throat as her gaze arrested on one female sitting on a sofa, squashed between two gentlemen. One kissed her whilst the other suckled at her bare breasts.

She and Aurelia stood frozen, eyeing the decadent scene.

"Ladies." A well-dressed woman in an elaborate peacock-feathered mask approached. She took Aurelia's hands warmly in her own. "So glad you could attend this evening. You both look lovely. So glad to see the dresses fit you so charmingly. And the wigs . . . very becoming. And this must be your friend." She turned a smile on Rosalie. "Hello, I'm Mrs. Bancroft."

"Delighted to meet you." Rosalie tried to smile, but her gaze continued to dart about the room at so many couples caught in amorous embraces.

"This is our sitting room, where everyone meets and greets each other," the proprietress explained. "There are several more specialized rooms throughout the house." She hesitated, surveying what must have been their astonished expressions. A female from some corner of the room let out a screech.

"What's that?" Aurelia asked. "Is she unwell?"

Mrs. Bancroft laughed. "Oh, she is quite well." Still grinning, she turned. "Come, my two wide-eyed little birds. Let us begin with baby steps, shall we? There is a room that might suit you on your first time here."

Rosalie released a grateful breath and followed Mrs. Bancroft and Aurelia from the room, side-stepping a man's hand that reached for her as she bypassed him.

In the quiet corridor, Mrs. Bancroft led them up another set of stairs. "We have private rooms upstairs for, as I mentioned, specialized activities as well as private assignations. Whatever penchant, we aim to satisfy here."

As they cleared the landing, Mrs. Bancroft motioned to the right. "These rooms are for those private assignations I mentioned." She motioned to the left and bid them to follow. She opened the door to a dim room suffused with deep red light from two red-screened lanterns. A large window opened to another bedroom where two people copulated.

"Oh, my!" Rosalie whirled around, presenting her back.

Mrs. Bancroft chuckled lightly. "This room is for people who like to watch. Don't worry, this couple enjoys being observed . . . they crave an audience."

"I—I don't think I want to see this," Rosalie hastily murmured.

"Good heavens," Aurelia breathed, facing the couple, her eyes enormous in her face. "I—I . . . I had no idea . . ."

"I think one of you appreciates the view," Mrs. Bancroft murmured with a wry twist of her lips beneath her vibrant mask. The mask was elaborate and riveting and almost the sole point of focus in her face. For some reason, in that moment Rosalie suspected that Mrs. Bancroft valued anonymity as much as they did. Very curious indeed for an owner of a house such as Sodom.

The proprietress fully faced Rosalie then as Aurelia continued to watch the scene through the window with her mouth agape. "What is it you hoped to experience tonight? Everyone's desires vary . . . they come to Sodom for different reasons. What is your desire, my dear?" Her voice was throaty and low, an intoxicating purr that simultaneously enticed and put one at ease. Rosalie could only imagine that served her well in her particular brand of business.

"I . . ." She shook her head, unsure of herself. What did she want?

The lady's keen eyes studied her for several moments before saying kindly, "Perhaps you wish to leave—"

"No," she said quickly, certain she did not want that. "For the first time in my life, I'm doing something . . . bold." Something brave. She came here looking for a taste of adventure. She would not flee now. "I don't want to leave before I've experienced anything for myself."

"Ah. You wish for an experience. You've come to

the right place." Mrs. Bancroft nodded as though she understood, which was bewildering since Rosalie had yet to fully understand what it was she was looking for. Or perhaps she did know. She simply could not put it into words. Embarrassment and modesty and inexperience stopped her.

The woman in the adjoining room cried out suddenly, a great shuddering moan that reverberated on the air and sent a ripple of gooseflesh across her skin. It was like a whole army of butterflies erupted there, set loose from a cage.

"I . . ." Rosalie paused, moistening her lips. "I think I should like to be kissed . . . by someone . . ." Her voice faded beneath Mrs. Bancroft's knowing regard.

"By someone who knows how?" she finished for her.

She nodded. "No more than that, I think . . . I've no wish to be ruined . . ."

"Am I to assume you've never been kissed before?"

"No. I haven't."

"We shall rectify that, then."

"I don't want to go beyond—"

Mrs. Bancroft nodded with alacrity. "Understood. We can find an accommodating gentleman, I'm sure."

"Someone handsome," Aurelia chimed in, glancing over at them as if this sudden important thought had just occurred to her. She looked at Rosalie with raised brows. "You don't want an Archibald Lewis slobbering all over you." She shuddered before dragging her attention back to the trysting couple, her mouth parting with continued astonishment at the scene.

"Of course." Mrs. Bancroft nodded. "For your first kiss, we wouldn't settle for less than a handsome man who knows what he's about."

Rosalie nodded as well, her face overly warm.

"And what of you, dear?" Mrs. Bancroft queried of Aurelia.

"I'm content to watch. For now."

"Very well." She fluttered her fingers at Rosalie, beckoning her forward. "Come along."

With one last glance at her friend, Rosalie followed the elegant lady from the room and down the corridor to the private rooms. Mrs. Bancroft opened one door and motioned her inside.

"If you'll wait in here, I'll return shortly."

Rosalie nodded, her shoulders knotting tensely.

Mrs. Bancroft hesitated at the door. "Don't worry. I guarantee, you will enjoy yourself. That's the promise of Sodom. Pleasure only."

With those parting words, she slipped from the

room. The door clicked softly behind her. Rosalie rotated where she stood, eyeing her room. Like the last one, dim red lighting suffused the cozy space. A bed overflowing with pillows and an inviting-looking fur blanket sat in the center. Coal glowed in the grate. After a few moments she moved to sit on the edge of the bed, folding her shivering hands in her lap, wondering how long she would have to wait . . . wondering who Mrs. Bancroft would bring with her.

Wondering if she had the courage not to flee through the door before Mrs. Bancroft returned with the man who would be her first kiss.

Dec prowled restlessly through the second floor of Sodom, moving between rooms, searching for something to satisfy the ache, the need . . . to dispel the numbness. He'd been here for a while now and was on the verge of giving up. So far, nothing had enticed him. No one. For once it did not appear he could chase away the numbness in a female's arms. A matter of some concern, as the only thing left for him was to take another pounding in the ring.

He stepped from a room where three women had just invited him to join him on a bed. He didn't know what he was in the mood for, but it wasn't that.

An image of Rosalie as he'd last seen her outside his bedchamber door flashed across his mind, but he quickly dismissed it. She was not an option.

"Ah, Banbury. How good to see you."

He smiled as Mrs. Bancroft approached. He took her hand and bowed over it, kissing the back. "Mrs. Bancroft, how good to see you and how lovely you look." A statement both true and untrue as he had never fully seen her face. Several ladies donned masks at Sodom, but the proprietress herself was perhaps the most veiled. Her masks were always elaborate and covered half of her face. A fact that only made her more intriguing. As was the fact that her gowns were stylish but as modest as the most conservative old dames of the *ton*. She was a contradiction. The proprietress of a house of sin disguised and garbed modestly. Her voice was youthful, as was the trim figure covered from neck to ankle. Every man here wanted a peek under her skirts.

"You flatter, Banbury." Her hand fluttered elegantly. "Have you not found a diversion to occupy you this eve yet?"

"Still on the hunt." He grinned. "No worries. I shall find something to amuse myself." Even if that something meant returning to Jackson's for another taste of abuse.

"I may have something for you." She smoothed a hand down the flat front of his jacket. *"Someone."*

"Indeed?" His gaze skimmed her consideringly. "Would the infamous Mrs. Bancroft finally be interested in entertaining one of her patrons herself?" As attentive as the lady was to the needs of all her guests, she never once offered herself up as part of the menu. As far as he knew, no patron had sampled her favors.

"No." Her lips curled beneath the edge of her feathered mask. "As tempting as you are . . . no, I have another proposition for you. One that I suspect might intrigue a man of your select tastes."

"You have my attention. Continue."

Turning, she headed down the corridor, past rooms that barely contained the cries and moans of the people within. He fell into step beside her.

"There is a young lady here . . . a novice, quite untried. She seeks nothing more than a kiss."

He hesitated. "A kiss. Seems a bit tame for—"

"A first kiss," she qualified. "And nothing more."

He fell back in pace with her. He needed more than a kiss to assuage his needs.

"You would be doing me a great favor. I know your tastes run to the more experienced encounters, but does not the idea titillate? A woman's first kiss."

"It . . . intrigues," he admitted. At least it would be different. Unpredictable. Little surprised him anymore. The kisses of an experienced lover had become predictable. As common in flavor as honey in his tea.

"And who knows? She might change her mind. She might want more than a kiss if you sweep her off her feet." She slanted him a challenging look. "There is some challenge in that, is there not, Your Grace?"

His skin tightened, thinking about that. He wasn't one of those men who relished breaking in untried misses. At least he never had been before. But the idea of Rosalie had perhaps altered his perception. Breaking *her* in? She'd tempted him this night. Fed his hunger in a way he had not felt in a long time. Too long.

"Why not?" He shrugged. Perhaps this would warm him up and he could sate himself on another female later.

"Brilliant. She's waiting in here." She stopped at the door, one hand on the latch. "I trust you to be a gentleman, Banbury. When she wishes to stop—"

"I've never forced my attentions on a woman. I won't begin now."

She smiled widely, as if he had just impressed

her. "Just as I thought. You are a true gentleman, Your Grace."

He stifled a snort. He did not count himself a gentleman, but considering the ilk of gentlemen to run through this house, perhaps in her mind he was.

She cracked the door, motioned for him to enter, and then backed away with a little flutter of her fingers, her smile somewhat secretive and bemused. As though she knew something he didn't.

When he pushed the door open and took his first view of the female he was to kiss—he at once understood the reason behind Mrs. Bancroft's smile.

Rosalie pushed up off the bed, rising to her feet as the door opened and a man stepped inside.

And then she lost the ability to stand. Her knees gave out and she sank back down bonelessly on the edge of the bed. Her eyes ached from staring so hard. She couldn't even blink.

How had he found her?

Her heart slammed in her chest, panicked at what he would do with her now. Would he denounce her? Cast her out?

She struggled to speak but her mouth was suddenly as dry as bone, speech impossible.

He stood for a moment, staring back at her as well, unmoving as he scanned her from her head to her slippered feet.

"You require a kiss, madame?"

The deep timbre of his voice sank through her, pooling like lava in her veins, starting a low simmer in her blood. The significance of his words penetrated. He was here. To kiss her. She angled her head, studying him. He was much as he'd appeared just a short time ago, in the corridor outside his bedchamber. Except now he looked at her as a stranger. He did not know her. The tightness in her chest eased. She resisted the urge to run a hand over her hair. She was safe from recognition. Aurelia had secured the wig carefully. Never was she so grateful for a decision in her life. Aside of the wig and domino, the hazy red glow infusing the room distorted everything.

Careful to speak low, fearful that he might recognize the sound of her voice, she tentatively spoke in hushed tones, "Yes. Mrs. Bancroft sent you?"

Although it seemed evident that Mrs. Bancroft sent him, she wanted to be certain.

A slow smile curved his mouth that made her stomach flip. He'd never smiled quite like that at her before. It was somehow . . . free. Charming. There was nothing guarded about him as he stood before her. "Yes. She did. A fact I will most heartily thank her for later."

He was flirting with her. Her pulse trembled at her neck at the strange sensation. Dec smiling at her, his eyes bright with invitation. It was a definite first.

His hot gaze skimmed her, bringing back to mind the scandalous gown draping her body like a second skin, clinging to curves she had not known she possessed. A fresh onslaught of embarrassment washed over her to know that Dec was seeing her like this. Her stepbrother and not a stranger that Mrs. Bancroft picked out for her. A stranger would have been preferable. It would have been simpler to forget herself with a stranger.

With Dec? She didn't know if she could. She'd always felt something for him. He'd been so handsome even years ago. He had radiated . . . something. The maids, even the housekeeper, had been helpless to his appeal, tittering whenever he entered a room. Even her mother had been fond of him. Always smiling and laughing at him. Rosalie remembered because it had made her jealous. She thought her mother liked him more than her own daughter. Not that she blamed Dec. She'd been under his spell like everyone else.

Granted, she had just been a child then. But now

. . . face-to-face with him all these years later, nothing had changed. He smiled less, but he was still heart-stopping attractive. He still drew her. The only difference? She was no little girl anymore.

And he was here now. With her. She could act out her every fantasy with him.

And yet she couldn't.

How could she forget herself like that? He was her stepbrother. She was living under his roof. How could she accept a kiss from him and then face him on the morrow?

"I'm sorry," she murmured softly, striding forward, her dress sliding languorously along her body as she moved. "I c-can't do this."

She gave him as wide a berth as possible, but it didn't matter. His hand reached out and seized her wrist. "What?" His eyes were dark and fathomless in the muted light of the chamber. His fingers brushed against her wrist, five electric points of contact that sent sparks up her arm. "Am I so displeasing that you've changed your mind?"

Her breath escaped in a choked gasp. Was he serious? "No. Of course not. You're . . ." She waved at his person as if that gesture said it all.

"I'm what?" His mouth curved, seductive and new once again. Totally unlike any smile he had ever given her before. This smile . . .

This smile was devastating. It was clearly the type he reserved for women he liked in a certain way. Women he met here. At Sodom. His previous smiles had all been mocking and cruel, conveying his dislike of her. Well, save for the smiles he had bestowed on her in the garden. And yet that had been fleeting. *This* smile, the hot look, his over-familiar touch. It was all new and made her feel a little breathless. Like how she felt as a child slicing very high through the air on a swing. Euphoric. Her stomach twisting and dipping.

"You're perfectly . . . pleasing." She could have choked on that understatement.

"Perfectly pleasing?" he echoed, still smiling. His gaze roamed over her again, missing nothing, not one inch of her outrageous gown—or rather the body of which the gown hid so very little. She felt naked before him. "I could say the same of you. Or how about simply perfect? That might better apply to you."

Heat scored her cheeks at the compliment. "No one's perfect," she quickly countered, speaking in low, deep tones she hoped did not sound too unnatural.

"True." His eyes flickered with something akin to surprise. "But there are people perfect for each other. Perfect for kissing? Don't you agree?"

Her chest squeezed. Oh, he was deadly charming. How did women resist him?

What made her think they did?

What made her think she could?

"You require a kiss. Why are you fleeing?" His thumb started moving in tiny circles against the inside of her wrist, the gentle friction tantalizing and distracting at the same time. He addled her thoughts.

She shook her head. It was truly mortifying. He might not know who she was behind the mask, but *she* had not forgotten. She recalled with painful clarity who she was. And what he thought of her. She could not forget. She wished she could. She wished she could sink into a kiss from him and forget. Except this morning he had agreed for her to marry another man with no more consideration than one might give in selecting blackberry or blueberry jam. That's how little he thought of her. That's how badly he wished to be rid of her.

A dim room and mask were the only things that protected her from discovery. It was risky and dangerous—*too* dangerous—and utterly beyond what she was willing to do.

She gave a tug on her wrist, but he didn't let go. Somehow the effort invited him closer. He stepped in until the breadth of his chest almost brushed her body. A mere hair separated them.

"I confess to a little confusion." His heated gaze slid over her again, skimming the sleek fall of dark hair past her shoulders. He angled his head thoughtfully. "Are you certain you've never been kissed? You don't appear the type of female to lack opportunity." His stare fixed on her bodice, on the expanse of bare skin between her breasts— and she knew precisely what *type* of female she appeared.

She swallowed. Dressed thusly and drawing breath within the walls of Sodom, no less. Her appearance was like the rest of the scantily clad near-naked females populating the house. Of course, he doubted her alleged inexperience.

She plucked at the gossamer-thin fabric. "I borrowed the dress from Mrs. Bancroft."

"Ah. She is ever helpful, is she not?"

"Indeed." Rosalie glanced to the door, anxious to be through it.

"But my confusion is not completely alleviated."

"No?"

"You chose this place for a first kiss? Rather extreme measures for a mere kiss?" His grip loosened around her wrist, sliding down her hand until his fingers laced with her own, their palms flush. It felt shockingly intimate . . . and nice. Her breath fell a little faster. She'd never held a man's hand before. His palm was big and warm, and he was virile and handsome and young. His hand, this moment, *him* . . . it was the dream she had imagined when she envisioned coming to Town and being courted.

But this was Dec.

She took a step back, severing the heady sensation of his fingers wrapped around hers. This time he let her go. "You're correct, of course. My actions are extreme." She moved for the door. "I've changed my mind." Turning her back on him, she grasped the latch.

He stopped her, flattening a palm against the door, killing her escape, his chest a hard wall at her back. "Don't go."

She inhaled sharply, staring at that broad hand and tapering fingers on the door. "I beg your pardon?" her voice rasped.

If she didn't know him, she might have been alarmed, but she knew him well enough to know that he was not the sort of man to harm a female. Even a female at Sodom. She had once watched him save an injured bird from his father's hounds. He'd nursed it until it could fly again. The years did not change one's soul. He would never be so beastly as to force his attentions where they were not wanted. She knew that.

"Let me kiss you." The words gusted near her ear in warm breath. His deep voice felt like a physical caress. A tremor rushed through her. She turned. Not because she agreed, but because she had to see his face. She could not withhold that pleasure from herself.

He looked down at her, his face so close to her upturned one. They hardly needed to move for their lips to meet.

Oh God. She wanted . . .

She *wanted*.

"No. I can't." Anyone else and she could. Anyone but him.

Yet her sudden jarring and disappointing thought was that she wouldn't want anyone else. Not like him. Not like this ever again.

At that bleak thought, her hand found the latch behind her and pushed down. This time when she tried to leave, he let her go.

Chapter 11

She stumbled out the door and hurried down the hall, determined to find her way back to the room where she had left Aurelia, not daring to look over her shoulder. Her chest hurt from lack of breath and she realized she had forgotten to breathe. She sucked in air, filling her lungs, but still felt breathless. As though she had run a great distance.

She was moving so quickly, she didn't have time to stop when a man stepped suddenly from one of the private rooms.

She collided with him, crying out in surprise from the impact. Arms came out to wrap around her waist, steadying her on her feet.

"Ho there!" he exclaimed, his eyes traveling up and down her. "Have a care there. Where are you off to in such haste?" His hand came up to rest on her chest, fingers splaying wide on the bare skin between her breasts.

She gasped at the intimate touch. It came so suddenly and automatic from him. As if he had every right to touch her. She supposed it was the nature of Sodom. What people did to each other here . . . willingly. A stranger's touch was welcome.

She arched away, but he didn't unlock his arm from around her waist. She pushed at the mass of his soft, yielding chest.

"What have we here? An eager little dove looking for her next conquest? I'll gladly offer myself."

"No, unhand me. I'm not—"

An arm shot over her shoulder, a fist connecting with the stranger's face.

Immediately the arm dropped from around her and she was free. Her gaze shot to the fallen man. He clutched his nose, glaring over his fingers up at Dec. "Banbury, what in bloody hell—"

"She asked you to unhand her, Hendricks." Dec

stood with legs braced apart, looking ready to tear the man apart.

Hendricks's glare narrowed on Rosalie. "Since when do you mind sharing?"

Dec took a menacing step forward. Rosalie quickly jumped in his path, pushing a hand against his chest. A brawl in the hall of Sodom was calling more attention to her presence here than she wanted.

Dec stopped, looking down at her with glittering eyes. His hand came up to cover hers on his chest, his fingers warm over her own. Her gaze dropped to her hand against him. It looked small. Fragile. Or perhaps he was simply big.

Hendricks lumbered to his feet and marched past them, muttering under his breath. His tread faded down the corridor and still they stared at one another.

"You should not wander unattended through Sodom."

Rosalie nodded, soaking in his handsome features as he stared down at her. She released a rattled breath and moistened her lips. His gaze followed the movement. Her belly fluttered.

"I'm trying to find my friend," she said a bit desperately. *So she could flee this place . . . him.*

"I'll stay with you until you do."

She nodded. How could she refuse? She just discovered firsthand how unwise it was to stroll unescorted throughout the house. Still, neither one of them moved right away. She was achingly aware of their proximity. Of her hand still on his chest, the press of his hand over hers, his heartbeat thumping beneath her palm.

Voices sounded at the end of the hall, and they both snapped to action. He moved to the side, pulling her with him, tucking her hand into the crook of his elbow to allow the individuals to pass.

A trio of ladies, faces as hidden as hers, headed in their direction.

"Banbury," the woman at the center called. "How good to see you, Your Grace. It's been almost a week. Wait. More than that, I think. Where have you been, you naughty lad?" She glided forward and ran a familiar palm over his chest. She wore a brilliant gold gown and a powdered wig that looked heavy and headache-inducing. "I was just telling my friends they needed to meet you."

"Lady X," he greeted.

An alias, obviously. And she was a regular here and well acquainted with Dec. For some reason, this made her hand tighten around his arm.

Lady X turned her attention on Rosalie. "And who is your companion?" She lifted her hand from Dec's chest and lowered it to Rosalie's bare arm, stroking lightly. "I haven't seen you here before, dear."

"She's never been here before, so tread easy." There was humor in his voice, but a warning, too, however softly worded.

Lady X laughed and dropped her hand. "I see. I'll let you introduce her to Sodom, then. Perhaps we will meet again. Once you've broken her in and she is feeling more adventurous."

Rosalie's face heated. She doubted she could be any more adventurous than this.

The ladies sidled past, their happy chatter fading away. "Friends of yours?" she asked.

"We're all friends here." His mouth twisted into a smile. "Until we're not."

"Until it doesn't matter, you mean."

He waved a hand idly. "Here? It never really matters."

She couldn't help the stab of disappointment. She knew Dec was a rake. Perhaps she wanted to think that she—an anonymous female who had come here for a first kiss—would mean something to him. She wanted it to matter. She wanted to be different for him.

She couldn't imagine ever having a liaison with anyone and it not mattering, but he did it all the time. And yet buried beneath her disappointment was curiosity. The same curiosity that had led her here in the first place. She wanted to know what all the fuss was about. She wanted more. That's what she had told Aunt Peregrine. She might not be able to find it in marriage, but could she not find a taste of adventure? Passion?

She didn't want merely a kiss. She wanted a kiss that she would never forget.

Sliding her hand from his arm, she stepped back. She glanced down the corridor and pointed to a door. "This looks like the one. I believe my friend is in this room."

He smiled, but there was a grim set to his lips, as if he understood. This was good-bye. "Don't come back here."

"I won't." Turning, she moved toward the door, feeling his gaze on the back of her dress, and she knew he would wait until she was safely in the company of her friend. Her hand dropped to the latch. Turning, she pushed it open and peered inside. The room was empty. A quick glance at the window revealed the same couple still preoccupied on the bed in the adjoining room. But no Aurelia.

Frowning, she stepped back out into the corridor.

Dec approached. "Your friend?"

"She's not there."

"She likely moved on to other diversions. There's much to see and do in the house."

She nodded, beginning to feel the stirrings of concern. She hoped Aurelia was all right.

"No worry," he murmured, plucking her hand and dropping it back on his arm, no doubt sensing her concern. "We'll locate her. Or Mrs. Bancroft. Surely she knows where your friend is. She knows the comings and goings of everything in Sodom."

They didn't move right away. It was as though a string stretched between them, keeping them connected. Keeping them from stepping too far from each other.

"Never been kissed?" he mused, clearly in no hurry to sever the string. "Interesting. You can't be married, then?"

She laughed lightly, nervously, touching her domino, making certain it was still in place. "Of course not. I wouldn't be here if I were married, would I?"

His smile was slow and sensuous. Amusement was etched in the well-carved line of his bottom lip. "You think that so absurd? That a married lady would frequent this place? You really have strayed from the flock, haven't you? How did you even hear of a place such as this?"

"Rest assured, it was quite by accident." She thought of Aurelia, imagining his expression if she happened to inform him that his cousin was the one responsible for her presence here.

"A happy accident, then. For me."

"Is it? Even though I've changed my mind and wasted your time? You could be with a more willing female right now."

His gaze skimmed her, a physical touch. "None nearly as interesting as you."

"Are you complimenting me because you think it will win my favor?" A coy smile lifted her lips. "I'm certain a gentleman . . . a nobleman, no less . . . who looks as you do can have anyone he wants." She waved a hand at him.

He leaned in, propping a hand on the wall above her shoulder. His body pressed close but stopped just short of meeting hers. And yet his warmth radiated, reaching her, touching her in spots that she never even knew could feel sensation. She inhaled. God, he smelled good. Like clean man and something else that was entirely him, imprinted on his skin. Wind and salt and heat. "It's not always 'anyone' that I want," he whispered, his warm breath sending a rush of goose bumps across her arms.

"Oh." The single word escaped her in a breath. He was good. Heat swallowed her face. "Me?" She shook her head. Swallowing, she whispered, "You can't . . . You don't—"

"I want the one who isn't so easily affected. By my title. By pretty words. Like you, yes." He considered her for a moment, his gaze roving over her bare shoulders, the swells of her breasts. She sucked in a breath, remembering how very nearly transparent the bodice was. The action forced her breasts higher against the thin bodice and his eyes darkened. "I'm going to hazard a guess that you're surrounded by nobility. Only that explains why you are so unimpressed. Your father perhaps? Is he titled?" At her silence, he shrugged. "Keep your secrets. If it makes you feel comfortable."

Oh, her secrets didn't make her comfortable . . . they made her a wreck of nerves.

They proceeded back down the hall in the direction of the stairs. She heard them before she rounded the corner, spotting the boisterous group of men and women hovering in the threshold of a room.

Dec gestured. "Perhaps your friend . . ."

Rosalie scanned the gathering. "I don't see her among the spectators."

They stepped closer and Rosalie peered between the bodies to the scene within the chamber.

"Oh," she choked as she spied four people sprawled in the middle of a massive bed. A man was spread out naked in the center. Three equally unclothed women hovered over him, kissing him . . . everywhere. One even kissed him directly on his—

With an inarticulate sound, Rosalie whirled past the crowd and ran blindly down the hall. Mortified and feeling decidedly . . . *overheated*, she rounded yet another corner.

She heard his voice behind her, calling her to wait, but she didn't stop. She had to flee from the shocking display she'd witnessed. From how it made her feel. And perhaps, most importantly, from him.

She was almost to the stairs when he caught up with her. His hand came down on her arm and yanked her back around. "Where are you going?"

She shook her head. "I should never have come to this place. I'm sure you think me foolish and irrational—"

He cut her off with a swift shake of his head. "I

think you're a girl far out of her ilk here. Nothing more."

A *girl*. Indeed. A girl on the brink of marriage whether she liked it or not. She had insisted on choosing, but what would her choices be? She gulped with the bitterness of that realization. Choice was an illusion. She had no choice and little control.

Of course the irony wasn't lost on her that the man standing before her happened to be the one pushing her into marriage. The one controlling her fate.

And yet she didn't want to be that *girl*. A girl led. A girl without choice. She wanted to be in control even if it was fleeting.

Even if only for one kiss.

His dark eyes flicked back and forth over her face as if awaiting her response. She could not fathom what he saw. It could not be much in the dim light of the hall. With over half her face hidden by a domino and framed in the black wig, he could not see much. Just her eyes peered out, drinking in the sight of him.

"What are you thinking?" she whispered.

"That you need to go home and forget about this place." He lifted a hand, and she held still, resisting the instinct to pull away. He brushed one of the tendrils of hair that fell across her shoulder. "Forget me."

Impossible. She held herself still for a moment, savoring his hand on her hair, the heat radiating from his body, so close to her own. *This*. It was supposed to be like this between a man and woman.

He smelled good, like soap and male. He was so handsome that it hurt to even look at him. A first kiss should be this. Or rather the moment leading up to the first kiss should be like this. The pull. The heightened awareness. A man whose mere closeness, his face, his eyes, his lips, made her ache.

She would have this. The moment before the kiss.

No. *More*. She would have the kiss.

Standing on her tiptoes, she circled her hand around his neck and pressed her lips to his. They felt warm, firm but soft. Softer than she had expected from such a hard man. A small breath escaped him, and her stomach fluttered at the gust of warm air in her mouth.

She pulled back, hand loosening on his neck.

He stared down at her, his eyes dark and fierce. "I thought you changed your mind."

"I changed it back."

"Why?"

"I decided I wanted my first kiss after all." She dropped her hand from his neck and started to pull away, satisfied that she had come here to do what she set out to do.

His arm came around her waist, hauling her back, pressing her intimately to his chest, holding her up so that her feet came off the ground. She felt her eyes go wide.

"Then let's make it count." His head dipped, and when his mouth came over hers, there was nothing hesitant about it. No, his lips were commanding and thorough, both soft and hard, slanting over hers. It was nothing like that first press of her lips to his. "Open your mouth," he rasped against her lips.

She obeyed, and gasped at the thrust of his tongue, gliding across hers. He tasted of heat and scotch and male.

He backed her into the wall and she clung to him, relishing the sensation of his strong body sinking against hers. She wrapped both her arms around his shoulders, her fingers delving into his hair.

His kiss deepened, grew harder, his tongue bolder, lapping at hers. She kissed him back, moving her tongue, mimicking his movements and tasting him as he tasted her. She marveled that a kiss could be so consuming. How it could set all of her ablaze.

"Wrap your legs around me," he instructed. The command made her shake. She hesitated, unsure how to go about that, but before she could speak or move, he grasped one thigh and guided it around his waist. When he reached for her other thigh, she understood and hopped up to meet him.

The thin fabric of her gown fell like a waterfall around her legs, offering no real barrier. She felt him between her legs, his lean hips wedged between her thighs. And that part of him. The bulge of his manhood rubbed at the core of her, where all sensation seemed to begin and end.

She moaned as he thrust himself against her. Her belly clenched.

How did one begin a kiss and not want more? Not *do* more? Or was it simply that this kiss was better than most?

Yes. That was it. It had to be. It had to be because it was him. *Dec.*

She grabbed his face with both hands, reveling in the bristly stubble of his cheeks against her palms. She slanted her mouth and licked her way inside his mouth, her thighs tightening around him, instinctively angling so that she felt him even better, harder, right over the throbbing core of her.

"That's it," he growled. "Take what you want."

His guttural voice was like a dose of cold water.

She'd had what she wanted. She'd had her kiss. A kiss with Dec, no less. This needed to stop. Before it became impossible to stop. She knew that point couldn't be far from now. She ached and quivered so badly. She was certainly already close to that point.

She tore her mouth away, panting, both heartened and alarmed to see that he was panting, too. He wanted her. He ached and quivered for her, too.

They stared at each other in the murky corridor. His features were cast in gloom, but it didn't matter. She had them memorized, and she could see what was lost to shadow. Every line. Every hollow. She could see him so clearly, so perfectly. And now she had the taste of him to forever go with his image.

She brought her gloved fingers to her lips, brushing the tender flesh. "Oh. My."

"For first kisses, I'd say you have received a thorough education."

She nodded once, speech impossible.

"Did it meet your expectations? Your hopes?"

"I . . . yes." Beyond that.

He brushed her cheek with his hand and his head inched closer again, coming back for more. Her gaze fixed on his mouth, hungry, wanting him, and she realized she might not have the power to resist, to stop this from happening.

"Ah, there you are."

They jerked apart. Rosalie snapped her attention to the figure approaching them up the stairs. Mrs. Bancroft held her skirts as she ascended. "I was just returning to check on you, my dear." Her gaze, shadowed and unreadable within the bright plumage of her domino, fixed on each of them in slow turn.

Rosalie moved down one step to meet her. Dec stopped her, stalling her with one hand on her shoulder.

She looked from him to Mrs. Bancroft uncertainly.

The proprietress nodded as though understanding that they needed a moment. "I shall await you at the base of the stairs."

The desire to call out to her and ask Mrs. Bancroft to return and accompany her warred within

Rosalie's chest. It was cowardly perhaps, but what was left for them now? More kisses? That would only lead to ruin. It was one thing to toe the line, another to dive headlong over the side.

And there was the fact that every moment in his company put her at risk.

But Rosalie said nothing. She let the proprietor of Sodom drift away, leaving her alone with the man whose kiss still burned on her lips . . . on her very soul.

"I must go," she whispered in her carefully modulated voice.

"You won't return." It was not a question but a statement—which he only confirmed by adding, "This place is not for you."

But you are. You are for me.

The wretched thought snuck into her heart, unbidden.

She nodded in agreement, panicked at the foolish direction of her thoughts. "I won't be back."

Slowly, he lifted his hand from her shoulder. Everything about him seemed resigned, and perhaps that was regret in his eyes.

Satisfaction curled through her. It was a dangerous thing . . . this feeling that he had enjoyed their kiss, that he regretted its end. That he enjoyed *her*. That she was somehow different than the multitude of women to pass in and out of his life. In and out of his bed. Dangerous indeed.

She was an indiscretion. She was his stepsister. Two factors that meant this would never happen again.

"Your name, then. At least leave me with that."

"No names," she murmured, trying not to choke on the idea of giving him her true name.

"But you know mine. Banbury. If you . . ." He paused and sliced fingers through his dark, unruly hair. As though he did not know quite what he was doing or saying. "If you ever have need of me, or wish to see me again, you may contact me. Directly . . . or send word through Mrs. Bancroft."

She blinked. Was he truly inviting her to see him again? That feeling that she was somehow different, special, reasserted itself. It lightened her heart and made her wish. Made her wish she was someone else so that she could be with him.

"Thank you, but that's not necessary." She inclined her head. "I received what I came for. Thank you for obliging me."

She turned without lingering for his reply. Mrs. Bancroft waited for her at the bottom of the stairs.

"Well. I trust you are satisfied?" she asked as she looped arms with Rosalie.

"Quite so. Thank you. Have you seen my friend?"

"I believe she's engaged in a game of whist. Let's fetch her before she gets in over her head."

Rosalie frowned. "Is it a high stake game?"

"Oh. Indeed. The only games to be had at Sodom are high stakes, but not in the manner you are thinking. So let us fetch her while she still has her clothes and hasn't wagered away her virtue. I think that might be more than she bargained for at her first night at Sodom, don't you agree?"

With a gasp, Rosalie quickened her pace, alarmed at the very prospect of Aurelia now naked in a room full of strangers.

Fortunately, when they found her she was still garbed and sitting at a table with none other than Lord Camden. Shirtless. She couldn't see below the table to detect if he still wore his trousers, but he did not look too happy as he sat there— ostensibly losing at cards.

Rosalie stopped in the threshold. This room was better lit than the upstairs. Even with the wig and domino, there was a slight possibility he might recognize Aurelia.

She couldn't hear what they were saying from across the room, but Aurelia's lips were moving and her head was in that cocky angle of hers. Rosalie knew it meant her ire was up. Aurelia was annoyed, and if she wasn't careful, the viscount would guess her identity, disguise or no disguise. They were quite familiar with each other, after all. Camden was one of her brother's closest friends.

"Mrs. Bancroft," she said, "would you mind having my friend meet me at the front door?"

"Of course."

Rosalie watched for a moment as the proprietress made her way across the room, stopping at intervals to exchange pleasantries. She was the consummate hostess. She stopped at Aurelia's table finally, patting the well-muscled shoulder of the viscount fondly. Of course he was a regular here, too—just like Dec—and the lady would know him.

Rosalie glanced over her shoulder, almost like she was expecting to find him there, conjured by the mere thought of him. She really needed to make herself scarce. If he saw her in this lighting, he'd take one look at her and know.

Suddenly, Aurelia was before her, face flushed and eyes bright with merriment. "Rosalie, how did it go?"

She shook her head. "We have to leave. I'll tell you on the way home."

Nodding, Aurelia followed her, holding her

questions until they were in a hack and headed across town.

"Well?" her friend pressed, settling back on the squabs. "Did you have your first kiss then?"

"I saw Lord Camden was at your table," Rosalie countered, not ready to talk about her kiss. "Did he recognize you?"

Aurelia made a snort and her flush deepened, creeping all the way down her throat into her décolletage. "That boor. Max only sees what he wants to see."

"Did he recognize you?" she demanded. "Do you know for certain?"

Aurelia shrugged. "Possibly, but he wouldn't have dared say anything. He wouldn't risk ruining me. I'm Will's sister. And Dec's cousin. He wouldn't be that inconsiderate of his friends." This last bit was said with something of a sneer. As though she didn't think he would refrain from ruining her reputation simply for her sake—only theirs.

Dread closed in on Rosalie, tightening her throat. If Camden mentioned seeing Aurelia at Sodom that night, Dec might walk down the path to concluding that she had been there, too.

Aurelia saw her expression and patted her hand reassuringly. "Max will not utter a word to anyone. Don't look so sick. Trust me. Now tell me. Did you kiss—"

"Yes."

The squabs squeaked as Aurelia adjusted her weight on the seat across from her. She fairly bounced in her eagerness. "Ohh, do tell. What was it like? What was *he* like? I'm sure Mrs. Bancroft wouldn't have selected anyone for you short of—"

"He was like—" she cut in, pausing before adding, "Declan."

Aurelia stopped bouncing where she sat on the squabs, her mouth dropping in a small O of shock.

"You kissed my cousin?"

Rosalie nodded. She needed to confide to someone, and as Aurelia was the only who could ever know about tonight, she was it.

"You and *Declan* kissed?" she pressed, as though that clarification were necessary in addition to this name.

Rosalie gave voice to her confirmation this time. "Yes." Then she winced. "Or rather *I* kissed him." She had flung herself at him.

"You did?"

"Well, the first time. And then he kissed me." Properly. Thoroughly.

"But you initiated it?" If possible, Aurelia's eyes grew even larger.

"I know," Rosalie groaned, burying her face in her hands. "I shouldn't have let it happen. I don't know what I was thinking." Yes, she did, but she wasn't sharing with Aurelia that she found her cousin irresistible and the perfect candidate to act out all her wishes for something *more*.

"Well this is an amusing turn of events."

Rosalie looked up from her hands and cut her a glare.

"Sorry," Aurelia replied without an ounce of repentance. Clearing her voice, she attempted what she must have deemed to be the suitable amount of seriousness. "Did he know it was you?"

"Good God, no! No!" The idea made her skin itch. "And he can't! He can't ever know it was me."

Aurelia nodded. Untying the strings from her mask, she dropped the fabric on the seat beside her. "Of course not." She fell silent, her gaze speculative across the carriage.

"Why are you looking at me like that?"

"Simply considering."

"Considering what?"

"You and Declan."

"There is no me and Dec. He's trying to get rid of me, as you are well aware."

"Yes. Rather desperately. Too desperately perhaps? I wonder why that is?"

Rosalie shook her head. "You read too much into this. He hates my mother and I am merely an extension of her."

"I think that is a rather simplistic view. He might have thought that way in the beginning, but I'm sure he no longer does. Or he no longer will once he comes to know you better."

Rosalie shrugged. Her gaze drifted to the small crack in the curtains and the passing buildings. "Really, this is moot. There is nothing more to say about it."

"Well," Aurelia continued. "You'll be under his roof for the rest of the Season. Anything can happen. Perhaps you need to open yourself to the—"

Her gaze snapped back to Aurelia. "Nothing will happen."

"But it already did."

"And he doesn't know that," she reminded tartly.

Aurelia sniffed like it was a debatable point. "He wanted you tonight . . . I'd wager he wants you, Rosalie. That on some level, he knew it was you tonight. He just needs to realize it."

Rosalie stared at her, stunned. "No. He does not need to realize it." *He must not.* "Please do not attempt to match-make me with your cousin."

Her friend settled back in her seat, her lips flattening into a mutinous line.

"Promise me, Aurelia," Rosalie pressed, drawing out her name in warning.

"Very well. I promise to do nothing. Only because there's nothing I need to do. You're under his roof. I predict proximity and frequency of said proximity shall take care of matters."

Rosalie swallowed.

A cold sweat broke out over her at the idea of Dec realizing she was the girl he'd been with tonight. If it was the eventuality Aurelia predicted, then perhaps she needed to hasten all her efforts toward matrimony. Because, despite what Aurelia suggested, she knew that Dec discovering the truth of this night's deeds would not end well for her.

She sucked in a deep breath and resolved that it wouldn't happen. As though sheer will alone could prevent it from occurring. Her mind worked, shoring up her defenses against the possibility. It was clear there was only one thing to do, and she was already doing it. Perhaps halfheartedly. But no more. Now she would seek a husband in earnest.

Dec lingered another half hour at Sodom's. He

moved from room to room, looking for something to divert himself, hoping even though he knew it was fruitless that he might spot his mystery lady. He joined Max at the tables just as his friend was shrugging back into his clothing.

"You lost your clothes, man?" he asked on a chuckle. "Never knew anyone to out-wager you."

"A cheating, barbed-tongue hoyden got the best of me." He yanked his jacket angrily back into place. "Not to worry. I'll have satisfaction."

Whoever the chit was, Dec felt sorry for her in that moment. Max was rarely given to anger or ill temper. He was all smiles and jests, which gave those rare moments when he was in a temper all the more weight. He was no one to trifle with when he was in a mood.

"Are you heading upstairs?" Dec asked.

Max hesitated, a scowl still etched on his features. "No, to home. You?"

Dec nodded, understanding as he thought of what awaited him at home. He'd had his fill of Sodom for the night, too. He rubbed his mouth. His lips still felt warm.

Strange. He'd come here looking to erase all thoughts of Rosalie, and had succeeded for a short time. Too short. Now he was back to thinking of her again. And a lady whose name he did not even know. Damned vexing night. He was still returning home with an aching cock. Precisely the state he had been in when he arrived at Sodom.

"Should have stayed home," he muttered.

Immediately he knew he didn't mean it. If he had stayed home, he wouldn't have claimed her first kiss. He would not have been the one. Some other bastard would have taken that from her. His hands curled reflexively at his sides.

He wouldn't have the memory of her taste. He wouldn't have experienced the way she came alive in his arms, waking to passion, to his touch, his mouth—to him. His only regret was that he would have nothing more of her.

He couldn't stop himself from scanning the room yet again as he took his departure, hoping for one last sight of her. But no. She was gone.

The two men walked out into the night.

Max looked at him. "Will you be at the Waverley ball?"

He frowned. "Should I know about it?"

Max gave his cuff a tug, as if he could not quite get the fit right after undressing in Mrs. Bancroft's parlor. "Only the biggest event of the Season. Thought with your stepsister on the market, your aunt would insist that you make an appearance. Lend your support and all that."

He shrugged, marveling at the slight tension running through him at the mention of Rosalie. The chit had the temerity to dress him down outside his bedchamber. After everything he had done for her. After he had taken her in even though her mother was responsible for ruining his childhood, taking away everything good and innocent he once had.

And then she had gone and bewildered him with her concern for his injuries. He couldn't recall a woman ever attempting to play nursemaid to him, but she had been quite ready to the task.

"I don't see why that's necessary," he said. "My aunt is doing a fair enough task of ushering her about. What of you?" he inquired.

Max barked a laugh. "That's amusing. Might have dinner at the club. Who knows from there?"

A lone hack clattered noisily down the street. The hour was late, and he felt decidedly reluctant to return to his bed. "I'll meet you for dinner."

"Brilliant." Max clapped him on the back, the force of which made him wince. Max caught sight of his expression. "Sorry, there. You spar today?"

Dec nodded.

"You know there are other ways to exert yourself. Some far more pleasant than fisticuffs. Perhaps you need to spend more time at Sodom."

The suggestion only made him scowl. He hadn't found release tonight as he had hoped.

"Perhaps," he agreed. Perhaps tomorrow he'd find a chit to shake him from his odd mood. A pleasing female with eager lips and yielding flesh. Or one that wasn't his stepsister. One that was agreeable to more than a single kiss. How difficult could it be? It had always been easy enough before.

Chapter 12

*R*osalie did not have long to worry about coming face-to-face with Dec and suffering his presence. There would be none of his overwhelming nearness with the memory of that blistering kiss between them.

Because her mother came for her the next day.

Melisande stood before her in the drawing room with her hands on her hips, putting a swift end to Rosalie's concerns regarding Dec. There was no warm greeting. No hugs. No kisses or happy words at their long overdue reunion. Rosalie could dredge up very little happiness at seeing her mother. Likely because her mother made no effort to disguise her annoyance with her.

"Are you satisfied, Rosalie? You've made me a laughingstock about Town!"

"I thought you were in Italy."

"Not that it matters, but I was visiting a friend in Bath before leaving for Italy. That's where I received word of your machinations here in Town!"

"And how have I made you a laughingstock, Mama?"

Melisande winced. She had always winced at being called Mama. As though being a mother pained her.

"Everyone assumed my daughter was still in plaits, and you show up on the marriage mart, clearly a schoolgirl no longer!"

Ah. Of course. It was an affront to her vanity. Now Rosalie understood the problem.

Melisande continued her rant, barely pausing for breath. "How dare you leave school without my permission?" She paced the drawing room in a swish of muslin skirts. Rosalie watched her in rapt fascination. She hadn't seen her mother in years. She couldn't take her eyes off her, noting all the changes . . . all the little things she had forgotten over the years. Her hair was several shades darker than she recalled, and she could only suspect her mother tampered with the color of her hair through artificial means. Perhaps the dark strands had started to gray. She was still beautiful. With high cheekbones and slashing dark eyebrows. Stunning in a way that she knew she would never be. Her mother's face was one sculptors would wish to mold in clay. Almost severe in its perfection.

"I couldn't remain at Harwich," she finally cut in. "The tuition—"

"Don't you be so crass and vulgar as to discuss finances with me, Rosalie. I can see your years there taught you nothing of decorum. I shudder to think how you're faring about Society without me."

She bit her tongue, mightily tempted to say she had fared through life these many years without her.

Melisande dropped down on the settee with a weary gust of breath. " 'Tis done. We shall make the best of it. At least Albert's brat has seen fit to do his duty and provide you a dowry. I shall take over from here."

Rosalie blinked. "Take over?"

Melisande leaned forward to inspect the items on the tea service, wrinkling her nose. "What are these?" She poked at a biscuit. "Lemon iced?"

"Mama?" Rosalie scooted to the edge of her chair. "What do you mean you're taking over?"

Melisande looked up, blinking her blue eyes. "You'll come home with me and I shall oversee the rest of your Season. Of course, you don't think I'm leaving you here with Declan." She snorted indelicately.

Rosalie narrowed her eyes on her mother. "Why should you suddenly care?"

"Of course I care. Curb your tongue. I'm your mother, dearest. It is my duty. Everyone would expect me to usher you through the Season and guide your way on the marriage mart, not Declan. What does he know of young debutantes?"

Rosalie nodded slowly, understanding her mother's motives. Expectations. That would weigh on her mother. That would matter. Enough, apparently, for Melisande to take a sudden interest in her.

"And you don't know the first thing about men, either. You will need my help in wading through the waters of the *ton*, trust me. I won myself a duke for a husband, did I not? I can help you snare the perfect husband. We don't want a miser who clings to every farthing and fails to understand our relationship."

"Our relationship?" Rosalie echoed, shaking her head in some bewilderment.

Melisande finally selected a biscuit, nodding as she nibbled on the corner. "Hm-mm. You and I are a package, darling. Any man that chooses you gets me, too. That must be understood straight away."

She blinked, a sick feeling twisting its way inside her as everything came together like pieces of a puzzle. Of course. Melisande wanted a son-in-law who would be agreeable to supporting his mother-in-law. Someone who wouldn't mind her dipping into his pockets.

The door opened suddenly and Dec strode in, his face hard as stone.

Melisande seemed to freeze, her eyes widening with the biscuit halfway to her mouth.

Dec looked from Melisande to Rosalie and then back again, his eyes chips of ice. "I believe I told you that you were not welcome here that last time you called."

Melisande recovered herself. Squaring her shoulders, she lifted her chin. "You have my daughter. That gives me the right—"

"The daughter you conveniently forgot about for years?"

Rosalie flushed, not appreciating the reminder of how little her mother cared for her. It was one thing for this to be a known fact . . . and another thing to speak of it so boldly directly in front of her.

"I did what any mother would do and sent her to a proper school—"

"From which she completed her studies two years ago. You made it clear you have no wish to resume responsibility for Rosalie. Why attempt to act the role of doting mother now?"

Melisande flung the biscuit down on the tea service. "As though you give a bloody hell about her. You've only placed a dowry on her head to get rid of her. Like you got rid of me."

"And yet here you sit." His lip curled back like her very presence tainted the room.

"Oh, you act like such the moral prig, but we know the truth about you. All of Town hears of your deviant—"

"Enough!" Rosalie set her teacup down with a sharp click. She glared at the both of them. They were bickering children and she'd had enough of it. "I'll go pack my things." She turned for the doors. Really. What else could she do?

Dec stopped her with a hand on her arm. "Rosalie—"

She looked up at him, the sound of her name on his lips sending a shot of sensation directly down her spine. She waited. He merely stared, saying nothing, his eyes deep and dark, conveying some silent message that she was unable to comprehend.

What could he say? Her mother had come to fetch her. She had no valid reason to remain here.

She inhaled. "Thank you for your hospitality . . . thank you for everything." Without him, she wouldn't even have a hope for marriage. Now she would go home with her mother and finish out the Season—likely, hopefully, with a marriage proposal soon in hand.

She glanced at her mother's smug expression. Melisande had won and she knew it. Rosalie did not relish going home with her but it was the thing to do. Perhaps the next time a gentleman made an offer, she would accept. Indeed, reflecting back on Strickland's offer, he was not a poor prospect. He more than likely wouldn't have bowed to her mother's whims . . . and suddenly that became a new goal. She didn't want to find a merely tolerable gentleman, but one who would stand firm against her mother and not let her run roughshod over him.

Dec slid his hand from her arm. He gazed down at her, his bearing stiff and correct as he tucked his hands behind his back. "No thanks necessary."

She fled then, leaving them alone together. Hopefully the pair could remain in a room without murdering each other.

A lump rose in her throat that she could not credit as she hastened toward her chamber. She had worried about staying overly long beneath his roof. That he would eventually realize she was the one he kissed at Sodom's. That she would give herself away in some small way.

She had worried that perhaps . . . she *wanted* him to remember.

Now she was leaving and there would be no chance of that.

Dec watched through the window of the upstairs drawing room as Rosalie's last trunk was loaded onto the coach. Aurelia embraced Rosalie on the stoop as Melisande climbed inside the conveyance, no doubt impatient to be off. She'd gotten precisely what she wanted in coming here.

His jaw clenched.

"Are you mad?"

He turned to find his aunt directly behind him.

He'd been so lost in thought he hadn't even heard her approach.

"I've been accused of much, but that particular allegation? Never."

She waved one thin arm toward the window. "You know why she came for Rosalie. She doesn't give a fig about her daughter. Never has. Never will." She snorted and adjusted her obscenely fat cat in her arms. The beast looked annoyed to be handled about and let out a low rumbling growl.

"Hush, Lady Snuggles," his aunt said distractedly, looking beyond him to glare out the window. "All those years she left Rosalie to rot at that school, and suddenly she's here. *Pffft*. It's the dowry. Nothing more."

"I'm aware of that," he said evenly. He knew Melisande. He knew her perhaps better than anyone.

His aunt's gaze yanked back to him. "You are? Then why are you allowing her to leave with that wretched woman?"

"Because it's not my place to allow or disallow her to do anything. And because she's Rosalie's mother. Nor does it appear that Rosalie wishes to stay here. She left willingly."

"Well, did you tell her she could remain here?"

His lips pressed flat at this.

Aunt Peregrine shook her turbaned head. "Of course you didn't. Men never dare do something as foolish and weak as announce their thoughts or feelings."

He squared his shoulders. "Need I remind you that I never wanted her here? She has a dowry now. *Rosalie* does. Not Melisande. It shall go to her husband upon her marriage—"

"And you know Melisande shall steer her toward less than ideal candidates that *she* can control with no thought to what is best for Rosalie."

He shrugged, his hands still tight at his sides, belying the casual air he was struggling to affect. "The final decision rests with Rosalie—as she explained to me just yesterday when I dared to presume to accept a proposal on her behalf. If she's foolish enough to let her mother choose her husband and rule her life, then so be it."

"So be it?" Aunt Peregrine looked affronted.

Just then his cousin blasted into the room full force, her cheeks flushed and artfully arranged brown ringlets bouncing over her shoulders. "How could you have let her go?"

He sighed. "Why do the women in my family seem to think I have any right to keep her here?

She chose to leave." He waved at his aunt's fat cat. "She's not some pet to be lugged about without a by your leave!"

"A word from you and she would have stayed." Aurelia stabbed a finger at him accusingly.

He shrugged. "This is for the best. I am certain of it. She is with her mother. Better that than residing here with me and—"

Aurelia shook her head. "Oh, you're not certain of one bloody thing."

"Aurelia," Aunt Peregrine cried in outrage. "Language!"

She ignored her mother and continued, "You cannot see what's directly before your eyes."

"What does that mean?"

She looked at him so earnestly. Like she wanted to say something but was fighting it.

"What?" he pressed.

"It means," she began, "that perhaps you should consider wedding Rosalie. There!" She flung her arms wide. "I said it."

Dec and his aunt stared at his cousin as though she had sprouted a second head.

"Aunt," he said after some moments. "I fear it is not I whom you should fret over. Clearly your own daughter is the mad one."

"Clearly," she echoed in agreement, and then

added gently, "Aurelia, Rosalie is Declan's stepsister. That's highly unseemly."

"But not illegal. They're no blood kin to each other."

He sliced a hand through the air. "The point is moot! Even if I wished to marry, which I do not, I could not imagine a more unsuitable match for myself."

"Suitable? Suitable?" Aurelia looked close to apoplexy. "Do you hear yourself? You're such a dolt!" That said, she stormed from the room without a glance back.

Aunt Peregrine hugged her evil-eyed cat close, kissing the top of its head as she looked at Dec with blatant disappointment. "Suppose I'll go oversee the packing of my luggage. No need to stay here any longer."

He nodded absently. "Thank you for coming when I needed you."

"Of course, Declan-dearest." She patted his arm as she passed him, leaving cat hairs on his sleeve.

He beat at his sleeve, scowling and wondering when his life had become such chaos. Weeks ago it had been calm. Peaceful. *Dull.*

He'd have that again. Standing there, he let that sink in. A return to dull existence. To when he no longer felt things. When no one affected him.

His aunt and cousin were leaving.

This paled beside his second realization. He moved toward the window and stared out at the quiet street, only one fact ricocheting around his mind with the speed of cannon fire.

Rosalie was gone.

Chapter 13

*L*ord Peter Horley was the son of an impoverished Cornish viscount and French émigré. He was also Melisande's current lover. All of which Rosalie inferred throughout the course of dinner that evening. It was in the intimate language between them, their knowing glances and lingering touches. It was in the many references to their shared trips. Everything from their recent travels to Bath to shopping expeditions on Bond Street. Horley was well entrenched in her mother's life, Rosalie gathered with some bitterness. Melisande had room enough for him in her world. Just no room for her.

Over glasses of claret, Melisande toasted her return home like it was something she was truly happy about. As far as homecomings went—not that Rosalie had many to reference—it was a dismal and uncomfortable evening.

Home. It felt strange to consider Melisande's modest town house across Town from where she had stayed with Dec and Aurelia and Aunt Peregrine as home. She supposed she didn't possess a home at all. And yet this place was her mother's home, and she should think of it thusly. She had more claim to it than Dec's town house at any rate.

However, accepting this place as her home . . . *feeling* at home here, was difficult to do as she sat at the dining table, watching her mother and Horley drink deeply from their cups and eating with a gusto that bordered on gluttony.

"Spain," Melissande declared as she cut into her pheasant. "We should winter in Spain, Peter."

Horley nodded, wiping a dribble of claret from his chin with the back of his sleeve. "Indeed. Hate these bloody winters here. Feel the wretched cold and wet in my bones. My bloody teeth ache from it." He lifted his cup again, watching Rosalie over the rim as he drank. He'd watched her all night.

She stabbed at the peas on her plate, pretending that he did not unnerve her and wondering how much longer until she could excuse herself without appearing rude.

"Perhaps you could join us, Rosie? Eh? Would you like that?" He tore a hunk of bread and swiped it around his plate, gathering up all the juices from the pheasant.

He'd already nicknamed her. As if they were close . . . intimate. As if he had the right. She tried not to curl her lip, determined that he not see his effect on her.

They were close in age. He was perhaps four or five years her senior. Approximately the same age as Dec if she were to hazard a guess. *Dec*. The thought of him brought a pang to her chest.

The age difference between Horley and Melisande obviously didn't concern either one of them. It did somewhat surprise Rosalie upon meeting him, although it shouldn't have. She knew her mother's reputation. She'd probably run out of options in men her own age or older. She had to look to the up-and-coming generation. She knew her mother would never consider remarriage. She'd not risk losing her title.

As the evening wore on, the pair became overly free with their hands, constantly touching each other. Horley seemed to especially enjoy stroking her mother's bare shoulder—all the while watching Rosalie, his eyebrow lifted almost defiantly. As though he knew it made her uncomfortable.

She loathed him already.

Melisande snapped her fingers for the servant to fetch more claret. "I think not, Peter. It's doubtful her future husband will be willing to depart with her so soon."

Horley smiled widely. She supposed some women would find him attractive with his big-toothed smile and fair, pomaded hair that gleamed as though it was wet. "No. I imagine not." His eyes slid over her again, and she shivered. "Her husband will want to keep her close for some time." He brought his cup to his lips again and drank deeply, his eyes never leaving her.

Her mother looked up and watched him, following his gaze to Rosalie and then back to him again. Her forehead knitted. "Now, Rosalie," she said in an almost overly loud voice. Horley looked at Melisande, thankfully distracted from her. "I want you well-rested for tomorrow. We shall be going to the opera."

Horley grinned an oily smile. "You'll be on proper display there."

"And we're guests of Lady Willcox. She conveniently shares a box with her cousin, the Marquis of Hildebrand's, so that is quite a coup."

Horley wagged his eyebrows. "The old goat is senile, but randy. Should be easy enough to lead him by the nose."

Rosalie looked back and forth between the two of them, understanding at once their plans. They wanted her to wed someone malleable . . . and they expected to benefit from the match. She reached for her drink and took a long sip as if she needed fortification. From these two, she no doubt did.

Strickland was looking better and better. She bit her lip, wondering if she should make an overture toward him. She recalled his temper that day when she rejected him, and knew that opportunity had passed. Even if she could stomach being married to him.

"Peter, don't be crass." Melisande smiled without any real heat. "You'll frighten the girl. My daughter is still an untried miss. Are you not, Rosalie?"

Her mother held her gaze for some moments, and Rosalie realized her mother was awaiting a response. She actually wanted her to answer to her level of experience. Horley looked avidly intrigued as well.

Rot the both of them! Rather than satisfy her question with a response, Rosalie set her napkin on the table, stopping just short of flinging it. "If you'll excuse me. It's been a long day."

Melisande fluttered her fingers in the direction of the doors. "Off with you, then. I'll see you in the afternoon and we'll evaluate your wardrobe. You must look your best."

She rose from the table and departed the dining room, making her way up the short staircase. Once in her chamber, she rotated in a small circle. Her clothing had already been put away—her mother present to inspect every garment and exclaim over the lavish wardrobe with admiration and a fair amount of jealousy. Her only criticism had been the modest cut of many of the gowns. She insisted they would have to make some alterations. *If you want to catch a husband, you need to show the merchandise to full advantage.* Of course her mother would view her as mere goods. She would serve as wares to Melisande, to be exchanged for benefit. It was a bitter pill and one that did not go down easily.

She pushed the thought away and turned her attention to her surroundings. Her bedchamber was half the size of the room she had occupied at Dec's home. Instead of a mammoth fireplace, a single coal grate sat in the corner. She blinked back the sting of tears and hugged herself as she sank down on the edge of her bed. She couldn't escape *all* her thoughts.

She missed Aurelia. And Aunt Peregrine. And yes. She missed Dec.

She had leapt upon the opportunity to leave because she was afraid. Afraid of her attraction to him. Afraid that she might not be able to hide it. Afraid that she might give herself away—that he would guess that it had been her at Sodom's. Perhaps her biggest fear of all was that she might start to love him a little bit . . . that she already did. Which would make her one grand fool, considering he would never love her back.

But now here. With her mother. With Horley's leering face. She had never felt so alone.

High-pitched laughter drifted from below-stairs, and she knew her mother was far gone in her cups. She recalled that wild laughter from her childhood. The few times she had stayed with her mother following her stepfather's death, Melisande had laughed like that. There had been countless dinners and parties, and always her mother drank. And laughed. Some mornings, Rosalie would rise to find her mother with several of her friends, asleep in some room in the house. The dining room. The drawing room. It was as though they had simply dropped where they stood. The reek of wine clung about the room and their persons. And other smells, too. Rosalie would stare her fill until one of the household staff found her gawking and ushered her away.

Now, she undressed herself without ringing for the maid. Slipping into her night rail, she paused and inhaled the fine lawn of her sleeve. It smelled of Dec's house. That indefinable scent was there. She settled beneath the covers with a deep breath. Staring blindly into the shadows, she willed herself to sleep. Every once in a while a burst of laughter would flow over the air. Usually it belonged to her mother, but sometimes it was Horley, and she would envision his too pretty face with its toothy smile. The man made her uneasy. He reminded her of a shifty-eyed dog that used to lurk around Harwich. Cook always fed him scraps. The mottled-brown mutt always watched the girls, even approached them in the hopes of more food. One day he bit Rachel. He had turned from sniffing dog to snarling beast in a blink. Indeed, Horley reminded her of that dog.

Sitting up, she stared at the door on the other side of the room. Across the long shadows of the chamber. She itched to lock the door. Only there was no lock.

She stood and skirted around the heavy trunk she'd brought from Dec's home. The bureau hadn't been large enough for all her belongings and was brim full with shoes and other items Aunt Peregrine had insisted she needed to complete her wardrobe. Even empty, however, the trunk was heavy. She grunted as she used all her force and shoved it across the rug until it was flush with the door.

Satisfied, she exhaled a great gust of breath and stood back. There. That should at least alert her if someone attempted to enter her bedchamber. Someone like Horley.

Not that she was certain he would, but the need to take precautions was a compulsion she couldn't ignore. Settling back in the bed, she reminded herself that she was better off than she had been a month ago—stuck at school with no prospects and a mother who would not acknowledge her. She had prospects now. She had a dowry. She even had her mother.

Closing her eyes, she pretended that was enough.

She woke to a darkened room. The smoldering coals in the grate had faded to a dim red glow, and she blinked against the near black, wondering with consternation what had woken her. She held herself still, listening to the hum of silence, and then she heard it again.

A faint creaking click.

She turned her head slowly in the direction of the sound, squinting at the hazy outline of the door. Even in the dark, she recognized the sound of the door latch. Someone was trying to enter her bedchamber.

She flung back the counterpane and padded quickly across the room on her bare feet, stretching out her hands so she would touch the trunk first and not run into it. Well-worn wood and a sharp metal hinge met her palms. She curled her fingers into a tight grip just as the latch started to rattle with more force.

Her heart jumped to her throat and she dug in her heels, bearing her weight into the trunk, determined to create as much of a barricade as possible.

Her pulse hammered against her throat. She adjusted her grip, her palms suddenly slick with perspiration.

Her stomach twisted sickly. She doubted her mother would be at her door in the middle of the night. Not after likely consuming that full bottle of claret. She wouldn't crack an eyelid until well after midday. She couldn't imagine any of the household staff would be bothering her either. They were likely comfortable in their beds, exhausted from a long day of catering to the whims of Melisande and Horley.

That left only one possibility. Suddenly the latch ceased to rattle. A hush fell like a blanket over the room. There was no sound save for the harsh fall of her breath.

She didn't relax her grip on the trunk. She held her pose, her shoulders straining, muscles burning. She swallowed, trying to steady her breath. Her gaze peered into the gloom, narrowing on the latch. It didn't turn. Her breath quieted. The rush of blood in her ears was louder now. Still, she couldn't budge. She wouldn't. Not yet.

Her ears strained for the faintest sound. She almost thought she could hear someone else's breath. Just on the other side of the door.

"Rosalie." Her name drifted through the door, whisper-small, taunting in a singsong voice. "Rosie . . . Rosie."

A shudder racked her at the hated nickname. No one called her that. No one except him.

She bit her lip, her knuckles aching where they clutched the door.

"Open . . . open, Rosie."

The coppery tang of blood trickled over her lip and she unclenched her teeth. Terror licked down her spine. It was a combination of the dark, of that frightening voice, of knowing who it was and that he relished his torment of her.

She moistened her lips. Clearly, he knew she was awake and nearby. Just on the other side of the door. She could hear that in his whispered voice.

If this was to be her lot for the duration of her stay here, then she would have many sleepless nights. Cold resolve filled her and she steeled her spine. She needed to let him know he would not bully her. She was not weak.

Swallowing, she flattened a hand against the surface of the door and found her voice. "Go away." Thankfully, the words rang out with confidence.

His slow chuckle floated through the door. "Good night, sweet Rosie. See you on the morrow."

Silence. She waited, unwilling to leave the door just yet.

She bowed her head. Her breath fell slow and raspy. As long as she stayed here, she'd never feel safe. This only deeper cemented in her mind that she could not remain in this house, under this roof. Every moment was a risk. And yet she had nowhere else to go.

She darted to the bed and yanked the counterpane off with two hard tugs. Dragging it after her, she returned to the door and curled up in front of the trunk, wrapping herself in the counterpane. Even if she fell asleep, she would feel if someone tried to force their way into the room. She would wake.

With the trunk at her back, she stared straight ahead, seeing nothing and yet seeing everything.

She needed a husband. Posthaste. It was the only way out of this house. Preferably a husband her mother could not manipulate and one whom she herself could stomach. Would that be too much to ask?

Snuggling into the blanket, she wrapped her arms around her still shaking knees, seeking comfort even if it only came from herself. She needed to take care of herself. No one else would. It was with some grimness that she realized it had always been this way. She came into this world alone. And she was still alone. No one to rely on but herself.

Dec's visage rose in her mind, and she squeezed her eyes tight against the darkness as if that would somehow rid her of his image. Dark was dark, and he was still there.

She couldn't help wondering what he would think of her dire situation. As though he would care that her mother's special friend was making himself a nuisance. As though he would do something to help. *Stupid*. He'd never wanted her underfoot to begin with. He'd done far more than necessary already. She still had her dowry. Why did she think he might care about her miserable fate? He hadn't uttered an objection when her mother collected her.

He might have stepped in and stopped her from being accosted when she'd been disguised at Sodom, but that was a far cry from actually caring about what happened to her—*Rosalie*, his unwanted stepsister.

No. No one could help her but herself.

With that determined thought, she rested her head back against the trunk and settled in to wait for morning.

Chapter 14

After three nights of dozing in and out of sleep in front of her bedchamber door, Rosalie was an exhausted wreck. Horley had made no attempt to return, but she was unwilling to lower her guard and go back to her bed. She continued her vigil, wrapped up in the counterpane in front of the trunk each night, telling herself that it wouldn't be forever.

In addition to these restless nights, her evenings were a whirlwind. She was led about Town by her mother and Horley. He never strayed far, of course.

She'd met the Marquis of Hildebrand at the opera, and he was just as senile as Horley claimed. And as lecherous. He actually invited her to sit upon his lap, leering at her newly altered neckline. Melisande merely smiled in encouragement. As though he had invited Rosalie to tea and not to a seat on his lap. And then Melisande invited *him* to tea. And dinner. Rosalie quickly realized that her mother accepted invitations, almost exclusively, to events she knew the marquis would be attending.

Rosalie was having none of it. Her mother could throw them together all she liked, but she would not marry Hildebrand. Instead of allowing the old man to paw at her, she spent the evenings making herself amenable to other gentlemen who were present whom her mother did not recommend. Odds were, any of them would be an improvement. At least they wouldn't bow to her mother's whims. If they would, Melisande wouldn't scowl when she spotted Rosalie in their company. That soon became Rosalie's criteria. If her mother glared when she spoke to a particular gentleman, Rosalie made a point to continue conversing with him.

It did not take long for her mother to catch on to her game. "You're simply trying to vex me, Rosalie," she complained the evening they spent at a dinner party hosted by Lady Stanley, the marquis's goddaughter. Though her mother wished that she favor the marquis's attentions, Rosalie had instead taken an interest in Lady Stanley's nephew, a barrister from Bedfordshire. "Truly, Rosalie, a barrister?" Melisande demanded. "What could you be thinking?"

"I was thinking that he was very kind and an excellent conversationalist." And he did not make her skin crawl with a mere look. He was very circumspect, his gaze politely trained on her face and not her décolletage as he addressed her.

"Conversationalist? You have friends for that. Or you will. You need not rely on your husband for conversation. With any luck, he'll expect very little from you after he gets an heir or two off you. Then you can take a lover. With discretion, of course."

Such a future sounded bleak to her. She lifted her chin. "I'm thinking I shall have whatever husband I *choose* to have."

Melisande shook her head. "I don't know what's gotten into you. You never used to be such a rotten, willful girl. That school ruined you."

Horley had watched her through the entire exchange, his gaze narrowing as though he wasn't thinking particularly kind thoughts of her. As if her behavior somehow affected him. Rosalie would have preferred to talk to her mother alone, especially when the conversation turned to her taking a lover. Horley's expression had turned positively lascivious at that. Pointless wishing. He was always underfoot. No conversation was private.

She had hoped he might leave at some point, return to a home of his own. But his living with her mother appeared a permanent arrangement. Such flouting of convention was scandalous, but her mother claimed he was her protégé—a painter the like of Rembrandt—though Rosalie snooped about and did not find so much as a paintbrush in the house.

Her snooping did, however, lead her to Mrs. Potter. The garrulous housekeeper provided a wealth of information. Apparently, Horley had been with her mother for a year now. Mrs. Potter had never seen him pick up so much as a pencil to doodle on paper, so this claim that he was an artist? Complete fiction. He didn't possess two shillings to rub together. Money lenders often came in search for him. Following Melisande's orders, the staff always claimed ignorance of his whereabouts.

"Indeed, we're under strict instructions. Anyone comes looking for Lord Horley, we haven't seen him," Mrs. Potter explained one morning as she puttered about the kitchen, helping Cook prepare Melisande's afternoon meal—the first of the day. She set a plate full of biscuits in front of Rosalie, motioning for her to eat. "Got his claws in deep to your mama, that one."

The tight-lipped cook harrumphed as she cut into a fresh loaf of bread. Rosalie bit into the still warm biscuit with a satisfied moan. A dog slept before the crackling hearth, appearing content on a threadbare rug. The kitchen was the one place Rosalie felt safe. Horley would never think to set foot within its humble walls. Perhaps she should sneak in here at night. She could curl up with Cook's dog and sleep safely. Mrs. Potter poured fresh tea into her cup.

Rosalie took a sip, sighing in contentment as she eyed the kitchen fire.

"There you are now. Eat," Mrs. Potter chided. "You could use some meat on your bones. Might help with your color . . . you're too pale. Are you not resting enough? Perhaps you need a nap this afternoon, miss."

Apparently, her fatigue was noticeable. She couldn't hide the shadows beneath her eyes. A fact all the more problematic when Aurelia surprised her with a visit.

"Heavens, you look dreadful," she exclaimed when Rosalie joined her in the drawing room.

Rosalie laughed dryly. "Hello to you, too, Aurelia."

"Come now. You know I love you. Only a friend would be so honest with you." She took Rosalie's hands in hers and pulled her down next to her on the settee, her forehead knitted with concern. "Are you so very unhappy here?"

The sudden reminder that she actually possessed a friend—a very dear friend who cared about her—made emotion surge to Rosalie's chest. She hadn't had anyone she could call a friend since Rachel, her schoolmate at Harwich. "Oh, Aurelia." She flung her arms around her.

"There there." She patted her back. "I'm here now."

Rosalie hugged her for several moments longer, taking solace in her friend, in the warmth of another person who actually cared for her. She had felt so very alone the last several nights and knew she would be alone again in the nights ahead. And perhaps beyond that. Even after she made a match for herself. She fought down the lump that rose in her throat.

"It was good of you to come." She pulled back finally, still holding Aurelia's hand. She didn't want to let go. She wanted that small contact, at least.

"Of course. Now tell me what you have been up to. From the look of these shadows—" She gently brushed a fingertip beneath Rosalie's eye. "—I would say your mother has been keeping you up nights. I heard you were at the opera earlier this week. And at Lady Stanton's. Rumor has it you've been spending time with the Marquis of Hildebrand." Aurelia wrinkled her nose. "Tell me your mother isn't considering him for you. He's ancient, not to mention revolting."

Rosalie shrugged, not answering to the matter of Hildebrand. "I haven't been sleeping well."

"Well, if my mother was shoving me at Lord Hildebrand, I wouldn't be sleeping well either."

Rosalie tried to smile and failed. Tears threatened and she blinked them back, hating that she should feel so emotional.

"What? What is it?" Aurelia's gaze flitted over her face. "You have me worried now. Please tell me what is wrong."

"Oh, Aurelia, if it were only my mother shoving me at Lord Hildebrand, I shouldn't feel half so wretched." She gulped back tears then and told her friend everything. Her sleepless nights guarding her bedroom door, and her need to accept the next offer that came her way to simply get out from beneath her mother and Horley.

"That is intolerable, Rosalie," Aurelia said. "You cannot stay here a moment longer. We will go to Dec—"

"No," she bit out with a shake of her head. "He wants nothing to do with me. Or my mother." He'd let her go with nary a blink. "I will not drag him into this."

Aurelia shook her head, her brown eyes deep and anxious. "It's a little late for that, isn't it? And you cannot think to remain here—"

"I can manage. Horley simply enjoys his cat and mouse game with me. He is no threat. My mother, and thereby me . . . we're all he has. He's penniless. He won't abuse me. He merely wishes to torment me for his own amusement."

"And that is why you guard your door at night? Because you think he is no threat?" Aurelia pressed.

"I'm cautious."

"And how long can you continue to do that?"

Aurelia angled her head, her expression both earnest and sympathetic.

"As long as necessary."

"Hm." She fell back on the sofa, clearly unconvinced. "Perhaps you need to call upon me at home. We can put you up in my chamber and you can sneak in a little nap." She touched Rosalie's cheek. "Look at you. You need a good rest, sweet girl."

Rosalie pulled her friend's hand from her cheek. "Thank you for letting me unburden myself, but you needn't worry. It is good of you to come. You make me stronger. Just the sight of you . . . knowing I have your friendship."

"You daft girl. I've been starved for a proper friend for an age. It's just been Mama and the girls she thinks I ought to be friends with." Aurelia rolled her eyes. "All little beasts, with their simpering smiles and thinly veiled insults." She lifted her voice an octave. *"Oh, Aurelia. I wish I could wear that but such a style would overpower my slight frame."*

Rosalie laughed. "I'm certain they are no match for you."

"You know what we should do?" Aurelia bolted upright on the settee, and then dropped her voice to a hush. "We should return to Sodom."

Rosalie shook her head. "I was an absolute wreck the last time. It was far too, too—"

"Scandalous? Debauched?" Aurelia nodded, smiling widely. "Yes. Indeed."

She shook her head. "No. What if I bumped into Dec again—"

"Then you can kiss him again."

"Aurelia!" Despite her outburst, her heart tripped at the suggestion.

"You know you want to."

Rosalie couldn't deny this, so she held silent.

After a few moments, Aurelia sighed, taking her silence for denial. "Very well. I suppose once was risk enough." She glanced away, looking a little dejected. A little sad. Rosalie well knew how she felt. Trapped in a life that seemed to be moving without any guidance from her.

For whatever Sodom was, however depraved it had been, Dec had been there. He had wanted her. And it hadn't felt sordid or depraved. It had felt special. She had felt special. Like someone was seeing her perhaps for the first time in her life. Ironic, considering she'd been wearing a mask and wig, but there it was. That kiss had felt . . . it felt like *everything*. It had consumed her. It haunted her still. When she sat awake at night, propped against her bedchamber door, his lips, his mouth on hers, tracked through her mind again and again.

She had trembled when he touched her. And for one moment, she'd thought his hand trembled, too.

Perhaps she could have that again. Just as Aurelia suggested. If only for one more night. She'd had that kiss—lived it. She wanted to have it again. She wanted to *live* more.

As much as she knew it was wrong, she missed Dec. Seeing Aurelia only drove that home, made her think of him, ache for him. She felt her loneliness even more acutely.

That night at Sodom . . . she hadn't felt quite so lonely. In Dec's arms, with his mouth and hands on her, she had felt alive and free. Free to choose. Free to feel. She wanted that again. Even if it could go nowhere. Even if it changed nothing.

She wanted more.

Chapter 15

𝒯he parchment crinkled in Dec's pocket where he had stuffed it earlier. Not a half hour ago the missive had arrived, intruding on his solitary dinner. His appetite had fled at once and he'd pushed back from the table.

Not that he had much of an appetite lately. He'd taken his meals alone the last couple of nights, shrouded in the silence of an empty house. Strange how he suddenly noticed that emptiness, that silence. He'd never been especially conscious of it before. He had never minded, but now he felt the absence of his aunt and cousin and Rosalie keenly. Ah, hell, Rosalie. He felt her absence most of all.

He had come to expect the soft sound of her voice, her laughter . . . glimpses of her throughout her house, sitting in his garden, her bare toes peeking out from the hem of her gown. He still saw her even though she wasn't here. Her image was imprinted on his mind. Even her scent seemed to trail him, that faint scent. Nowhere else more than at the door to his room, so close to her old room. Honeysuckle, he thought. How did she come to smell of honeysuckle in the midst of London?

He'd let her go with Melisande, telling himself it was for the best. It was right. They were mother and daughter. Rosalie belonged with her.

He'd always viewed Rosalie as an extension of Melisande. Never as her own self. Never her own person. She was part of the woman who had destroyed his youth and robbed him of his father and left him a shell. Melisande had taken so much from him that he could never get back, and he had simply viewed Rosalie as cut from the same cloth.

Until he saw them side by side in his drawing room.

It dawned on him then how entirely different

they were. Rosalie was nothing like her mother. She wasn't Melisande. The evidence had always been there, but not until that moment had he faced it.

As much as he told himself letting her go was right, he felt guilty. He worried. Even though he told himself he needn't. Rosalie still had the advantage of her dowry. She would not be with her mother for long. She'd have her pick of suitors. Her future was bright. He'd seen to that.

So why did that rationale not make him feel better? Not that it mattered how he felt. It was done. She'd been eager to leave, and he had no cause to keep her. He was nothing more than a stepbrother who had not even been in her life for years.

He looked down at the parchment again, flexing his fingers around the edges. The missive could not have arrived at a better time. The distraction was much welcome. The single sentence, neatly scrawled on a blank sheet of parchment, took his thoughts to a kiss that had affected him more than the seductions of any expertly experienced female. There had been something about her. Her utter lack of guile and artifice. His body responded at the memory, recalling her soft mouth, so warm and responsive to him . . . and the little sound she made when he had lifted her against him.

Meet me at Sodom tonight.

It wasn't signed, but he knew. The possibility of seeing her again made his skin tighten and mouth dry. He hadn't returned to Sodom since the night he kissed the masked girl. Nor had he touched another female. He simply wasn't in the mood. In the past, any willing woman would suffice. A night's pleasure, a few hours losing himself, and the numbness faded. For a short while. Until the next time. But *any* woman wasn't what he wanted anymore, and the realization troubled him more than he wanted to admit. None of them appealed in the slightest.

The only other woman to even tempt him had been Rosalie, and since she was out of the question—and wisely out of reach—this opportunity was one he would not pass.

He changed his jacket quickly and departed.

Sodom was crowded tonight. He spied Max at one of the tables. This time wearing clothes. A woman sat on his lap, her arm draped around him, fingers playing in his hair, but he seemed more interested in his cards. In fact, he looked almost annoyed, stretching away from her delving fingers.

Mrs. Bancroft greeted him with a warm smile. "Your Grace, how good to see you. We've missed you." Dressed modestly in a canary yellow gown with black beads at the hem and cuffs that reached her neck, the proprietress was an anomaly among the rest of the women present, which only added to her allure. Men in the room followed her movement across the room with hungry eyes. She was as unattainable as the queen. She was untouchable and every man wanted to conquer her. Every man but him. He was here for one reason.

"Mrs. Bancroft." He bowed over her hand. Despite her charm, there was only one woman he wanted to see tonight. He opened his mouth to inquire if she had seen her.

As though she read his mind, she volunteered, "This way. She is waiting for you."

His blood quickened. She led him to the second floor at a sedate pace that drove him mad. If he knew which room she was taking him to, he might have actually rushed past her in his eagerness.

He inhaled, chiding himself to not behave as a green lad. His hands opened and curled at his sides as he fought for his composure. He wasn't even certain she wanted more than another kiss from him. That, quite clearly, had been all she was willing to sample the last time. It would be torment, but he would take it. He would take whatever she wanted to give.

Mrs. Bancroft stopped before the door. "I think you can manage this from here."

Alone, he actually hesitated, his hand on the latch. He took a moment, gathering his composure so that he didn't come at her like some randy goat.

He opened the door then and she was there. His eyes adjusted to the dimness of the chamber. She popped up from the edge of the bed where she had been sitting, her hands falling to her sides. Her midnight-dark hair slid like a waterfall around her shoulders.

She was wearing a darker gown, but in the shadowed chamber, he couldn't identify the precise color. The bodice was sleeveless, leaving her shoulders bare save the veil of her hair. It was another form-fitting dress, and he wondered if she had borrowed it again from Mrs. Bancroft. He felt only relief that she wore it for him. That she had come back to Sodom for him and not to experiment with another man.

He shut the door behind him and leaned against it. Even in the murky gloom, even through the eyeholes of her domino, her gaze seared him. The way she looked at him was devouring and intimate.

"You came back," he murmured.

"I wanted to see you again." Her low, husky voice was like a physical stroke on his skin. She rubbed her palms against the sides of her gown, and he could only think of that hand rubbing down his chest in that same manner.

He glanced around the room and his lip curled. It was well-appointed but he couldn't help think about how many people had used this room before them. As glad as he was that she wanted to see him again, he regretted it was here, in this place. The idea rose, surprising him. Sodom had always been good enough for him before, but for some reason he wanted more for her. He wanted her in his bed. At his home.

The idea was novel to him. Perhaps it was time to take a mistress. Random women flitting in and out of his life, his bed, had been good enough before, but if he could find one woman to satisfy him for a spell, that wouldn't be so bad. There was something appealing to the notion. Except the only one he could imagine in that role stood before him.

Rosalie's face was there, a flash across his mind before he thrust it away. She could not even be considered.

"What's your name?" He knew no names were required here. It was understood at Sodom, but he could not continue without knowing what to call her.

Her tentative smile slipped, and he knew he had crossed a line. He pushed off from the door and advanced on her. "Come. I must call you something."

She shook her head, her mouth pressed shut, and she looked around the chamber as if suddenly reconsidering.

He stopped before her and cupped her face in both hands, his thumbs resting on the stiff brocade of her domino. He loathed it. He wanted to rip it off, but he knew such an action would send her bolting from his arms faster.

"No names," she whispered in that low, guttural scratch.

"But you know mine."

"You've no need to protect your identity." Her tongue darted out to moisten her lips. "If who I am is so important to you, then we should put a stop to this—"

His mouth silenced her, muffling the words he refused to even entertain. There was no ending this. No stopping.

He needed it. Her. An ease to the ache that plagued him. That he'd been unable to appease in weeks. He tasted her with lips and tongue. She was ready for him, opening her mouth and meeting his tongue with less hesitancy than the last time. There was no awkwardness. She'd made up her mind before she came here. He felt that at once.

Her hands crept around his neck and he deepened the kiss, growling when she slid her fingers into his hair and pressed her slim body against his.

She moaned into his mouth. "I missed—"

Her lips froze, as though startled by her own words.

He pulled back to look down at her. "Missed what? Me?" He smiled slowly.

She dipped her head, and he knew she was embarrassed. He could guess her thoughts then— that a single kiss with a stranger shouldn't warrant her missing him, and she was correct. If a woman had announced she *missed* him before, he would have walked as fast as possible in the opposite direction. Yet hearing the words from her made something swell inside his chest.

He smiled and brushed a tendril of hair that fell across the hated domino hiding half of her face from him. Her eyes were dark pools, like the night sea. Again he wished to tear the offensive fabric from her face so that he could see her eyes. Her face. Bloody hell, he wished for enough light so he could see all of her and rid himself of the mystery. Was this even her hair or a wig?

She blinked slowly. "N-No. I . . ."

"But you came back. You sent me that note."

"You must think me terribly forward."

"A girl who gave me her first kiss?" He cocked his head, watching the movement of her lips. "That's a far cry from what I think."

He leaned down and pressed a lingering kiss to the corner of that mouth. Her breath escaped in a sharp hitch. Another one of her little sounds he well remembered. "You can say you've missed me. Because I've missed—" He kissed the next corner. "—this mouth. The little sounds that escape it."

He dragged his thumb across her bottom lip, his other arm pulling her closer, one hand gliding down her back. He spread his fingers wide. He could feel her through the thin fabric of her dress. The small bumps along her spine. The twin indentations directly above where her cheeks started to swell. "Have you kissed anyone else since that night?" he asked without deliberation. He had to know. He couldn't stand the thought that she had come back here and taken with another man. That some man might have kissed her. Or done more than kiss.

"Have you?" she was quick to rebut.

He laughed lightly, knowing he deserved that. He had no right to inquire. He had no claim on her. "No. I haven't."

Her eyes widened. Apparently she didn't expect that answer from him. Her gaze roved over his face. "You haven't kissed anyone . . . since me?"

"You don't believe me?"

"I merely find it hard to believe. You're . . . Banbury."

"And what do you know of me?" He angled his head, something sharpening inside him. A sense, an awareness, that maybe she knew him. "Wait. Do you . . . *know* me?" His heart beat a little faster at the possibility. Did he know her? Had they met before?

The idea that their paths had crossed . . . that they might cross again, outside the walls of Sodom . . .

She shook her head fiercely. "Merely by reputation. We do not move in the same circles.

"That is unfortunate."

She angled her head and he felt her curious stare even if he couldn't clearly see her eyes in the shadow of her domino. "Why? Out there. In the real world." She motioned in the general direction of the door. "We could never have this."

"Perhaps we should make a standing appointment, then." He brought his hand lower, cupping her derrière with one hand and drawing her fully against him. Partly so she could feel his desire, his cock hard against her belly. Mostly so he could just have her softness cushioning the part of him that throbbed to sink inside her.

"Here? At Sodom again?" Her words floated on a little gasp. Her chin lifted slightly, indicating the chamber.

"It doesn't need to be here." He would prefer it *not* be here.

She bit her bottom lip, mulling over his words. "I don't know that I can do that. This . . . was hard enough to arrange. It's tricky leaving the house."

He frowned, not liking that this might be all they had. Deciding he needed to make this night count, he brought an arm around her waist and lifted her off her feet, bringing her mouth up to his and kissing her as he carried her across the room.

She moaned against his lips, her hands flying

to his shoulders as though frightened he would drop her.

"Don't worry. I've got you."

He lowered her down on the bed, wedging himself between her thighs. Her skirts fell back, exposing her legs, deliciously stocking-clad legs with lacy black garters that he wanted to remove slowly. With his teeth.

He sat back, gazing at every inch of her displayed like some decadent feast for him. Those eyes of hers were dark and unreadable in her mask, peering up at him. Her lips were swollen from kissing, parted in a small O of wonder.

He ran his palms up her calves, over the curve of her knees, along her thighs, stopping just at her garters. Her breathing grew louder, raspy.

He took her hand, guiding her to him. He pressed her palm directly over his breeches, against his cock, groaning at the sensation of her hand, hesitant at first, and then bolder, molding to the shape of him. Her fingers flexed and traced him. He shuddered. Unable to help himself, he showed her what to do, grinding the base of her palm against him in rhythmic strokes.

"Oh," she gasped. "It's growing . . . bigger."

He dropped over her until his mouth grazed the tender skin of her neck. "That's what you do to me." He kissed his way down her throat, fastening his mouth over her breast through the sheer fabric of her dress, sucking until her nipple beaded hard and she arched into his mouth.

"M-More."

He wasn't even certain what that meant, what *more* even was. He wasn't even certain if she knew. All he knew was that he needed her, too.

He released his grip on her hand, leaving her there, fingers splayed over the length of him. She continued to explore, her slender fingers pressing and stroking his straining cock. His skin pulled tight at the base of his skull and his breath fell faster. He bit lightly, nipping at her breasts through the wet fabric, cupping them with both hands, his thumbs rolling over her nipples until she was shuddering and crying out sweetly in his arms.

Her hands still caressed him through his trousers. If he didn't compose himself, he would lose himself like some green boy. He locked hard fingers around her wrist, stalling her movements.

She lifted her mouth to his neck, her lips moving as she spoke. "Please. May I touch it . . . you?"

The whispered request undid him. He froze for a moment, holding her gaze, wondering how he could stand much more of this. And then the answer came swift and resounding in his head . . . in the hard pump of blood in his veins. *He couldn't. Not anymore.*

He pulled up, yanking open the front of his breeches, briefly severing the sweet torture of her hand on him. And then he was free, his cock jutting between them.

Her eyes fixed on him, her mouth parted in wonder. Neither one of them moved or spoke. Indeed, it seemed neither one of them breathed.

He couldn't move. He didn't trust himself. Her gaze alone felt like a caress. He inhaled, holding himself in check.

"Oh . . . I've never seen . . ."

He smiled, almost in pain. Of course she hadn't. He almost wished she wasn't so inexperienced. It wasn't his habit to debauch virgins. He felt like the veritable scoundrel stealing away with a maiden's virtue. His arms strained, holding himself in check over her.

Then she touched him. Those slight fingers wrapped around him. Her bare hand to his manhood, skin to skin. His cock pulsed and he forgot everything except sensation and mind-obliterating need.

Chapter 16

*H*is mouth crashed over hers and she could only think that it wasn't enough. The pressure of his lips and tongue ravaging her wasn't enough. She mewled, writhing and wiggling under him, her hand never releasing him. She loved the feel of him. Like silk over steel in her hand. She reveled in the way he shuddered and groaned as she worked her fingers on him, rubbing her thumb over the tip of him until she felt moisture rise there to kiss her skin.

Her other hand moved up, touching his bare

chest. She ran her hands over his abdomen and then higher up his chest. Because she could. Because she was free to do so. She savored the cut of heavy muscle under the warm, contracting skin. The tight nipples that shrank under her questing fingers.

"I have to touch you," he growled. "It's my turn."

Before she understood fully, he slid down her body. His hands found her thighs, splaying them wider, and then his face was between them.

"What are you—"

"Ssh. Trust me. I won't do anything you don't like. Nothing that won't give you pleasure."

And then his fingers were there, sliding against her wetness, parting her. She started, startled at the hand there, touching her in ways she had never touched herself. His hand drifted up, finding and pressing on a spot that had her crying out and arching.

"There you are," he said in a deeply satisfied voice. There was a shifting of his weight, a rustling of fabric as he moved, and then his mouth! Dear Lord, he placed his mouth on her.

She cried out, sitting up, her hands seizing his head buried between her thighs. He pressed a hand to the flat of her stomach, forcing her back down with a deep, guttural groan as he feasted on her, his mouth sucking on that tiny nub, drawing it between his lips and flaying it with his tongue. Instantly she came apart, flying into a million little pieces. He eased his mouth then, licking at the over-sensitized little button even as he slipped one finger inside her, stretching her.

"Oh, so bloody tight," he moaned against her, his finger working in and out. In and out. Again she felt the pressure building. She panted, her fingers still flexing in his hair. He raked his teeth against that nub again and she cried, pushing herself against his mouth, greedy for more, stunned that any of this was possible. He shifted his wrist then, did something marvelous with his finger, brought it up, hitting some hidden, secret place within her, and the pressure inside her burst.

Again she shook and flew apart.

He came over her again and she felt him. The hardness of him against her thigh. Instinctively, she sought him, arching, wanting that hardness thick inside her. He dragged his mouth against her neck, biting and sucking at the tendon there. She wiggled until she felt the head of him at her opening.

"God," he gasped. "You're so wet. So ready."

She nodded dumbly. Past thinking. Feeling only.

"Tell me. Ask for it," he pleaded.

She opened her mouth. It was there. On the tip of her tongue. The engorged tip of him prodded the opening of her channel, and her eyes flew wide. His hand moved between them, and she felt him grasp himself, better positioning that part of him against her, ready to slide within.

Good God! She had not meant to go this far. No. *No!*

He stiffened over her, and she realized she must have uttered the words out loud.

She grabbed his wrist, her voice ringing out desperately in the air, which was thick with the smell of them. "Wait. Stop."

He froze instantly, sucking in a deep breath.

She sat up and shoved her skirts back down over her legs. He backed away, needing the distance to stop himself from touching her, from hauling her back into his arms again. He expelled a deep breath and dragged his hands through his hair, stopping when he saw that his hands were shaking. He folded his fingers into fists and sucked in more air, reaching for restraint.

"This is too much." She shook back the sleek fall

of hair from her shoulders and pressed her hands to her cheeks as if that would somehow help her cool them. "I didn't mean for this to go so very far."

"A week ago I had to steal a kiss from you." His voice shook a little as he said this, and he swallowed. "You may not believe me, but this was not my plan."

"Of course. That was not my thought. I sent you the letter, after all, requesting your presence."

Nodding, he inched away . . . although a part of him felt like lashing out like a petulant child at her. Had she lured him here only to torment him? If that were the case, she could count herself successful.

"And you didn't steal it." Her fingers brushed her swollen mouth as though still feeling him there. "Tonight . . . this was all me. I initiated this. I'm to blame." Her throaty voice broke at that, and he looked to her sharply, wondering at the thread of emotion he heard.

"Why did you send me the note?" What had she expected? What did she want? She clearly wasn't a girl willing to forget herself in an illicit liaison, so what was this about, then?

She scooted to the edge of the bed, curling her fingers around the side and hunching her shoulders. "I'm sorry. You must think me contrary. I merely wanted something for myself before . . ."

Her voice faded.

He moved to the edge of the bed, tucking himself back in and fastening his trousers. "Before?"

She turned her face to him. "Before I'm gone." Her voice was hoarse and whisper-soft, as though she was afraid saying it aloud would make it happen—would make her disappear right then. "While I'm still me."

He angled his head. She made no sense. Who else would she be? Instead of asking, he settled for: "Are you leaving Town?"

"No. Yes . . . I mean, I don't know." She gave her head a small shake. The black strands swished sharply. Her hand went to her hair self-consciously as though checking it, and that's when he knew it was a wig. "Perhaps, I will. I didn't mean . . ." A pause fell before she continued, admitting, "I'm to be wed."

Everything came together then, clicking. "Ah. Now I understand," he murmured, feeling unaccountably angry. He stood in one swift move and turned, towering over her. "So you wished to have a little fun first for yourself. Was that it? Or, wait." He held up his hand. "Are you honing your skills so that you might please your husband? Learning what to do while stopping short of the full act?"

She stared up at him with her eyes wide through the eyeholes of her domino. "You are angry." It was part statement, part question.

He knew he had no right to snap at her. There were no promises or expectations between them. Those things didn't exist at Sodom. So she was to be married. Half the women who frequented this establishment were already married. He'd never cared about that before. Why did he care now?

Even as he asked himself this he knew. *Because she was the second female to stir something in him. The second one that he could not possess. First Rosalie and now her.*

She rose from the bed. "You can't possibly understand. What would a man in your position know about being helpless and vulnerable, subject to the whim of others?"

Everything. He understood helplessness and vulnerability. In a way he would never admit. His throat tightened but he refused to give voice to the sudden dark thoughts swirling through him.

He followed her, stalking really, feeling dangerous in mood. "You're here, are you not?" He looked her up and down in her gown that invited a man's touch. The shape of her breasts through the fabric was clearly outlined. He could discern the pebbled tips of her nipples, and the distraction, the urge to taste them again, only angered him. "Women who come here know what they want. That's why they're here. They're in control. They're not vulnerable. This isn't the place vulnerable or helpless females frequent. Someone should have made that clear to you."

She made a sound that was part snort, part growl. "Oh, you're insufferable. Clearly it was a mistake to reveal anything of my true self—"

He laughed roughly. "You want to reveal something of yourself?" He stepped closer, and she took a step back. His hands curled into fists at his sides. The temptation was there, to rip the mask from her face. "Let's begin with your name. Your face. Your bloody hair!"

She drew a hissing breath. "This has gone far enough." She turned and reached for a cloak draped on the corner of the bed that he had not noticed before. She flung it around her shoulders, her movements jerky. "You know I cannot—"

"Go home. Marry. Show him what you've learned from me. He should count himself very fortunate indeed." She froze at his deliberately cruel words. Her back still to him, he moved behind her, pressing his body against hers, letting her feel his hardness against the small of her back. "But know that when you're with him, you'll be thinking of me."

A shudder racked her body. He stroked a hand down her false hair. He picked up the mass of it, brought it over her shoulder and grazed his mouth over the tender skin of her neck. She made that sound again. That delicious hitch of her breath. He bit down softly where her shoulder and neck met, let his teeth scrape the skin he knew was so very sensitive. She jerked a little, making a soft, strangling sound low in her throat.

She lurched away from the press of his body and bolted for the door, fumbling for the latch.

He watched her go, his hand dropping to his side as she slipped from the room without a backward glance.

She made her way to Mrs. Bancroft's private rooms where she quickly shed the scandalous plum-colored gown she had borrowed from the proprietress. Once again in her own modest clothing, she kept the domino just to be safe, repositioning it on her face and covering herself head-to-toe with her cloak. She wrote a hasty note of thanks to Mrs. Bancroft, knowing she would never be back. Tonight had to be the last time. Satisfied, she headed back down the stairs, still shaking, *still* longing.

She moved blindly, seeing nothing of her surroundings. The need to flee pumped through her blood with urgency. If she didn't leave now, she'd lose everything. She'd lose herself.

She had only thought of her desire to see him again. Nothing else had mattered. She had not considered how much worse, how much harder, it would be to walk away this time.

The doorman fetched a hack for her and saw her safely inside. She managed to hold on until she was safely ensconced in the hack and on her way back to her mother's house. She smoothed a shaking hand over the skirts of her familiar sensible gown before bringing both of her hands up to her face. With a ragged exhale, she released a choked sob into her curled fingers.

Coming to Sodom had been a selfish, desperate act. She had sent the missive to Dec because she felt drowning and helpless beneath her mother's roof. Lonely and aching . . .

She wanted to escape her existence even if for just a little while. And she couldn't stop thinking about Dec. She missed him. She couldn't stop remembering his kiss and thinking how she would never have that again.

It had been rash. She'd very nearly given everything to him tonight. And not just her virtue—although that very nearly happened. She had actually toyed with the idea of removing her domino and tossing her wig aside that moment at the end when he had come up behind her.

When had she become so foolish? A girl who thought that the stepbrother who never wanted anything to do with her might actually want her? *Her.* Rosalie. She lifted her face from her hands. A tear rolled down her cheek and she dashed it away with clumsy fingers.

The house was silent when she crept around to the servants' entrance. She rapped twice at the door and Mrs. Potter appeared as promised, opening the door for her. The housekeeper hadn't asked for details when Rosalie requested her help, simply agreed with a smile and a wink.

With a nod of thanks, Rosalie slipped inside and fled to her chamber, pushing the trunk back into place against the door. A precaution that might not be necessary anymore, but one she wouldn't neglect, nevertheless.

She'd taken enough risks for the night. She was quite finished with living on the edge, reaching for things that weren't to be. She needed to get out of this house. And she needed to forget about Dec.

She wasn't certain which would be harder to do.

Chapter 17

The swish of his bedchamber's drapes dimly registered as sudden light punched his eyelids. Dec groaned and reached for a pillow, quite certain that someone was on the verge of death. He'd played cards with Max late into the night and imbibed too freely of brandy. At the time, it seemed a good idea. Better than going home to an empty house where he would sleep in an empty bed.

A dull throb pounded at his temples. He cracked an eye to peer out at the person who dared to interrupt his sleep.

Aurelia stood beside his bed, hands propped on her hips.

He groaned. "Aren't you in the wrong house?" He hadn't seen her since she and Aunt Peregrine packed up their things and moved. "What time is it?"

"It's early. I couldn't sleep last night, and I vowed I would see you as soon as the day dawned."

He sat up, shielding his eyes with a hand. "What's so bloody urgent? And would you mind closing the drapes again?"

"No. I need your attention."

"You have it," he growled.

"Have you seen or spoken to Rosalie?"

"Not since she left. No." Not that her absence had stopped his thoughts from straying to her. Max had mentioned seeing her at the opera in the company of old Hildebrand. The man was a letch. Clearly Melisande wasn't looking out for Rosalie's best interests if she let him court her. Not that he expected her to. He might have been concerned for Rosalie if he didn't already know she was determined to marry a man of her choosing. She had made that abundantly clear to him.

"Well, you need to."

He looked at her sharply. "Why? What's wrong?"

Aurelia waved her hands wildly. "I told her I would not come to you—"

He sat up. "Too late for that. You're here. Out with it."

She nodded once, her lips pressing into a firm, resolute line. "Your stepmother has a lover living with her."

He made a snort. "Unsurprising. She's never been overly concerned with her reputation." Melisande still had the weight of her title, fortunately. And while it wasn't seemly, he'd placed a large enough dowry on Rosalie's head that most suitors would look beyond her mother's indiscretions.

"It's not that . . ."

"What is it?"

"It's him. Melisande's lover. He makes Rosalie . . . uncomfortable."

The hairs at his nape prickled. He fought to swallow against his suddenly constricted throat. "Has he harmed her?"

"No. Not since I spoke with her. He just makes her feel . . . anxious, I suppose."

He well remembered what it felt like to be uncomfortable in your own home. *Hunted.* "Turn your back," he snapped.

Aurelia blinked. "What—"

"Unless you wish to see me without my clothes, turn your back."

"Oh!" She whirled around and he flung the counterpane back from the bed and strode to his armoire on the other side of the chamber. He jerked on clothes with angry movements. "You may turn around," he said, tucking his shirt into his breeches. "His name? I'll have it."

"It's Horley. He's a viscount."

"I've never heard of him."

"A penniless viscount, apparently. Several years younger than your stepmother."

His lips curled with distaste. She always did prefer them young. "You should have come to me at once with this."

Aurelia nodded, looking miserable. "I know. She made me promise. And she sounded so certain that she could handle the situation, but she looked exhausted. She's not sleeping. He tried to enter her room one night, and now she's keeping vigil."

He uttered a profanity that made Aurelia's eyes widen. It was as much directed at him as anyone else. He'd known. In his gut he had known that he shouldn't have let her go. He was as much to blame for this as Melisande. Rage filled him at how helpless she must feel. How alone.

Just then the words from last night drifted back to him: *What would a man in your position know about being helpless and vulnerable?*

He knew, and he'd let that very thing happen to Rosalie when he could have prevented it.

Over a day had passed since she confessed her situation to Aurelia. Anything could have happened since then. "Damn it, Aurelia. You should have told me."

She nodded, her eyes gleaming with moisture, and he realized she was on the verge of tears. In three strides he was across the room and folding his cousin into his arms. "I'm sorry. This is not your fault. I'm angry and taking it out on you. This is my fault for letting her go. You told me, and I thank you for that."

She nodded, sniffing back the threat of tears. He moved away and slipped on his vest, not even bothering with the buttons. Grabbing his jacket from where he had discarded it last evening, he shrugged into the rumpled garment. "Go home. Fetch your things and Aunt Peregrine. Inform her that I will need her again."

"What are you doing?"

He paused only a fraction of a moment at the door. "Bringing Rosalie home."

He rapped on the door fiercely until an annoyed-looking butler opened it. Dec strode past him and into the foyer. "Miss Hughes," he bit out. "Where is she?"

The butler shook his head. "Your pardon, sir? You cannot simply walk in here unannounced—"

"I'll announce myself. I'm the Duke of Banbury." He waved a little finger. "This house. Your wages. All are due to me." He snapped his fingers. "Like that, they can be gone."

The butler's eyes widened.

"Now where," he continued, "is Miss Hughes?"

The butler pointed to the stairs. "I believe she is in the dining room with Her Grace."

He didn't wait. He took the stairs two at a time, the butler following.

He marched on the large double doors, assuming it was the dining room. He was correct. His stepmother sat at the head of the table, Rosalie to her left and a man to her right. Presumably, Horley.

"Declan?" Melisande stood, dropping her napkin to her plate. "This is a surprise." She motioned for an empty chair, a glimmer of unease in her eyes. "Would you care to join us?"

He didn't acknowledge her. His gaze zeroed in on Rosalie. She looked pale. Dark smudges marred the skin beneath her eyes. "Rosalie. Get your things."

She blinked, angling her head uncertainly. "My things?"

"Or leave them. They can be sent over later."

"Now just a moment, Declan. You can't charge in here and demand Rosalie leave with you—"

He avoided looking at Melisande even as her voice continued at a shrill pitch. Instead he focused on Rosalie. "I never should have let you walk out. This place is poison."

"See here now!" Horley surged to his feet. "You can't walk in here and say such—"

Dec turned, took the three strides necessary to reach Horley, and struck him with one swift blow to the face. The satisfying smack of his knuckles into Horley's jaw made him feel slightly better.

"Peter!" Melisande screamed and lurched from her chair to where he dropped to the floor. She lifted Horley by the shoulders, cradled him in her lap as she glared at Dec. "You beast! What is wrong with you?"

"What's wrong is that your *special* friend here has been paying particularly close attention to Rosalie. And then he dared to open his mouth in my presence. He's lucky he's still in possession of his teeth." He waved a hand at Horley where he moaned, clutching his jaw.

Melisande flicked her wild-eyed gaze toward her daughter. "Did she tell you those lies? Peter would never even look twice at Rosalie!"

Rosalie stood now, her hands buried into her skirts. Her unblinking stare fixed on Dec.

"I'm sorry," he said to her, then shook his head and swallowed past the lump in his throat. "I should have stopped you. I should have told you that you could stay."

She looked down with a shaky sigh that lifted her shoulders before meeting his gaze again. "I didn't ask to stay, either. I did not give you much chance to say anything on the matter."

"Rosalie," Melisande said sharply. "I'm your mother. You *will* stay here. Don't you dare think of leaving with him."

Dec said nothing. He merely waited, looking at Rosalie. It was her choice. He held out his hand, offering it to her. "Come with me, Rosalie. Come home."

*   *   *

Come home.

It was crazy, absurd, but the words resonated deep within her. Perhaps because she never really had a home of her own.

Home. Dec's house. That town house in Mayfair had come to feel like home to her. Or perhaps it was simply that this place felt so much like a prison. Whatever the case, she couldn't refuse him. She didn't want to.

He was offering her an escape from Horley and her mother's miserable machinations. She'd agree to almost anything in order for that to happen. And yet as he stood there holding out his hand to her, she could only think of last night. For one moment she felt confused, thinking he had come for her. That this was a continuation from the previous evening. That somehow he had figured out the truth and had come for her . . . that he wanted her for himself.

Despite the reason she had so readily agreed to go with her mother in the first place—because she was too afraid he might realize she was the girl from Sodom—she couldn't refuse. Not this time. This time she had to stop herself from racing into his arms.

"Yes." She nodded. "I'll go with you."

"Rosalie!" Melisande cried.

"I'm leaving," she asserted, staring at him as she uttered these words, not even glancing at Melisande.

"How can you do this? I'm your mother."

Only when it's convenient for you.

The thought entered her head, but she didn't give it voice. Instead, she took her cue from Dec and ignored her mother, circling the table toward him, giving Melisande and Horley wide berth.

She stopped beside Dec. He offered his arm and she took it, allowing him to lead her through the house.

In the foyer, he addressed the butler. "Send all of Miss Hughes's belongings to this address." He presented his card. The butler nodded as he took it.

Dec led her to the carriage out front and assisted her inside. Once seated across from her, he knocked on the ceiling. The carriage lurched forward.

She carefully angled her legs, avoiding his longer legs. "Thank you," she murmured after several awkward moments.

He shook his head, not wanting her gratitude. Not feeling he deserved it. "I'm sorry—"

"You already apologized and it's really not necessary." She smoothed her hands over her skirts.

"You were my responsibility—"

"But I'm not." She plucked at her skirts. "We're not even kin. Melisande is my family. Just like she said. She's my mother. Why are you even doing this for me?"

He turned his attention from the window to stare at her. "I agreed to see you married. I settled a dowry on you and agreed to sponsor you through the Season. That's why. That's why you are my responsibility."

She swallowed, nodding. She opened her mouth to thank him again but stopped herself. She had already thanked him. "I assume Aurelia came to you and told you."

"Yes. Don't be vexed with her. She was worried about you."

She nodded, understanding. Aurelia was a friend. The first she had since leaving Harwich. She couldn't be angry with her. "I owe her my thanks. I didn't want to come to you. I wouldn't have."

His words came quickly. "Why not? Why didn't you? Something—" He stopped hard and took a breath before continuing. "Something could have happened to you. Do you understand that?"

He meant Horley could have happened. If she had been weaker. Or simply more trusting. More naive.

"I was embarrassed. And maybe I was afraid that you wouldn't care." It was embarrassing to even admit *that*, but she did. "I was afraid that you wouldn't want to help me." She stared down at her hands. "That you wouldn't come."

He sighed, and she wasn't sure what she heard in that sound. Resignation? Disappointment? In her or himself? "I care."

Her gaze flew to his face at that.

"And I'll always come when you need me, Carrots."

Did he mean that? It was more than any one person had ever promised her. She most especially had not expected it of him.

The intensity in his green gaze struck her hard, and anxiety skittered along her nerves. What if he knew the truth? What if he learned she was the same masked girl he had kissed? For the first time, she was tempted to tell him. And only to see if perhaps he would kiss her again. Her lips ached. The memory of his mouth was forever imprinted there.

The temptation to confess the truth to him lasted only a fraction of a moment. As soon as the thought entered her mind, it fled. He would not forget who she was and take her in his arms to pick up where they left off. He was honorable.

Despite his unsavory reputation, he would never cross that line with a female under his protection. Rest assured, her virtue was safe under his watch.

And why did that fill her with such hollowness?

Chapter 18

She did not see Dec for the rest of the day. Shortly after returning home, Aunt Peregrine and Aurelia arrived, luggage and a growling Lady Snuggles in tow once again. They hugged her warmly and chattered happily, making her feel like she had, in truth, come home.

"Aurelia." Rosalie pulled her aside while Aunt Peregrine went off in search of a treat for Lady Snuggles. Apparently the beast deserved a reward after her jaunt across Town yet again. "I—"

"I'm sorry," Aurelia blurted, grasping her hands. "I know I abused your trust by going to—"

"Thank you," she cut in, looking her friend squarely in the eyes. "You did me a favor I shan't ever forget."

Aurelia smiled in relief and released her hands to hug her. "I'm so glad you came to be here. How terrible if you never came to be in our lives."

Dinner was a leisurely affair. Rosalie dined with Aurelia and Aunt Peregrine. Dec was conspicuously absent. They discussed which social engagements they should schedule into their agenda. She chimed in, but her gaze continually strayed to his empty chair, wondering at his whereabouts. She didn't inquire despite her curiosity. It was better if he was scarce. His proximity made her too nervous by far.

She knew it was likely he wouldn't guess it had been her at Sodom. Not if he hadn't already done so. But she didn't trust that she wouldn't give herself away with a touch, a lingering glance. After being so intimate with him, she found it difficult to resume as though they were polite acquaintances.

After dinner, she enjoyed a warm bath before changing into her nightgown. The sky was just purpling into dusk, but she slipped into bed, exhausted, her muscles melting into the mattress. A pleased sigh shuddered from her lips. She was so relieved that she could sleep without fear. In peace that no one would enter her room uninvited.

She was asleep almost the instant she closed her eyes.

Rosalie woke to a darkened chamber. Her mind groped in the darkness for a moment, struggling to remember precisely where she was. She inhaled, but there was no scent of the lavender rushes that Mrs. Heathstone always framed the windows with. No sound of howling wind on the moors outside. Gradually, memory returned. Along with all that had happened. Where she was. What she had done and with whom. She was a long way from Yorkshire. It felt a lifetime since Mrs. Heathstone unceremoniously dumped her on her stepbrother's doorstep.

She wasn't certain the precise hour, but she knew it was not yet morning. She lay in bed for several moments longer, expecting to fall back to sleep. She had been tired enough to sleep well into tomorrow afternoon. Or so she thought.

After half an hour of staring into the dark, she pushed back the counterpane, donned her night rail and left her room, giving up on sleep. Nothing stirred as she made her way to the library. She pushed open the door and stepped inside. The remnants of a fire burned in the hearth, the crumble of incinerated wood cracking softly as it cast a dull glow throughout the room.

Well familiar with the library's layout by now, she made her way to the wall of shelves housing the novels. Squinting, she peered at the spines. She was debating rereading one of her favorite of Mrs. Radcliffe's novels, or something called *The Black Tulip* that looked relatively new.

"Looking for a little late night reading? I thought you would be asleep by now."

She spun around, clutching the book close to her chest. Dec stood in the doorway, jacketless, without his cravat, wearing only his shirt and breeches.

She sucked in a breath. She could well imagine his muscled chest. Her heart kicked hard against her ribs. "I was asleep. I'm afraid I woke and can't seem to fall back to sleep again."

Nodding, he walked fully into the room, his hessians whispering softly over the rug. "This is my favorite room in the house." He moved to the hearth and lifted the guard away so he could add several more logs to the fire. She studied his movements, appreciating the hard lines of his body. Straightening, he waved to the plump sofa before the hearth. "I've spent many a night on that sofa. Reading a book, staring into the flames until I fell asleep. Perhaps you should try it?"

"I cannot sleep down here. What would the servants think if they discovered me? Your Aunt Peregrine? It would not be seemly."

He stopped before her. One stride separated them. "I thought we agreed this is your home. Do you not feel comfortable here?"

"I do." She nodded vigorously. "It's only that it is not *only* my home. It's yours, too. I cannot simply spend the night on the sofa."

"So proper," he mused, brushing the hair back off her shoulder.

Her breath caught. Everything inside her jumped and reacted to that small touch.

His eyes locked on her face. Several moments passed before he murmured, "Who would have ever thought? It's a marvel to me."

"What is?"

"That you are your mother's daughter."

Nothing he said could have turned her blood cold faster. It always seemed to go back to her mother. He hated her so much. She lowered her gaze, seemingly finding the pattern in the rug of utter fascination.

"So innocent," he murmured, placing a finger beneath her chin and tipping her face up.

She thought of Sodom and what had transpired there. Heat swamped her face. Between *them*. She was not *wholly* innocent.

"I'm not . . ." She stopped, her voice fading. Was she actually arguing with him about her state of innocence? *Brilliant, Rosalie.*

His lips quirked. "Not so innocent? I think you are. Or did Strickland manage to steal a kiss." He was mocking her now, and that only pricked her temper.

"No. Not Strickland," she blurted.

His smile slipped, not missing the emphasis she placed on her words. "No? Someone else, then?" He stepped closer and closed his hands around her shoulders. Suddenly he wasn't smiling. "Did Horley—"

"No!" She shook her head. "No! I'm merely trying to say that I'm not such the innocent. I'm not that little girl that tagged after you like some sad puppy all those years ago."

"I never thought of you that way."

"Indeed?" The idea that he had thought of her at all inordinately pleased her. More than it should have.

His gaze moved from her eyes to her mouth

then. It was disconcerting. Her breathing grew shallow, her chest tight and almost pained. He couldn't be considering kissing her. It was absurd. She was his charge. His stepsister. She might have looked at him with stars in her eyes for years, but he had never looked at her that way. If he even looked at her.

He certainly wouldn't be looking at her that way now.

She held herself still, achingly conscious of how close they stood. It was familiar and strange all at once. They weren't at Sodom. She wore no mask. He was gazing at her. *Her*. Rosalie. Just as she had fantasized.

He leaned his head down a fraction, and then stopped hard, his mouth hovering over hers. His eyes were so close she could see the dark ring around the green depths.

"Rosalie?" Her name was just a breath fanning against her lips.

"Yes?" Her voice was warbled and hoarse. She swallowed, attempting to regain sound.

"I'm going to kiss you."

She inhaled. There was no mistaking his intention. Despite who they were to each other, he was going to kiss her. She nodded once, reeling at the declaration.

She felt elated and angered simultaneously. What about her? The other *her*! Obviously the girl from Sodom was forgotten. Obviously she meant nothing as he was ready to kiss someone else. It was madness, she knew, but she still felt betrayed. And also thrilled. Yes, it was illogical. She was jealous of herself.

All this considered, she didn't command him to stop. She didn't try to duck or push him away. His head dipped and his mouth slanted over hers with unexpected gentleness. His warm lips teased at hers, exerting only the slightest pressure.

Not at all what she was used to from him. He hadn't kissed her like that at Sodom. At least not beyond that first touch of his mouth. By the end his kisses had been raw and consuming. Fierce. His mouth had claimed and ravaged hers. She wanted that again. She ached for it.

And it was aggravating. She'd already had her first kiss from him. She wanted more. She wanted what she knew it could be. With a moan, she dropped the book she clutched and grabbed his head, spearing her fingers through the thick strands of his hair, tugging him down even as she stood on her tiptoes and arched against him. Anything to get closer. To have more.

She nipped at his bottom lip and then licked at

the seam of his mouth just as he had taught her, seeking entrance. He groaned his approval, and she took advantage of his open mouth, thrusting her tongue inside, searching for his, needing to taste him.

His hands stole around to clutch her back, pulling her even closer. She could actually feel the thump of his heart in his hard chest.

He sucked on her tongue and she moaned, fingers tightening in his hair. He shuddered, his hands sliding down her shoulders to grasp her arms.

Suddenly, he wrenched her from him and held her at arm's length.

His gaze blistered her. "Rosalie," he gasped.

Panting, she nodded and made another dive for his mouth, but he kept her at a distance, his hands firm on her arms. "You."

She didn't understand. She strained toward him, but he held her at arm's length. Her body was alive and humming. She couldn't think at all. There was only feeling. She could scarcely register him.

"It's *you*."

Something in his voice made her freeze and stop pulling against his hands. His gaze skimmed her. All of her. Missing nothing. From the top of her head to her bare feet peeping out from her hem. His gaze came to a stop on her hair, lingering over the loosened mass, and she realized with some dread that he was probably imagining it black.

She stepped back completely then, bumping the bookcase behind her. Her gaze darted over his shoulder, contemplating making a mad dash for escape.

His eyes burned a pale shade of green. "It is you. You were at Sodom."

Denial seemed futile. It was not a question. He spoke with conviction.

A long tense moment stretched between them. Finally, she nodded. Just once. A hard jerk of her head. And there was some relief mixed in with the dread swirling through her. Finally, he knew. No more secrets.

His expression twisted, and she knew she had lost him then. Whatever softness there had been for her vanished. Whatever had motivated him to want to kiss Rosalie vanished. She saw something in his eyes. Her stomach churned sickly. Something hard and bitter that she had only seen when he looked at her mother.

"Is there more?" he demanded. "Anything

else I should know? What other secrets do you harbor?"

"None. Nothing."

He looked skeptical. "You've had no other rendezvous at Sodom? I needn't fear any other gentlemen recognizing you? Come, I need to know what ruin might at any time befall."

"It was only you. Only those two times."

He inhaled, his shoulders pulling back at the reminder of them together. She was sure that was it. She had tricked him into doing things with her that he would never have dared otherwise. It stung. He was angry. She knew he would be. And yet a small part of her was hoping he remembered their connection . . . and how good it had been between them.

He dragged both hands through his hair, sending the dark strands in every direction. "How did you even learn of such a place, much less gain an invitation?"

She opened her mouth and then closed it with a snap. She could not throw Aurelia to the wolves. She needn't be dragged into this.

He held up a hand, shaking his head. "Let me guess. It involves Aurelia."

"This doesn't have anything to do with her."

He angled his head, his gaze on her sharp, feral. "So this was all you."

She gulped, wishing she could deflect his wrath, but she deserved every bit of it. She had deceived him.

"Very well," he bit out. "It's clear that we need to continue on our present course and see you wed before it's too late and you bring ruin upon yourself."

She nodded. "I—I—" She stopped and looked down at her hands, twisting her fingers until they were bloodless and numb.

There was nothing to say. No argument. She would not protest. She would not drag her feet. Dec knew of her masquerade. Just as she had feared. It was mortifying. She could scarcely look him in the eyes.

"Say something," he demanded.

She moistened her lips and searched for her voice. "What do you want me to say?"

Everything was out in the open between them. She had said enough. Done enough.

The look in his eyes . . . it was too much.

He didn't want her. Now he knew it was her, the woman from Sodom he had practically begged for, and he didn't want her. She wasn't enough.

He was already talking about her marrying

someone else even though she had stood before him with her heart in her eyes.

"What do you want me to say?" she asked again.

He stared at her so intently, his eyes jade-dark, searching, reaching inside her, touching that part of her she had worked so hard to hide and protect. He saw it now. He saw *her*. "Why? Why did you do it?"

She shook her head and looked up at the ceiling, squeezing her eyes tightly. Her chest ached from the pain of it all. From him looking at her, hating her, not understanding. "I don't know," she whispered.

It was easier than the truth. Easier than explaining that she had needed something more than the life he was arranging for her with such cold calculation. An empty future without excitement. Without passion.

Without love.

She had wanted love. She claimed it was merely adventure she was seeking . . . a taste of life. A first kiss. But it was more. And she had found it. She had found it in him.

The thought struck her like a slap. *Love.* She loved him. *Dear God.*

Her legs suddenly felt wobbly. She gripped the edge of a shelf behind her for support.

"Was it all a game?" he demanded. "Was *I* a game? Were you laughing at me this entire time?"

"No!" The word choked from her lips.

It was never a game. Those nights it was *him*. And it was *her*. Nothing else. Nothing more. That was enough. That had been everything. She fought to swallow the lump in her throat.

How couldn't he know? He had to know. Didn't he feel that it was *her* on those nights? Hadn't some part of him known when he looked into her eyes that it was her? Somewhere, buried deep? Had her shaking fingers on his skin revealed nothing?

He shook his head swift and hard. "You would risk everything . . . a chance for a good marriage. Your reputation . . . for dim-witted sport."

The words sliced deep. She couldn't breathe. It had not been sport to her. She loved him. And he despised her.

She turned to flee the room, panicked at her thoughts.

"Where are you going?" he demanded, catching up with her at the door, forcing her around. She resisted, struggling, and that only brought them closer. He wrapped both arms around her, hauling her close. His body, this nearness, was familiar and foreign at the same time. It had never been the two of them, so honest and exposed before. That was new. His eyes swept over her face, piercing and intent.

"Let me go," she muttered. "I'm leaving."

"Where? Where will you go?" he bit out, his lips curling in a cruel smile that was no less devastating to her senses. She felt it all the way to her toes.

She shook her head. "Anywhere but here."

He laughed then—the harsh sound stung her like needles to the skin.

"There's only *here*, Rosalie. There is only *me*. You have nowhere to go. You have no one else."

"I have my mother. She'll take me back if for no other reason than to spite you."

His smile slipped. "And you'd want that? To go back to her . . . to suffer the advances of her lover."

She raked him with her gaze—at least what she could see of him from the shoulders up. Too much of him, really. The square jaw and straight, sharp line of his nose over well-carved lips. He was too beautiful and well he knew it. She shivered in his arms. Wasn't Satan said to be the most beautiful of God's angels? "Some poisons are worse than others."

His nostrils flared. "Meaning I'm poison?"

She nodded despite the tightening of his jaw. His eyes sparked fury. "You've the right of it. I am poison . . . brewed at the hand of your mother. I am to be feared and avoided."

She ceased to breathe as his words sank in. He was hard and merciless and she had fallen in love with him. How was it possible?

Because you saw another side of him. You saw something other than this spiteful creature.

So which one was real? This man or the other?

He was holding her tightly, practically lifting her from the ground. Her slippered toes grazed the carpet. Her arms were trapped between them, mashed into his chest.

"Let me go," she whispered, trying to pull her hands free.

Something indecipherable glinted in his eyes. He angled his head, studying her oddly, his dark eyebrows drawn tightly.

"Unhand me," she added, relieved her voice held steady even as sensation slithered along her nerves. She was achingly conscious of his bigger body. Her softness melded into all his hard angles.

"So you can leave. Run away to your mother?"

"Or I can leave with Aurelia," she snapped defiantly, knowing she couldn't stomach being under that roof again. "She'd take me—"

"She's my cousin, subject to her brother, and he will not go against me."

Outrage bubbled up in her chest, blinding her to reason. "If I want to go, I will. I'll find a way—"

"Fine. Go," he practically snarled, releasing her abruptly.

She stumbled back a step, staring at him as he swung around and stalked toward the massive mahogany desk. She gazed at him uncertainly. His back was to her, his head bowed like he was reaching for something deep inside himself—like he couldn't stand the sight of her.

And that hurt most of all maybe. That she was something he could not even bear to look at anymore. Shaking her head, feeling battered and a bit broken inside, she turned to leave.

And then she stopped. Took one staggering step and froze.

Turning around, she stared hard at the back of him, resolve firing through her. She would not leave him. Not like this. Not without at least trying to dispel whatever awful thoughts he harbored of her. He wanted to know why she went to Sodom. Then she would tell him.

Lifting her chin, she approached slowly, her slippers whispering over the carpet.

"I went to Sodom," she began tentatively, her voice growing stronger as she drew closer, "because for once in my life I wanted to do something

. . . I wanted to make a decision that was my own. I wanted to choose who I gave my first kiss to."

His back stiffened and she knew he was listening. He lifted his bowed head and stared straight ahead, still not looking at her.

She stopped directly behind him, almost tempted to touch the rigid expanse of his back but daring not. Talking to his back was easier. Cowardly of her, but there it was.

She sucked in a breath and continued. "I wanted to live for myself and not be at the mercy of others for once. Everyone else decides my fate . . . makes all my choices. I went there for me."

She knew what she described was the lot of every female. Well, most females at any rate. Debutantes like her didn't get to choose.

He swung around and she blinked at the sudden heat in his gaze. She stepped back quickly. The hard glitter in his eyes alarmed her. He didn't say a word. Simply stared. Several inches separated them but it wasn't enough space. She inched back.

He followed.

His movements were predatory. He backed her up until she couldn't move any farther and collided with the bookcase. Several leather spines dug into the back of her gown, but she didn't care.

She could scarcely feel them there with his eyes devouring her . . . with the encroaching heat of him enveloping her.

Neither one of them spoke. Neither moved.

Her palms flattened at her sides, brushing well-read tomes. There was nowhere else to go. No retreat at her back. No retreat at her front. Not with the hard wall of his body directly before her. His silence was killing her.

"Say something," she whispered, the same demand he'd made of her moments ago, her voice a broken little rasp on air that was stretched too thin around them.

"You went to the club because you wanted to live for yourself. Have your own experiences? Correct?"

She nodded jerkily, her eyes unblinking and so wide in her face that they actually ached.

"Then let's continue."

She couldn't react. Not with him looking at her that way. Not with him this close. Her gaze unerringly went to his mouth, and she knew. She already knew how good it could be. But this was different than before.

There were no masks. No disguises. Not that he had ever used one, but she had. She had clung to hers. Perhaps not so much for anonymity as for the sense of courage, however false, it imbued into her.

There wasn't even darkness. It was simply her. Rosalie. And Dec. Plain and simple. Well, perhaps not so simple, but they faced each other as a man and woman. Not strangers, hungry for a tryst at an illicit club. Not stepbrother and stepsister. Not guardian and ward.

His hand curled around the back of her neck, hauling her mouth to his. His tongue traced the seam of her lips and she shuddered, opening her mouth. Instantly, his tongue touched the tip of her own, tasting and stroking. She moaned, her hands coming up to cling to his shoulders. Everything changed then. His kiss deepened, grew harder, hungrier. Fast and desperate. She arched against him, those mewling sounds escaping from the hot fusion of their mouths.

"God, you taste so sweet," he growled against her lips, crouching for the barest moment to lift her, his big hands cupping her bottom through her nightgown. "Bloody clothes . . ."

"Take them off," she gasped as he worked one hand beneath her hem, gliding up her stocking-clad leg. She wanted this. Wanted his mouth and hands everywhere on her. She wanted him to do to her what he had done at Sodom. She wanted to fly apart in his arms again.

He froze.

Consternation washed over her. Had she sounded too brazen? Had she repulsed him with her forwardness? He stepped back. Her leg lowered, her foot dropping to the floor. He stared at her with an unreadable expression, his green eyes deep and fathomless. Impenetrable. Just as he was.

"Go to bed, Rosalie."

She flinched at the words. At the dismissal.

He didn't wait for her to move. She watched him with aching eyes, her heart a painful clenching fist in her chest as he turned and strode from the room, his strides eating up the distance. As if he couldn't be away from her fast enough.

Smoothing shaking hands down the front of her night rail, she followed several moments later, certain he was quite gone by now. And he was. She didn't glimpse sight of him as she made her way down the corridor toward her bedchamber. At her door, she hesitated, her gaze sliding toward the door leading to his bedchamber. Was he in there now? Regretting and hating that she had ever entered his life?

Pushing down on the latch, she entered her room, vowing that when it came to her, he would have nothing to regret again. She would be a ghost in this house. In his life. She would cause him no further worry or trouble. Somehow, some way, she would make herself invisible. It would be as though she didn't exist at all.

Chapter 19

The day dawned bright, the sunlight bringing with it the harsh reminder of last night. Rosalie was his girl from Sodom. No, he corrected himself. Not his girl. *Never* his girl.

Myriad feelings swamped him. Distaste that she had ever been there. Had ever stepped within its walls and seen the things she had doubtless seen. Guilt. As though he should have somehow known it was her in the shadows. As though he should have known it was her beneath his mouth, shuddering and coming apart under his lips and tongue and teeth.

Perhaps a part of him had suspected all along? Bloody hell, he didn't know. He'd lost perspective.

He only knew that he wanted the girl at Sodom. And he wanted Rosalie. They were the two women he had wanted for the last few weeks. The only two. And they were one and the same. It was a significant realization . . . even if he was not entirely certain what it meant and what to do about it.

He couldn't stop thinking about last night. About all she had said.

She'd gone to Sodom for adventure. A taste of passion. Her first kiss. By her own admission, she had wanted a choice in her fate.

And she had chosen him.

This continued to sink its way inside him. She'd chosen him for her first kiss. And then she had come back for more. He groaned and rubbed his hands over his face. How had he managed to break free last night? She knew how to kiss now. Expertly. Enough to leave him aching. She knew how to touch him. And those little sounds she made in the back of her throat—the very sounds that gave her away last night—drove him mad. He'd never been with a more responsive woman.

It was a dangerous thing, knowing she was beneath his roof. In close proximity. He'd thought of her for days, and now she was so close.

He expelled a great breath, knowing he'd have to venture from his rooms eventually. He had told Aunt Peregrine he would join them at the Collingsworth ball this evening.

He sank deeper into his armchair, circling the rim of his half-full glass of brandy with one finger. He would not be alone with her tonight. He needn't worry about repeating the incident in the library. He had come close then to forgetting. Who she was. Who he was.

He would not forget again.

They shared a carriage to the Collingsworth ball. This was the first time Dec had seen fit to accompany them to a social gathering. He usually joined them later at such events. It was awkward, to say the least. He shared the side with Aunt Peregrine, seated directly across from her. He trained his attention outside, through the cracked curtain, as his aunt rattled off the names of gentlemen Rosalie was to pay special attention to this evening.

He had not seen her since the night in the library. Somehow, they had managed to stay out of each other's way. He had not changed his daily patterns, so he could only think the effort was on her part. She was trying to avoid him.

"And Aurelia, George Snidely will be there. He's always paid special attention to you, dear. I expect you to return his attention in kind. This would be quite the triumph if I could see you both engaged by the Season's end."

Aurelia sighed and turned her head so that only Rosalie could hear her mutter, "Not with the likes of George Snidely, I won't."

Rosalie stifled a laugh. Dec must have heard the sound though. He turned his attention from the window to gaze at her with an inscrutable stare. She quickly sobered, feeling guilty. As though she somehow should not feel amusement.

She tried to offer up a smile, but it only felt weak and brittle. He held her gaze a moment longer and then turned his attention back outside.

Sighing, she crossed her hands in her lap, wishing she knew what to say or do to make things right between them again. They had been good. At least for a short while. After he'd fetched her from her mother's, there was something there between them. Something more than indifference or vague animosity. A friendliness, a truce of some sort, however fleeting. Now that was gone and she didn't know how to get it back again. If it was even possible.

The carriage pulled up before the glittering mausoleum that belonged to the Earl of Collingsworth. She was soon guided up the steps and into the grand foyer, escorted by Dec. It was all Aunt Peregrine's plan. For her to be *visibly* linked to the Banbury dukedom and no longer under her mother's shadow. For the bachelors of the *ton* to see her as beyond eminently eligible.

Her fingers barely rested on his arm as though afraid to exert any pressure. As though doing so was a presumption she dared not convey to him. It was already difficult . . . this sense that she was using him for her own gain. What did he gain from his association to her?

Following her introduction to the earl and his family, she soon found herself at the edge of the dance floor. A kaleidoscope of gowns in every possible color whirled past.

"Go on now," Aunt Peregrine encouraged. "Out there with the both of you. What better way for Rosalie to be seen than for you to lead her in her first dance?" She wagged her fan toward the dance floor.

"Oh, no." Rosalie shook her head. "That's not necessary—"

"Come." Dec took her elbow and guided them into the current of dancers.

She bit her lip and focused on not stepping on his toes. She was rattled. Finding herself in his arms, dancing so close with his hand wrapped around hers, the other at the back of her waist.

"I thought you enjoyed dancing," he said after some moments.

"I do."

"Then you have no wish to dance with me."

"No, that's not it," she said quickly, her gaze flying to his rather intense expression. She closed her eyes briefly. She was making a muck of things. As usual. "You've done so much for me. I didn't wish for you to feel further obligation."

"It's merely a waltz, Rosalie."

She nodded. "Of course."

They danced several more moments. He moved beautifully. With a grace that belonged to some jungle cat.

"You shouldn't have to stay too long," she said. "After this, your aunt should be satisfied and you can go."

"Trying to rid yourself of me? Am I such a poor dancer? Or is it my breath?"

"Not at all. I'm only certain there are other

places you would prefer to be." Places like Sodom. With women that were all they appeared to be. Uncomplicated.

He looked down at her, his green eyes intent and yet unreadable. As though he read her mind, he replied, "I have not been back there since you."

Heat flooded her face. There was no confusing where *there* was.

She was tempted to ask why and yet afraid to as well. It was none of her business.

"I only went that one night because you sent me that missive."

Her face burned at the reminder of the note she had sent him. It was blatantly brazen. She pushed past her mortification to what he was saying. To the implication of his words.

He had returned to Sodom only for her. He had not gone since.

The dance came to an end. She spotted Aunt Peregrine waving her over. Dec followed her gaze.

"It appears my aunt has need of you."

She nodded, feeling shaky inside. Not a new occurrence, but more so since he'd discovered the truth. That she was the woman he'd been with at Sodom. That he had kissed her. Touched *her*. She could hardly look at him without that knowledge making butterflies erupt inside her—the awareness that nothing stood between them anymore, no disguises, no hidden truths.

"Thank you for the dance."

Taking her elbow, he escorted her back to her aunt. Rosalie pasted a smile on her face as Aunt Peregrine introduced her to a young man fresh out of Eton who looked close to her own age. Mr. Fanning bent over her hand even as his gaze fixed on Dec. Clearly, he seemed in awe of the Duke of Banbury.

"A pleasure to meet you." He spared Rosalie only a glance as he uttered this. "My cousin is the Viscount Wescott. I believe you know him, Your Grace."

Dec nodded absently, flicking Fanning a glance before sliding his stare back to Rosalie. "I believe we are acquainted," he responded.

"He speaks very highly of you, Your Grace."

Dec's lip curled into a smirk. "Indeed? I can hardly recall his face." Mirth brimmed in his eyes. She looked away, hoping to hide her grin. This was a bit of the boy she remembered. Mischievous and incorrigible.

Fanning sputtered, no doubt feeling foolish. Aunt Peregrine pushed any awkwardness aside with her chatter. Before Rosalie knew it, Aunt Peregrine had persuaded them into a dance. Another waltz played. Fanning didn't dance half as well as Dec, but she doubted many gentlemen did. She would have to stop comparing other men to him if she was ever to marry anyone else and find any level of contentment with him.

"You must be very close to your stepbrother," Fanning offered in way of conversation.

"Yes. I suppose I am."

No sense denying it. That was the idea they wanted to give, after all. That whoever she married would also have the benefit of an alliance with the Duke of Banbury.

"You're very fortunate."

She looked sharply at Fanning's boyish features. Fortunate? Fortunate that Dec saw fit to bring her under his wing when she was no actual blood relation to him? Fortunate that he bestowed her with such a generous dowry?

"Yes. I suppose I am." Her gaze moved from the boy who held her hand limply in his moist one. She looked across the room, searching for the man who occupied her thoughts with such single, burning intensity.

She sucked in a breath when she found him. He stood at the edge of the dance floor, watching her. Tall, broad-shouldered and narrow-hipped in his black evening attire, he was easily the most attractive man in the room, and every woman knew it from the way they cast their eyes his way. She knew it, too. He was everything she desired, but he was beyond her reach.

Aunt Peregrine and Aurelia had moved off and he stood alone, with a face void of expression, watching her circle the dance floor with Fanning.

Fanning followed her gaze. "He seems a much devoted brother. I confess to hardly speaking to my sister when I visit home. Although she does spend most of her time in the nursery playing with her dolls. Perhaps when she is older that will change and I, too, shall stand protectively at the edge of a ballroom watching as she waltzes with suitors."

Is that how he viewed Dec? As a protective older brother? If he only knew that her alleged "brother" had kissed her until her knees went weak. Her face warmed at the memory. Until she recalled how he had stopped and pulled away. Then she felt only cold.

She dragged her gaze back to Fanning and smiled weakly, attempting to encourage him. That was the plan, after all.

Fanning smiled back at her, no doubt emboldened. "You're a fine dancer, Miss Hughes. A fine dancer indeed."

"Thank you, Mr. Fanning. It is easy with you for a partner."

They were merely words, pleasantries, but they felt so very final. The words settled like bricks in her stomach. As Fanning smiled widely, she knew he was hers if she would have him. And this time she must. If not him, then someone else. And soon. It might as well be him.

This time she couldn't run or refuse with all the haste of some spoiled debutante with the leisure of choice and time on her side.

She looked out at the dance floor again, searching for Dec. He stood in the same spot. As she whirled past him, she turned her head, her gaze locked with his.

His eyes were inscrutable, but she didn't need to wonder what he was thinking. She knew it had to be similar to her own thoughts. That she might have finally found her husband.

Chapter 20

Aunt Peregrine filled the carriage with her chatter on the ride home. She recounted every waltz Rosalie danced with particular relish. "That first dance with you, Declan-dearest, truly set the proper tone." She patted his hand where it rested on his knee. "Well done, nephew, well done."

He grunted a response. Now, he supposed, was not the time to confess that he had thought very little about prospective suitors when he swept Rosalie into his arms. It had simply been a valid reason to hold her. To touch her again. He hadn't thought at all. Need had guided him.

"I even saw you dancing this evening, Aurelia. With Lord Needleton and Lord Denton." Aunt Peregrine bobbed her turbaned head with happy approval. "An all around good evening, I must say. I count it a resounding success. Perhaps we shall have two matches to announce before the Season ends." She brought her hands together in a single clap. "Won't that be simply brilliant?"

Aurelia snorted softly. Rosalie's gaze flicked to him. Upon seeing him staring back at her, she quickly averted her gaze. She'd been skittish as a colt with him all evening, and he'd supposed that was understandable. He knew her secret. More than that. He knew her taste. It was imprinted on him. He wondered if she thought about everything they had done as much as he did. It was a problem. He could not stop thinking about her. And he wasn't thinking about her in the manner one thought of a stepsister. He saw her as a woman. A woman he wanted in his bed.

Aunt Peregrine's voice grated on his ears, droning on and on about the merits of a country wedding versus one here in Town. After seeing her tonight with the Fanning fellow, the prospect of

Rosalie's marriage to another man felt like a very real and impending thing. A sour taste coated his mouth at the thought of Rosalie in another man's bed . . . of another man kissing her, tasting her, parting her thighs—

"Declan-dearest? You look unwell. Is something amiss?"

He snapped his attention back to his aunt. She stared at him worriedly, her forehead creased. His cousin watched him, too. Even Rosalie had lifted her gaze. Her warm topaz eyes looked at him with a mixture of curiosity and concern.

His gaze dropped down to his hands clasped tightly on his knees. He loosened his death grip and tried to relax his features. Unclenching his jaw, he replied, "Not at all."

Aunt Peregrine looked from him to his hands and then back up to his face. There was mild skepticism in her eyes, and that surprised him. For the first time that he could recollect, his aunt looked somewhat cognizant. As though she might not only know he wasn't well, but she might know why. He held her gaze, swallowing against the uncomfortable knot in his throat. She slid her gaze to Rosalie before looking back at him again, arching one eyebrow.

"We're here," Aurelia declared unnecessarily as the carriage rolled to a stop in front of his home.

He descended first and then turned to assist each lady down, making certain his hands did not linger overly long on Rosalie.

"Well, I am exhausted," Aunt Peregrine declared as they entered the foyer.

"Me, too." Aurelia was already heading up the stairs ahead of them, working the pins free from her hair. "Don't look for me until the afternoon."

Aunt Peregrine grinned. "I echo that sentiment."

Rosalie sent him a hesitant smile. He waved for her to precede him. Lifting her skirts, she ascended the stairs after his aunt and cousin. He followed, the sway of her hips beneath her skirts mesmerizing him. His hands opened and closed at his sides, the memory of her filling his palms still present and alive for him. He'd never forget. Never stop wanting her.

Cursing beneath his breath, he walked a straight line for his room, murmuring a terse good-night as he passed her.

At his door, he looked sideways, his gaze colliding with hers.

"Good night, Declan," she said so softly he

scarcely heard her, but he read her lips. She slowly turned the latch to her door, smiling ruefully at him. That smile felt a little sad, too. A little like farewell.

His chest tightened almost painfully as he watched her disappear inside her bedchamber.

He paused in front of his door, listening for a moment to her voice and the voice of her maid. Shaking his head, he strode into his chamber, shooing his valet away and undressing himself. Climbing into bed, he folded his hands behind his head and stared into the dark, working on convincing himself that these feelings would dissipate once she was out from under his roof. Once she was married to another man. He'd stop caring. He'd learn to forget. Time. Distance. It would cure all.

Rosalie laid wide-awake a good hour after she dismissed her maid for the night. The evening had been agonizing. Dancing with Dec was the one bright light, but from there it had been merely banal conversation with gentlemen more interested in her dowry and the Duke of Banbury than her.

She rolled to her side, smiling weakly and tucking her hand beneath her cheek. She supposed she understood at least part of that. She was more interested in her stepbrother, too. A silly giggle escaped her in the dark. Dec clearly occupied the majority of her thoughts. Her foolish grin slid away as she wondered if it would always be that way. When she was married and old with grandchildren, would she still be full of thoughts for him? She rubbed her hands over her face. How had her life become such a mess? What happened to her days in Yorkshire? Reading to the younger students? Picking flowers on the moors in spring? Sharing a room with Rachel, who snored whenever she drank tea right before bed?

Two raps on her door broke the silence of her chamber. She sat up in bed. The low burning fire in the hearth cast the room in a warm glow. She didn't move for a long moment, staring in silence at her door. Perhaps Aurelia didn't go straight to bed after all and wanted to talk. Hopefully, she didn't want another go at Sodom's.

She pushed back the counterpane and started for the door, stopping when it swung open. Dec stood there, shirtless, wearing only his breeches. Her heart jumped to her throat as she devoured the sight of him. The hard chest. The stomach chiseled and defined. Her entire body tingled and came alive at his presence, at his nearness.

Still watching her, he entered the room, turned

slightly and closed the door. She heard the faint click of the lock and her stomach dipped.

He took several strides toward her and then stopped. A few feet separated them but neither spoke. His gaze swept her once before fastening on her face. Her pulse rushed in her ears. She opened her mouth to speak but couldn't manage to get out any of the words tripping through her head.

Why are you here?

What do you want?

He took one more step and stopped again, his bare chest lifting on a great inhalation, and she knew. There was only one thing that would bring him to her chamber in the middle of the night.

She released a breath of her own. This would be the time to demand that he leave. If she had any sense of modesty or self-preservation at all, she would point to the door. She wasn't certain who moved next. They came together in one motion, mouths colliding in a hungry kiss. He swept her up, lifting her off the floor. Her toes grazed the carpet as he walked her backward to the bed, one strong arm hard around her waist, his other hand cupping her cheek, their lips never breaking contact.

Her hands curved around his shoulders, his

back, smoothing over the firm skin, reveling in the play of muscle and sinew rippling under her palms.

Despite the intensity of their collision, he eased her down gently into the soft bed. His body was hard over hers. His weight slipped between her thighs, her nightgown billowing all around her, loose and insubstantial. No barrier at all.

His mouth consumed her. And his hands. His hands roamed everywhere. Her face. Her throat. She moaned as he kneaded her breasts through her nightgown.

She broke their kiss on a gasp as he yanked her nightgown down, exposing a breast so he could dip his head and take her nipple in his mouth. She sputtered inarticulate sounds, words that might not have been words at all. There was no thought. Just sensation. Just the wet heat of his mouth as he drew her nipple deep, as his teeth scraped the sensitive point and had her fisting his hair with a choked cry.

He came back up, his face hovering over hers, the angles and hollows more pronounced in the shadows, making him appear even more attractive, if possible. "I'm not fighting this anymore."

She nodded, understanding, relieved. *Glad.* That was the only description for it. It had been a fight, a struggle, from the very beginning. From the first night she arrived here she'd been at war with herself, running toward and away from Dec. And now the fight was over.

She touched his face with a shaky hand, tracing the rough scrape of his jawline.

"I may regret this tomorrow. You most assuredly will, but I need to hear you say that you want this." His eyes drilled into her. Everything seemed to slow and pause as he waited for her to answer.

She brought her hand back up his cheek, her fingers roaming over his strong features. "I want you."

The words were out, but he still hesitated, letting her touch his face, the delicious weight of him bearing her down. He stared like he was memorizing her, and everything inside her swelled with emotion. Without any more words, he simply let her hold his face, watching her watch him.

"I won't regret this tomorrow," she murmured as she traced his eyebrows, his nose, his mouth.

He smiled, slow and heart-stoppingly beautiful. Flutters erupted in her belly. "You can't know that right now."

"So you're changing your mind, then?"

His answer was his mouth on hers. His tongue teasing her lips open to tangle with her own. His fingers speared through her hair, pinning her head for his ravaging lips. She squirmed under him, her hips working, thrusting, seeking instinctively an end to this. To the hunger, to the ache. And she felt his desire, too. His hardness was there, pressing between them, prodding through the bunched fabric of her nightgown. She longed for him . . . felt the ache in her very teeth.

His hand arrived there, too, pushing the fabric up to her hips. He pulled back slightly and she mewled her disappointment but devoured the sight of him as he stripped his breeches. Perhaps the enormity of what was about to happen should have struck her then. When he loomed over her stark-naked, that part of him large and so very erect. And yet as he came at her slowly on all fours, she felt only heady anticipation.

His fingers curled around the nightgown bunched at her waist. His gaze didn't break with hers as he yanked it up and over her head. And then they were both naked. As never before. Her breathing fell ragged then. He swept her with a hot look. "You're beautiful."

A happy flush spread through her.

When his body came over her again it was different. Skin-to-skin, no part of them was shielded. His mouth found hers, kissing her until she was wound tighter than a coil, arching and straining against him. His hips nudged her thighs, spreading her wider. She obliged, too eager to harbor any fears.

His fingers found her, skimming up her thighs and parting through her folds to the core of her. She jerked at this first touch. He'd touched there before but she was hardly accustomed to such a thing, and this was different. They were both fully unclothed. Tonight there was no going back.

"You're so wet. I can't wait."

"Don't." She arched, digging her nails into his back. "Don't wait."

His hands left the core of her, and then he was there, his hardness nudging against her opening, parting her.

He braced his arms on either side of her head and bowed his neck until their foreheads touched. His breath gusted over her lips and mingled with her own.

His hands framed her face, fingers feathering against her hair. He eased in a little deeper, and she felt herself stretch, accommodating him even though he had yet to lodge himself fully. Still, it wasn't enough. She knew there had to be more.

"Please," she begged, wiggling her hips and pushing up, trying to take him in deeper. Ready. Hungry for more.

"Rosalie, I don't want to hurt . . ."

She dragged her hands down his back. Grasping his tight buttocks in both hands, she hauled him to her. He groaned a sound that could have been her name and buried himself deep, fully seating himself inside her.

She arched against him with a cry. It was more discomfort than pain. The sensation, the fullness of him so deeply within her, overwhelming. He was large and pulsing inside her.

"Oh, oh, oh . . ." Her breath escaped in broken little spurts. She had never felt particularly small. Or fragile. But he made her feel like the daintiest of females. Normally she would not have liked feeling so vulnerable, but she knew somehow if she didn't, then this wouldn't be what it was.

"I'm sorry, Carrots . . . give yourself a moment to adjust," he said through gritted teeth. "I can stop."

Stop? Impossible. She hadn't come this far to wait another moment. If there was more, she wanted it now.

She looped her arms around his neck and pressed her open mouth against his throat, biting down gently and then licking, loving the taste of him, the warm saltiness of his skin. He quivered under her mouth. "I don't want a moment."

"Rosalie—"

"*I* can't wait." She worked her hips, managing to move a little. She moaned at the sudden friction that sent sensation arcing through her.

His fingers dove through her hair, palms cupping her head as he pulled almost all the way out and then drove back inside her.

Her head fell back on the bed. "Yes, yes."

His hands slid from her hair. He tucked his forearms under her back and curled his hands around her shoulders, fingertips brushing her collarbone.

He repeated the movement inside her. The friction grew. Everything in her tightened, pulling and twisting and squeezing until she felt close to bursting.

His hips pumped between her thighs and a smacking sound filled the air as their bodies came together. It was feral and sent her hunger spiraling.

He wrapped a hand under her thigh and lifted her leg higher. She wasn't certain what that did or how that changed anything, but she thought she saw stars. She choked on a silent scream as all the tension inside her snapped and she felt like she flew from her skin.

Sinking back on the mattress, her arms fell limply above her head. She felt boneless, her muscles liquid. A silly grin curved her lips. He moved several more times, plunging into her until he stilled, until he released himself into her in a shuddered groan. He fell on her then, his arms still bearing most of his weight.

She'd never felt closer, never felt more linked with another soul. It was the most profound sense of intimacy. Being with Dec. Doing this with Dec. It awed her. He awed her.

After several moments he rolled to his side, taking her with him. He draped her long hair over her shoulder to press a kiss to her nape that sent shivers down her spine. She smiled idiotically, glad he couldn't see it. He spooned her against his body, sighing against her neck.

"That was nice," she whispered.

"Nice?" His deep voice purred against her neck.

"Very well. Better than nice."

"I should hope."

After a few moments his breathing slowed and evened behind her

"Are you falling asleep?" she asked.

"You should do the same," he murmured. "It's been an eventful night."

She turned on her side and stared down at him incredulously. "You can't sleep here. The servants—"

"All are in my employ."

She sat up, clinging the covers to her chest. "That does not mean we can totally disregard propriety."

He looked her up and down and attempted to tug the counterpane down to bare her breasts. He wore an infectious grin that made her stomach flip over. "Have we not already?"

She flushed. "We cannot do this so blatantly. There are rules—"

He kissed her. His lips claimed her, teasing at first and then growing firmer. She parted her lips and his tongue glided in, tasting, licking. Her bones began that slow melt again.

He wrapped an arm around her and pulled her against him, tugging the counterpane and wrenching it aside so nothing was between them. He rolled onto his back, dragging her atop him. Her breasts flattened against his hard chest.

His mouth moved, raining tiny biting kisses along her jaw. She gasped and shivered as his mouth nipped at her.

"You like that?" he murmured in a husky voice, licking the same area under her jaw. "Is that your spot?

Her response was a breathy little moan. She nodded twice, her hands traveling over his muscled chest. His hands skimmed down her sides, fingers locking around her hip bones, positioning her so his manhood rested directly at her opening.

Her eyes widened as she looked down at him. "Again?" So soon? Was it possible?

His hands dove into her hair, holding back the tumbling mass so he could better see her face. "We're just getting started, Carrots. We can do this as much as you like."

As much as she liked?

That was a dangerous thought indeed because right now she didn't think she would ever *stop* liking this.

She rotated her hips, grinding against him. His breath hitched. She grinned down at him and echoed his early query, "Is that your spot?"

His smile widened. "Saucy, aren't you?" He fisted her hair, wrapping it around his hand and wrist and tugging her mouth back down toward him. He feasted on her lips, licking, nipping, growling. "Do whatever you like. Take what you want."

What he was inviting her to do thrilled her. He wanted her to take command? Feminine power swelled inside her. She continued to grind over him, rotating her hips on top of him. Quite accidentally, she moved in a way that shot sensation from her core straight to every nerve in her body.

"Oh!" she cried out, pressing harder on that spot.

"Find your sweet spot, did you?" he murmured approvingly, his fingers flexing on her hips.

She whimpered, everything in her tightening as she worked herself over him.

"Rosalie," he gasped. "You're going to make me . . . I need to be inside you."

Nodding, she lifted herself and reached between them, closing her hand around his hardness. She guided him inside her, gasping as she lowered herself down on his shaft. He pushed into her, hot and pulsing,

She watched him, that feeling of empowerment swelling higher in her chest. And something else. Emotion too big, too intense to define.

He arched his throat, throwing back his head as she eased down, almost seating herself fully. His breath came in hard spurts.

She was sore from before, her stretching muscles burning in a good way, the friction making goose bumps break out over her flesh.

He groaned her name. His hands tightened and he pulled her the rest of the way, impaling her on him.

"Oh!" She arched her spine, certain she had never felt him so deep before.

He propped up on his elbows, taking her breast in his mouth. "Move," he growled wetly around her nipple. "Move or I'm flipping you over."

She moved, finding a rocking rhythm that brought her the most pleasure. She angled her hips so that every time she came down, she put pressure on that delicious, magical little spot that made her fly out of her skin.

"That's it." His fingers tightened in her buttocks and she moved harder, faster, driving toward that place he took her before. He watched her, the sight of her working above him, a slick sheen starting to glisten on her small, berry-tipped breasts, bringing him closer to release. Her fingers tightened around the nape of his neck and he bit down on one of her nipples.

Her entire body tightened, contracted, and she felt her channel clench around his cock.

Her mouth parted and he kissed her, swallowing her scream as she came apart, shaking and shivering over him. She collapsed on top of him and he flipped her over without severing the contact of their bodies. He moved then, pounding over her, racing toward his climax, his fingers digging into the swells of her bottom.

His release came, blinding hot. He dropped over her, burying his head in her neck. She relished the rapid rising and falling of his chest.

"Oh," she breathed on something that was part sigh, part laugh. "Is it . . . always like this?" She sighed in contentment, closing her eyes, thoroughly satiated. Soon she was asleep.

He lifted his head to gaze solemnly down into her flushed face. He smoothed sweaty strands of hair back from where they clung to her face and neck and removed himself from her body with some reluctance. Positioning himself against her side, he stared down at her, admiring the line and hollows of her face, the sweet curve of her chin, that delicious upper lip with its pronounced dip in the middle.

"No. Not every time." But a whisper meandered through him, settling with surety in his gut. *But with her it would be. It would be this way every time.*

He didn't know how he knew, but he did. He knew because he had never even thought such a thing remotely possible before.

Chapter 21

$\mathcal{D}$ec didn't know how long he watched her sleep. Propped on one elbow beside her, his hand would occasionally stray to touch her face, her hair, the curve of her shoulder. He was tempted to have her again. Only concern for her comfort stayed his hand from slipping under the bedding and finding her warm softness waiting for him between her thighs. He'd used her untried body well. She'd be sore. He'd let her recover before he took her again. For take her he would.

Somewhere in the back of his mind he had

thought maybe once he had a taste of her, it would be enough. He'd be enough. He knew instantly he had been wrong. He'd wanted her again. She made him feel. Hot sensation burned through him, shattered the usual numbness he felt. Nothing about joining his body with hers had been the usual. Everything had been more. Felt more.

And he wanted more.

Almost as soon as he finished. He did not think this desire for her would fade any time soon, and that left him with a bit of a dilemma.

She slept on blissfully unaware of his perusal, his touch, his thoughts. He would marry her now. There was no alternative. And he'd known that when he'd come to her room tonight. He knew and decided that he simply didn't care. Having her would be worth it.

And it had been. He wouldn't regret that even if he did feel uneasy over the prospect of marriage. Not unusual. He had vowed to never wed. To let the title pass to Will and his line.

But now everything had changed. He had changed. He didn't allow himself to examine that too closely. His thoughts shied from considering what it was about Rosalie, about them together, that made him decide he would have her, *this*, forever.

He only knew that he couldn't let her go. He couldn't endure her marrying another man. He wouldn't stand by as another man took her to his bed. He wouldn't watch as her belly swelled with the children of another man.

That would be him. Those would be his children. Something fluttered in his chest at the idea of a daughter with Rosalie's carroty-red hair. He wanted Rosalie. He wanted her children to be his children, too.

If she'll have you.

The whisper floated through him, revealing an insecurity he had not even realized he harbored. She had given herself to him tonight not once but twice. Why would she not take him for her husband?

He rose from the bed with silent movements, gathering up his clothes in the murky predawn air. He didn't want to embarrass her. And somehow he knew she would be embarrassed if her maid found him in her bed in the morning. At the door, he paused and glanced back at her one final time before slipping from the room.

Waking alone had been a disappointment. Until her maid strolled into the chamber. Then she realized that Dec had spared her the embarrassment of facing a servant while wrapped up in him. The maid arched an eyebrow as she reached for her night rail at the foot of the bed and slid it over her head.

"Good morning, Sally. It was rather warm last night," Rosalie murmured, tucking her unruly hair behind her ears.

"Of course, miss." Nodding, Sally moved to the armoire and selected a day dress. "Is this acceptable?"

"Yes. Thank you." She quickly dressed, noticing how different, how sensitive, her body felt beneath the brush of her fingers and weight of her garments. She frowned when she noticed the maid pulling out her luggage. "Sally?" she inquired, waving to the valise and trunk.

"His Grace said you're leaving today."

Her stomach bottomed out. "Leaving? For where?"

Sally averted her gaze, looking uncomfortable. "He did not share the particulars with me, miss. He merely instructed for me to pack all your things."

She nodded numbly. Suddenly it was hard to breathe. Was he rid of her now? Would he send her back to her mother? It seemed unlikely that he would do such a thing, especially after everything that had happened. She didn't understand. She knew last night would change things, but was he truly throwing her out?

She sat still as stone, stomach churning as Sally brushed and arranged her hair. Once the maid was finished, she hurried from her chamber, determined to get to the bottom of this. Aunt Peregrine and Aurelia were in the dining room, but not Dec. She managed to rattle off some excuse to them about not eating before hastening away.

She located Dec in his office with his man of affairs. His expression was unreadable, his eyes deep and intent as he looked up from his desk, and she flushed. Bent over with one hand pressed flat on the desktop, his hair falling low on his forehead, he looked rakish and handsome and made her belly churn for entirely different reasons than why she had sought him.

"Excuse me, Your Grace, but could I have a word with you?" Thankfully, her voice sounded even and calm, reflecting none of her inner turmoil.

He nodded at his man of affairs, dismissing him. The gentleman gathered up his ledgers and left the room with a circumspect nod for Rosalie.

Dec rounded his massive desk and leaned against it, crossing his arms. "You wanted a word?"

She nodded and approached, wondering how she could feel so awkward with a man she had just shared everything with only a few hours ago. At this point he knew her body better than she did.

His green eyes darkened to a stormy jade, and she suspected he was remembering, too. And yet he was sending her away. Her chest tightened and she looked down at her hands, hoping he didn't read her hurt and bewilderment.

She stopped before him, careful not to touch him where he stood, leaning so negligently against his desk. Inhaling, she looked up. "You're sending me away?"

"Under the circumstances, I think it's for the best—"

"You think putting me out of sight will erase last night?" She blurted the question before she could stop herself. Her emotions rode too high to the surface. She could not stop her temper from flowing free. "Sending me will not undo it—"

"Rosalie—"

"Perhaps it's easy enough for you to forget, but

it wasn't me who came into my bedchamber. That was all you."

"Oh? It was all me? Did this not begin at Sodom?" He cocked his head, his eyes sparking in challenge.

"It happened. You and me . . . Melisande's daughter. You never wanted me here, and now you—"

"Rosalie—"

"—regret it. Well, I won't!" She beat a hand against his chest, too overcome. "I won't regret it, damn you!"

He grabbed her flailing fist and hauled her into his arms, smothering her rant with a kiss that she melted into instantly. His arms locked around her, holding her tightly. She made a mewling sound in the back of her throat as she wrapped her arms around his neck.

"That's how I knew," he said, his deep voice making her skin shiver with goose bumps.

"Knew?" She blinked groggily, her lips brushing his as she spoke.

"That little sound you make. You made it at Sodom and it drove me mad. You made it in the library. You make it anytime I'm doing something you like."

She smiled idiotically. "Then I must make that sound constantly."

"It lets me know I'm doing something right." He nibbled on her bottom lip, his tongue flicking out to tease the swollen flesh.

When it came to her body, he was always doing it right. Suddenly, she recalled her anger, and that as delicious and distracting as his mouth felt on hers, he was sending her away!

"Why are you kissing me? You're kicking me out—"

"To my aunt's. I'm sending you and Aunt Peregrine and Aurelia to Will's. It's not seemly for you to stay here—"

"Why not?" Her fingers played against his jacket, beating a light patter against the hardness underneath the fabric. "No one knows about last night. No one *need* know of it. I've been staying here. You never thought it unseemly before."

"That was before we announced our engagement."

She stared. Her mouth perhaps parted on a gasp, but she couldn't be certain. She could only fixate on his face. On the utter seriousness of his expression. The deep green of his eyes.

"Our engagement?" she echoed.

"Yes. With all haste, I should think."

"You want to marry me?" Her heart swelled in her chest at the very idea, the notion she had not permitted herself to entertain. Marriage to Dec played out before her. Nights like last night all the time. Being with him when he wasn't looking at her like she was some unwanted visitor. It was too much to believe.

He smiled at her like she was some daft creature. "I should think after last night that was obvious." At her silence, his smile slipped. "Was that not obvious, then? Did you not think I would make an honorable offer? After taking your innocence? Did you think I would ruin you like that?" He looked almost offended.

She nodded weakly. "I'm not entirely experienced in matters such as these."

His expression softened. "Of course. Indeed you are not."

"Are *you* offering, then?" she asked pertly. "Because I've yet to be offered *anything* as far as I can recollect."

For a moment she thought he would simply shrug off the comment. After all, she had not exactly behaved in the manner of a proper debutante. Proper debutantes did not sneak out to houses of ill repute for illicit liaisons. Nor did they let men not their husbands into their beds. But then he stepped back. She watched in bewilderment as he bent on one knee at her feet.

"Rosalie Hughes . . . will you honor me . . ."

Understanding dawned. She felt her eyes widen in her face. Her hands flew to her mouth. Shaking her head, she reached for his hands in an attempt to urge to his feet. "You don't have to—"

" . . . by becoming my wife?"

She nodded mutely, unable to find her voice. She was in the process of tugging on his hands, urging him back to his feet, when the doors suddenly opened.

"Declan, have you seen— Ah!"

Aunt Peregrine looked on the verge of collapsing in the threshold as she took in the scene of Dec on bended knee before Rosalie.

Dec rose and stood beside Rosalie, his hand at her back as they faced his aunt and now his cousin.

Aurelia glowed. "I knew it!" She punched a fist in the air and gave a little bounce.

Dec chuckled. "Well, that takes care of that. I was worried it might be awkward announcing our impending marriage."

Aunt Peregrine sputtered even as Aurelia rushed Rosalie and kissed both her cheeks exuberantly. "I'm just so thrilled we never have to let you go! Now you don't need to marry some old goat!"

Rosalie laughed lightly, feeling dizzy from everything that had happened in the last few minutes. Was she really to be married? To Dec?

"Aunt, I'm certain you understand the need for Rosalie to relocate to your home until we've married?"

Her eyes widened. "Oh! Of course! We must pack!" She moved in a little circle before heading for the door at a speed Rosalie would not have thought her capable. She was almost out the door before she stopped with a jerk. She looked back at them both with wide, panicked eyes, waving one finger aloft in the air. "Oh, but the wedding! We must discuss! We've much to plan!"

"It's well in hand, Aunt Peregrine. We will discuss all the details later."

She bobbed her head and then plunged back out the door.

Aurelia remained, smiling at them both with a knowing, smug little grin. She nodded, her brown eyes bright. "You two." She pointed a finger at each of them. "I knew it. I knew you were mad for each other."

Rosalie shifted uneasily. *She* was mad for Dec . . .

"Indeed, cousin?" Dec's lips curled in amusement, his fingers moving in a small rhythmic stroke at the small of her back that made her think of the way he had touched her last night. The way those fingers had explored her body again and again.

Aurelia arched a fine dark eyebrow. "Indeed. Who would ever have guessed that when you called on us to help chaperone Rosalie, you would fall desperately in love with her?"

Instantly, his hand stopped moving on her back. He stilled so very completely beside her. Everything inside her seized tight, including her lungs. She couldn't breathe.

She was afraid to even look at him, afraid to see the denial of Aurelia's words in his expression. But she didn't need to see his face to know. She felt the denial in the way his hand slipped away and dropped from her back.

He didn't desperately love her. Of course not. She wasn't so fanciful and simple-minded to think she had stolen his heart.

He'd bedded her and now he would wed her because he was honorable. Somehow he had overcome his bias against her because she was Melisande's daughter, but he would not love her. She didn't even know if he _could_.

Aurelia was reading too much into it. She would

not make that mistake. She would not believe in what wasn't there. What didn't exist.

He would marry her but he would never love her. She understood that even if her heart didn't . . . even if that stupid lump beneath her breastbone ached for more.

Chapter 22

The week passed in a blur. Rosalie moved into the Earl of Merlton's residence. From there she was ushered into a flurry of activities in preparation for their wedding. Dressmakers. Long hours with Cook poring over the menu. Aunt Peregrine labored over the guest list until shadows rimmed her eyes. All names of people Rosalie didn't even know, so she had little to contribute in that arena. Then there were the rounds of parties, balls, routs. All carefully selected by Aunt Peregrine. Dec attended with her, dutifully at her side. The perfect fiancé. *Blast him*. Not so much as a stolen kiss. Not even the brush of his hand against her.

At first she told herself she was imagining things. He was not distant and quiet, but merely overwhelmed with the flurry of activity. But when she had tried to entice him out onto the balcony with her at a dinner party thrown in their honor by a friend of Aunt Peregrine and he politely refused, she knew. He didn't want to be alone with her.

She was careful from then on not to reach out to him. Cowardly perhaps. She was marrying the man, but she could only take so much hurt and rejection.

"Miss Hughes, you've a caller."

She looked up from the same page she had stared at blindly for the last half hour. Aunt Peregrine was out meeting with the milliner. Aurelia accompanied her. Rosalie had begged off and, for once, stayed behind. She should have guessed her solitude would be short-lived.

"Your mother, Her Grace, the Duchess of Banbury."

Her stomach sank. She had not seen her mother since Dec fetched her home. "Show her in." It was inevitable. She would have to face her eventually, and Melisande would have heard of the news by now.

Her mother breezed into the room, a vision in an emerald green day dress trimmed in black ermine. At least she was alone. No Horley. There was that.

"Rosalie," she exclaimed, kissing her on the cheek before settling into the armchair across from her. "So good to see you! I believe congratulations are in order." She nodded to the waiting maid. "Biscuits, please. Bring a variety."

With a nod, the maid curtsied and backed out of the room.

"Well." Melisande untied the strings from her bonnet, a confection that was mostly ribbons and black feathers to match her stylish dress. "You've won quite the coup. A duke! And my title, no less." She shook her head cheerfully. While her manner was all smiles and warm cheer, there was a certain light in her eyes that made Rosalie uneasy. "Seems you'll have my leftovers. In more ways than one."

Rosalie straightened. "I'm sure I don't understand."

"Well, I'll become the Dowager Duchess of Banbury. A dowager." She shuddered. "Can you imagine? It sounds so old."

Rosalie gave a wincing smile.

Melisande continued. "You shall become the

Duchess of Banbury. A title which used to be mine. And you'll have Declan." Her smile grew tight and wide then. "Who also used to be mine."

Rosalie angled her head, her folded hands tightening in her lap. "Your meaning still eludes me."

Just then the maid rolled into the room with the tray service. Silence fell as she positioned it between the two of them and poured them each their tea. Rosalie's foot tapped anxiously beneath her skirts.

"I'll serve, thank you," she said.

The maid bobbed her head and backed out of the room, once again leaving them alone.

Melisande leaned forward and selected several biscuits. She bit into a pink frosted one with a moan. "Delicious." Her gaze fastened on Rosalie. She licked a bit of icing from her finger with slow deliberation. "Just like Declan."

Silence stretched between them before Rosalie whispered, "You lie."

"Oh." Melisande feigned a wounded look and tsked. "A mother doesn't lie to her child."

Rosalie laughed. She held her side, rocking where she sat even though humor was the last thing she felt.

It cracked her mother's facade of composure. "What is so funny?" she snapped.

"You. Acting the loving mother." Her laughter died and she leveled her gaze on Melisande. "Let's end with the pretense of caring mother. Why are you here?" Clearly it was only to cause trouble.

Melisande blinked wide eyes. "I thought you should know the man you're marrying . . . well, I had him first."

Rosalie struggled to keep her expression blank, but her right eyelid flickered wildly. "Get out."

Her mother gathered her bonnet and rose with a satisfied sigh. At the door, she paused and turned in a half circle, smiling back at Rosalie. "Congratulations again." With that parting remark, she left.

Rosalie fell sideways on the sofa, burying her face in a pillow to muffle her cries.

Her mother was a beast. It wasn't true. It couldn't be. Dec hated her mother. He wouldn't have . . . he couldn't have *been* with her. Sitting up, she dashed the tears from her cheeks with the back of her hand, resolving to find out.

Dec looked up from his desk as Rosalie barged into the room. He stood at once, alarmed at the sight of her. She looked pale, ashen. Her eyes, however, looked haunted. Large topazes in her bloodless face.

"Rosalie? What's wrong? Why are you here?"

"Is it true? Did you—" She choked on the words, struggling, it seemed, to spit them out.

"Did you and my mother . . ."

Bile rose in his throat. He knew what it was that she couldn't say. He understood.

She continued, "Never mind. You don't need to say it. I can tell by your face it's true."

"Who told you?" Will and Max knew, but he couldn't imagine either one of them told her. That left one obvious culprit.

"She did, of course. She relished every moment in the telling."

He schooled his features to reveal nothing, donning the familiar mask he wore, carefully blocking out anything he might be feeling. "Of course she did."

"Not even a denial." She visibly swallowed. He knew she needed to hear him deny it. More than she even realized, she wanted him to say it wasn't true. It couldn't be true. They couldn't have been intimate. Not him and her own mother.

"I'm going to be sick." Turning, she started to flee, but he was there, his hand on her arm, forcing her around.

"And there you are. Just like my father," he snarled, his mask cracking. He could feel it slipping, emotion bleeding through. Just like it always did with her. "Thinking the worst."

"You deny nothing! What am I supposed to think?" She searched his face. "Am I wrong? Please, tell me! Is it not true?"

"You would believe me if I were to say it was not?" He snorted. "That would make you the exception. He never believed me either."

She hesitated, bewilderment flickering on her face. "*He* who? Who did you tell? Who didn't believe you?" Again she was wondering, doubting, hoping that perhaps it was all a lie, some twisted machination of her mother.

His heart slowed to a dull thud in her ears. "My father. I told him what happened." He laughed brokenly, bitterly. "I rather had to. When he walked in on us."

"*What?*"

"She hunted me, Rosalie. From the moment she married my father, she was always there with the smiles and long glances. The lingering touches. I was ten and four when she came to my room. I told her to stop—" He stopped to swallow.

He felt her stare, watching him struggle with the words, watching him remember it like it was some sort of bad dream. He gave a rough laugh. "I was just . . . inexperienced. It was rather bewildering . . . waking up with your stepmother's mouth on your cock."

She blinked at his harsh language . . . at the harsher, uglier image that filled her mind. He saw that. Saw it in the reflection of her eyes. She covered her mouth with her hand, speaking through her fingers. "She did that to you?"

His voice came out flatly, controlled and monotone. "I didn't understand what was happening at first. I had never—" Again he broke off, shaking his head, squeezing his eyes tight against the memory.

He reopened his eyes.

She stared at him, eyes so wide. "Fourteen. You were so young. When I was that age . . . I still slept with a doll." She looked down as though recalling herself then. "An old rag doll my father gave me." Her gaze snapped back up, fiery and bright, full of wrath. "You were just a boy."

"Man enough." His lips twisted. "In my father's eyes, at any rate. He said I should have known better. Hell, he saw me as the instigator. Rather absurd now when I think on it. When she was in *my* bed? Had I dragged her there? He was deluding himself." He shook his head and squared his shoulders. "No matter. It's all in the past now."

Except it wasn't. It was here now. Between

them. In her eyes and in the tension lining his shoulders. It was in the distance he felt welling between them.

His mind worked, thinking back to all those years, struggling with fragments of memory that he had fought to bury.

"That's when he stopped letting you come home from school."

He nodded. It was all falling neatly into place for her now. He had been fourteen when he stopped coming home from school. The duke's sudden disinterest in his son. The son he once doted on. His only heir. She understood why now.

Her face scrunched up bitterly. "My mother . . . what she did to you. That's why your father gave you the cut?"

"The cut? That's a gentle euphemism, but yes. I was dead to him after that. Your mother did nothing wrong, of course. She was his innocent young bride that his wretched beast of a son had abused. I was a monster in his eyes. If he could have disinherited me, he would have. You should have seen Melisande. She wept such copious tears. She really should have been on the stage. If he could have called me out and withstood the scandal of killing his own son, he would have."

She blinked at the shock of this. "No, that can't be. He would not have gone to such—"

"He told me that, Rosalie. That's not dramatic supposition. Those were his own words."

The last bit of color bled from her face as it all sank in for her. Her mother had taken so much from him. His youth. His father. The ability to feel, to touch a woman without the memory of her.

She shuddered. "How you must have felt when I turned up in your drawing room." He watched her throat work as she fought to swallow. "Dear God. You hated me."

He could practically track her thoughts crossing her expressive face as realization sank deeper, grinding into her. Her throat worked as she swallowed. "You must hate that you are marrying me. Her own daughter."

He stared at her for a long moment, feeling raw and battered inside. Exposed. Finally, he said, "I made my choice when I came to your bed."

Her face crumpled. "That's not a denial."

Turning, she fled the room. He watched her go.

Chapter 23

$\mathcal{P}$ushing back her hood, Rosalie strode past her mother's butler with hard, echoing steps. "Is my mother in the drawing room?"

"M-Miss Hughes," he stammered, hurrying after her. "Yes, she is. Shall I announce you?"

"That's not necessary, thank you." The drawing room's double doors stood ajar and she strode inside.

Her mother and Horley looked up from the tea service. Melisande paused, her cup halfway to her lips. Sunlight poured into the room from the window, bathing her in golden light. Her dark hair gleamed like ebony. She looked poised and beautiful, her porcelain skin ageless.

"Rosalie, what a pleasant surprise." From the way her lips curled into a smile, Rosalie's presence was no surprise at all. "Tea?"

Horley popped a biscuit whole into his mouth, watching her as he chewed, crumbs dropping from his lips to rain upon his trousers. She wished she could read the thoughts behind his hawk gaze, and then decided it was probably for the best that she could not. He slouched inelegantly in his chair, legs sprawled wide, one arm stretched along the back of the chair. Her mother. Once again with a younger man. Her stomach churned.

"I know."

Her mother arched a brow and took a dainty sip.

"But then you wanted me to know, didn't you?" she added. "Did you think I would blame him? Hate him?"

"I think it only right that you know the truth if you're going to enter into matrimony with—"

"The truth. That's quite amusing considering what you told me was more fabrication than fact. What you did to him . . . you're sick."

"Is that what he told you?" Horley snorted. "Of course. He wouldn't want to admit he dipped his wick in his stepmother . . . no matter how tempting a morsel she is. He was above such behavior, is that it? Unlike every other randy lad of his age."

"Peter," Melisande chided, although her eyes sparkled. She was enjoying this. Enjoying Rosalie thinking that Dec had been her *willing* lover.

Rosalie flattened her hands against her sides and strove for composure. "It never happened. Not like that."

Horley snorted.

Rosalie turned her glare on him. "This doesn't concern you. Why are you even here?"

"Rosalie." Melisande frowned. "Don't speak to Peter in such a manner."

She inhaled thinly through her nose. It didn't matter anymore. She didn't even want to argue the point with her mother. She didn't even want to be in the same room with her anymore—much less with Horley. It ended here. That's why she had come. She would have her say and then leave.

And never look back.

"You aren't part of my life anymore." She didn't bother adding that Melisande hadn't been for several years. All that time at school her mother had no use for her, and suddenly now, because she served a purpose, she wanted a place in her life.

Rosalie wouldn't let her. She wouldn't allow her mother's poison to contaminate her life—or touch Dec again. He deserved that much. She wanted them to have a chance—a chance to be something real to each other—and she had a better chance of that happening without her mother lurking around.

Melisande set her teacup down with a soft click. "You're pretty satisfied with yourself, aren't you? Soon to be Duchess of Banbury. You'll have my title. And Declan. And now you think you can tell me what to do."

She ignored the jibe, managing a calm tone. "This is farewell. Don't call on me again. If you see me on the street, keep walking."

Melisande laughed sharply. "You think he's yours? Has he already had his way with you? Did he whisper sweet words? He'll never love you, silly girl. In fact, I think the odds of your marriage happening are very slim indeed."

As the bilious words dripped from her mother's tongue, Rosalie ordered herself to turn away. To leave and not rise to the bait. Melisande had no power over her. She couldn't prevent her from marrying Dec. And yet she paused, her feet planted to the carpet. "What do you mean?"

Melisande's gaze slid to Horley. With a nod, as though sending him some manner of signal, he moved for the door.

At first Rosalie thought he was leaving, and she was glad. None of this was his concern.

"Well," Melisande continued. "If you were to marry someone else first, that would certainly impede your marriage."

The drawing room doors clicked shut, but Horley had not left. Instead he remained, locking his hands in front of him and positioning himself in front of the doors as though blocking her escape.

Her mother was still talking. "I think a marriage to another man would put an end to Dec wanting to marry you. For the obvious reasons. Men can be rather possessive. They don't want to share. Especially men like Declan."

"You're talking nonsense."

"No. Indeed not. I've given it a great deal of thought. Peter and I both have."

Her gaze flicked to him. Of course, he was involved in this. It should serve as no surprise that he had been plotting ways to make her life more difficult. Or rather ways to make his life *less* difficult.

She breathed in and out over the niggle of panic starting in her belly. Her mother was spouting empty threats. She shook her head. "I'm marrying Dec." Quite finished, she turned for the drawing room doors, stopping hard at the sight of Horley still standing there, blocking her way.

"No," he pronounced. "You're not."

She looked back between her mother and her lover. Her chest felt compressed, like some great weight was pushing down on it. "Mother?"

"I'm sorry, Rosalie." Melisande lifted her chin. "It's hardly a situation I wanted." Her eyes sparked almost angrily, accusingly. "But you've forced my hand."

Rosalie shook her head, utterly bewildered. Horley smiled a slow, slithering grin. He smoothed a hand over his slick, pomaded hair.

"I don't understand."

"I'm giving Peter to you." She waved a hand wildly. "He's unmarried. Titled. It's a perfectly acceptable arrangement. We'll leave for Scotland. Peter heard of a preacher on the border that doesn't ask too many questions . . . he doesn't even mind whether or not all the right words are uttered."

Cold washed down her spine. "Such as the bride saying 'I do'?" she asked through suddenly numb lips.

"Precisely."

Her stomach dropped. "Are you mad?"

"It's not the most ideal situation." Melisande's lips quivered at the corners. "But Peter has persuaded me that it's for the best. A perfect solution."

Peter. How she loathed his very name. "I won't do it!"

"You don't have a choice," Horley replied silkily, suddenly in front of her.

"So you will force me? Hold a pistol to my head and make me marry you?" She jerked back a step, yanking her arm clear of his encroaching fingers.

"Stop being so dramatic, Rosalie. We need your dowry." Melisande's lips pursed as though she loathed admitting it. "It's ridiculous how much Declan granted you. It will last us two lifetimes."

The blasted dowry. She wished Dec had never seen fit to announce that to the world.

"He'll never give the dowry to you," she argued. "This will all be for nothing."

"Oh, he will. He'd never let you suffer side by side with us in penury. Nor would he wish you shamed before the world." Her mother looked her up and down. "He cares too much for you. And he's too honorable."

The truth of her mother's words sank like rocks into the pit of her stomach. Melisande was right.

She tried to convince herself that even if she was forced into marriage with Horley, it would mean nothing to Dec. He'd still want her. If Horley forced her into consummating the marriage, Dec would come to her the moment he was able. He would rescue her. She told herself that.

Except she wasn't so convinced.

Would he want a bride who was broken? Broken in the way her mother had broken him? Could things ever be right between them?

She made a bolt for it then, only to have Horley grab her around the waist. She screeched, legs kicking, arms beating at him—anywhere she could reach.

She could hear her mother reprimanding her to behave herself over her own cries. As though she were the disobedient child.

"Peter, remove your cravat! Silence her with it. We don't need to concern the servants."

Horley yanked off his cravat and stuffed it into her mouth. Then her mother was there, too, Melisande's fingers working deftly at the back of her head, tying the cravat in an unyielding knot. "Come now, Rosalie! None of us are happy about this, but it's just the way it has to be."

Horley managed to pin her arms at her sides, grunting in her ear.

Panting, she glared up at his flushed face, at the smug smile. And she was quite certain that her mother might be unhappy with the situation, but he was not.

Aurelia met Dec at the door when he returned home that afternoon. Will and Max accompanied him. He had invited them home with him following a match at the club. In the back of his mind he suspected he wanted their company to keep him distracted from his encounter with Rosalie.

Somehow, absurdly, he now realized he had thought she would never have to know. That he could keep that bit of sordid history from her.

Will frowned at his sister as she stood in the foyer wringing her hands, her brown eyes deep with worry. "Aurelia, what's amiss?"

"I have not seen Rosalie in hours. We took breakfast together, and then her mother paid her a visit and she went out. But that was hours ago. Do you know where she could be, Dec?"

He processed her words, a sick feeling starting in his gut.

At his mulling silence, she cast a quick glance at her brother and Max. Shaking her head as if their presence didn't matter to her, she looked back at him and added, "We were supposed to go shopping this afternoon—Declan, where are you going?"

He was out the door, moving swiftly down the steps.

"Declan!" she called, her footsteps rushing after him.

He had a fairly good idea where Rosalie had gone. His stomach knotted to think of her back with her mother, in the same house, even for a moment, where she had felt compelled to barricade herself in her bedchamber every night.

Bloody hell.

He shouldn't have let her walk out. He had seen the knowledge of what transpired between him and her mother in her eyes . . . it was more than he could abide. He had not realized how much her good opinion mattered to him until then. The chance that she would somehow look at him differently, that things between them would not be the same again, was something he couldn't face, and so he'd let her walk away.

And now his cowardice had put her at risk. She was his to protect, and he had failed her. He should have made her stay. He should have told her what she needed to hear. He should have shown her that the past didn't matter anymore. Especially now. Now that he had her. Now that they had each other.

"Declan." Aurelia grabbed his sleeve and clung. "Where are you going?"

"To her mother's."

Aurelia frowned. "Why would she wish to go back there?"

"We'll take my carriage," Will announced, motioning to Dec's doorman to bring his carriage back around.

"We?" Will arched an eyebrow.

Aurelia nodded. "I'm going, too."

"Why are *you* going?" Max demanded.

Aurelia propped one hand on her hip. "She's my friend. Why are you going? Wait . . . what are you even doing here? Why are you *always* here?"

He jerked his head in Dec's direction. "He's my friend."

"This is a family matter," Aurelia informed him, lifting her chin, "and contrary to how much you're always lurking around, you are not family, Lord Camden."

"Small blessings," he muttered. "Not to have a brat sister—"

"Can you two sheath your claws for once?" Will snapped.

Dec shook his head. He didn't have time for their bickering. He spotted the carriage clattering his way and started moving toward it with long strides. Then he saw a heavyset woman in livery turning down the drive, puffing for breath.

She held up her arm, waving at him. "Are you the Duke of Banbury?"

He met her halfway, nodding. "Yes."

She stopped, pressing a hand to the generous swell of her stomach as if suffering a stitch. "They took 'er, Your Grace."

"Her? You mean Rosalie? Who took her? They who?" he demanded, even though he already knew. With a sinking sensation in his gut, he knew. He just didn't know why. Revenge? Were they that stupid? He'd hunt them to the farthest corner of the earth. If they hurt even a hair on her head, there was nowhere he wouldn't find them.

The woman nodded. "I was in the kitchen, but I came out when I heard the commotion. They shoved her out the door into the carriage. I tried to help, but they had Tom, the footman, and he's the size of a mountain—"

He shook his head. "I understand. Of course. Do you have any clue where they were taking her?"

She swiped several graying hairs back from

her sweating cheeks. "I heard Lord Horley tell the driver they were heading to Scotland."

"Scotland?"

"Aye, Your Grace. He means to marry her."

"What?" He blinked.

"Lord Horley means to marry Miss Rosalie."

Aurelia gasped beside him.

He froze. Everything in him turning cold. "He can't." He could think no other words.

He can't. He can't.

Rosalie was his. He couldn't lose her.

He vaulted inside the waiting carriage, hardly even aware of Will and Max hopping inside with him or Will forbidding his sister from joining them. His only thought was catching up to Rosalie. His hands opened and closed at his sides on the seat.

"Dec? Are you all right?"

He looked up and met his cousin's stare. "I have to get her back, Will." He had to. Somehow, in only a short time, she had come to be everything to him and he couldn't imagine a life without her.

Chapter 24

Stop looking out the window. There's no-where to go. Peter or the servants will overtake you if you try to run."

Rosalie let the curtain fall back into place on the window. Horley had left them in the carriage and gone to speak to the innkeeper—no doubt weaving some fanciful tale about her. How else would he explain when she opened her mouth to shout for help?

As though her mother could read her mind, Melisande said, "Now don't go doing anything foolish. Peter is letting them know that you're sick. Mad. And not to listen to a word you say."

"Why are you doing this to me?"

"If you had just done as you were told none of this would be happening to you. You think I'm happy that you're marrying Peter?"

"Then let me go. I love Declan. And he wants to marry me. I have a chance for happiness. You're my mother. Can't you want that for me?"

A flicker of something crossed Melisande's face, and Rosalie thought she might be reaching her. But then the carriage door was suddenly yanked open.

"Come. They have a room for us."

"Just one?" her mother asked as she offered him her hand and stepped down from the carriage.

"It's all he has, but it's for the best. We can better keep an eye on her." He held out his hand for Rosalie, but she climbed down without his help, holding her hands close to her sides.

"Did you speak with the innkeeper?" Melisande asked.

"Yes. No worry. He accepted my story of your mad daughter. I could have fed him any story so long as I lined his palm with coin."

Splendid. If that was true, she wasn't going to find much help from him.

The inn was crowded and the innkeeper hardly paid them notice. Indeed no one did as Horley ushered them upstairs. Only one bed occupied the room, barely large enough to accommodate two bodies.

Melisande motioned to the chaise near the window. "Perhaps the innkeeper can spare an extra blanket."

"Oh, I sleep there?" Horley queried.

Her mother looked back and forth between Horley and Rosalie, appearing uncertain and un-comfortable. A first since this whole nightmare began. "Where else . . ." Her voice faded. The arch of Horley's eyebrow suggested just where else he thought he could sleep. "You wish to begin your wedding night?" Melisande demanded in a tightly controlled voice. "With me in the room?"

"You're mother and daughter. Is it not right to share?"

Rosalie pressed a hand to her stomach, afraid she was going to be sick.

Her mother turned and started pulling the bedding back with angry, stiff motions. Only Rosalie saw that her hands shook, too. "I think you can wait until Scotland to do your 'duty.'"

Horley sighed. "I suppose." He moved toward the door. "I'll go see to our dinners."

As soon as the door clicked shut behind him, Rosalie whirled on her mother. "Mama, please. You cannot want this for me . . . or for you."

Melisande faced her, eyes suspiciously bright with what looked like tears. "What do you know of what I want? I want to be rich again. I want to be young and beautiful. I want men to want me again with the same desperation that they did before. What I don't want is an upstart daughter making me look a fool." She pointed at Rosalie. "Now you'll do as I say. You'll forget about Declan just as I'll forget that my own lover will share your bed."

"You speak as though I want this!"

Her face scrunched up, making her look almost unattractive. "How did such a stupid creature ever come from me?" She tugged the pins free from her dark hair as she moved toward the mirror. "I keep hearing that word come out of your mouth. Want, want, want. I *want* more than a paltry widow's settlement. I want a rich lover . . . a man who won't tire of me in a fortnight." She stopped in front of the mirror and speared her fingers in the dark mass of hair. "It's time you learned that you don't get the things you want in life. I don't." Her gaze lifted and collided with Rosalie's in the mirror. "And you won't either."

The dinner of roast hare was surprisingly good, but that didn't encourage Rosalie to eat. Her stomach was knotted and queasy. Horley ate with relish, gulping down multiple glasses of wine between mouthfuls of food. Her mother picked at her food, focusing mostly on the wine as she stared back and forth between Rosalie and Horley with ill-disguised animosity. She said very little, offering up only monosyllable replies to anything Horley said. He, on the other hand, grinned lasciviously over his wine cup, looking from Melisande to Rosalie.

Forgetting her scarcely touched meal, Melisande rose and undressed herself, heedless that Horley and Rosalie watched her. Dressed in her nightgown, she slipped beneath the sheets of the bed.

Horley looked at Rosalie. "What of you? You should get your rest, too. We have a long journey tomorrow."

Nodding, Rosalie moved to the empty side of the bed. Even with her mother in the room, she wasn't sure she could sleep in such close proximity to Horley. Sinking down on the mattress, she unlaced her boots and set them carefully on the floor beside the bed.

"You're not changing?"

She only had what her mother packed for the

both of them, and although they were of like size, she did not relish rifling through her mother's things to find something to wear. If her mother really cared, she would have pulled something out for her. Instead, Melisande was already snoring on her side of the bed, deep asleep with no thought to her daughter.

"I am quite fine in this." She settled down next to her mother without another glance at Horley.

With her hand tucked beneath her cheek, she listened to Horley's movements, his smacking lips and slurps. He made no move toward the bed, and gradually some of the tension eased from her shoulders.

She held herself still, waiting for him to douse the light, knowing full well that she would not sleep. Even if she did not intend to slip from the room and escape, she would not sleep with Horley so close. She wasn't that trusting.

The sound from the inn belowstairs had quieted by the time he finally put out the light. She listened as he settled himself on the chaise. His breathing steadied to a soft snore after several minutes, but still she waited. The night lengthened, but she held herself still. At one point, someone's tread thudded down the corridor, but silence soon reigned again.

Rosalie carefully pushed the counterpane off her and stealthily slid her legs over the side. Bending, she slipped her boots on.

Horley snorted and mumbled something. She froze, bent over in the dark, her hands on her laces. Satisfied he still slept, she finished tying off her boots and stood.

She worked her way around the room, moving slowly, wincing at every creak of the floorboards. Her palms were sweating by the time she reached the door. A thin line of light glowed beneath it, alerting her of where to go in the dark. She stretched out a hand and groped air until she felt the door latch.

The hinges let out a creak so loud as she opened the door, it sounded like thunder to her sensitive ears. Clenching her teeth, she shot a glance over her shoulder, her heart pounding so hard her chest ached. The flickering light from the sconces in the corridor sent a shaft of dim light into the room and she could see Horley sleeping on the chaise, snoring deeply, his features lax. Hopefully his wine consumption would keep him in a deep sleep for many hours to come.

Although the sight of him, even deep asleep, sent panic fluttering through her. In some ways, her stealthy escape had been easier to execute in the cover of darkness.

She dove out into the hallway, shutting the door behind her with shaking hands. The corridor stretched long and empty. She made it to the top of the stairs, half expecting to hear Horley crying out behind her.

But he wasn't there. There was no cry. No hard hand clamping down on her shoulder. She was free. She hastened down the steps and stepped out into the main room. There was no crowd as earlier. A couple of travel-worn customers sat at one table, nursing tankards. They didn't spare her a glance.

A serving maid looked up. "Can I help you, miss?"

This was her chance. She opened her mouth. And that's when the portly innkeeper walked into the room. His eyes widened at the sight of her. "You!" He looked around as though he expected to see her mother or Horley near. Finding no sight of them, he tsked his tongue and wagged a finger at her. "Now you didn't sneak out, did you? You're going to worry your family. You need to go back to your room."

He came at her and she backed up several steps.

She held up her hands in supplication. "Please. You don't understand. They've abducted me. My name is Rosalie Hughes and they're forcing me to Scotland with them."

He blew out a heavy breath, cocking his head to the side. "Not going to be difficult, are you, daft girl?"

"Papa," the maid, presumably his daughter, said. "What is amiss?"

"No worry, Frannie. Just not right in 'er head, this one." He tapped the side of her head. "Her family is upstairs. We just need to get her to them."

The words were all she needed to hear. They were enough. She bolted. They weren't even interested in hearing her out. As far as the innkeeper knew, she was some daft, out-of-her-head girl.

She raced through the main room, past the startled-looking men.

"Grab her, Frannie!"

Footsteps pounded across the floorboards. Adrenaline spiked through her veins, propelling her out the front door of the inn. The night air was chillier than when they had arrived, penetrating the sleeves of her gown and making her wish for a cloak.

She dove across the yard and into the trees, and instantly it was like plunging into a deep netherworld. The soft sounds of the woods were all around her. Whispering wind. Creaking branches and rustling leaves. An animal scampered nearby as she barreled into the brush.

She had no idea where she was going, only that she had to get away. Even if the girl, Frannie, couldn't catch her, she was certain the innkeeper was waking Horley even now. Horley, who was determined and persistent and maybe just a little bit mad. He'd come this far. He'd convinced her mother this insane scheme was a good idea. He wasn't going to simply give up. He was going to come after her.

With that burning thought, Rosalie pushed ahead into the murky woods surrounding the inn. She didn't even care that the trees seemed like ominous skeletons, dark and encroaching on every side. It was the stuff of nightmares, but being forced to marry Horley, facing life without Dec—that was the real nightmare.

She slowed her pace, trying to get her bearings. Her instinct had been to run. To escape. But now she realized she should have been mindful of her location in relation to the road. She would have to surface eventually and find help. She had no idea how dense these woods were. She didn't want to become lost, her body discovered weeks from now by some hunter. She shivered at the notion.

"Rosalie!"

She jerked at the sound of her name, close. Too close. Her heart leapt to her throat.

"You're really vexing me, Rosie! It's late and cold . . . and a branch just tore my jacket—my favorite jacket!"

With a gasp, she started running again. Unfortunately, leaves and twigs on the ground crunched as she ran. Stealth was impossible. She froze with a wince when a branch cracked beneath her foot and Horley shouted, "I can hear you! Stop this game. You've already worn my patience thin. Show yourself and I won't thrash you to an inch of your life."

She wasn't entirely certain he exaggerated. The man had abducted her. Who knew his limits? She didn't want to put him to the test and find out.

She rotated in a small circle, her gaze scanning all around her, desperately seeking something, *anything*—some way of escape to present itself.

There was nothing. Nothing but brush and trees and bramble.

And then that changed. She cocked her head, listening. She could hear him now. Not far, crashing through the woods.

"Have it your way, Rosie! When I find you, your pleas won't matter."

She took two careful steps, bringing herself flush with a giant oak. Perhaps it would hide her. If he didn't pass along the side where she stood.

Her hands pressed against the scratchy bark, scraping the sensitive skin of her palms. The solid feel of it seemed almost to absorb her shivering—or at least helped her feel more in control.

She dropped her head back and looked up at the canopy of branches. Turning, she practically embraced its width, seized with an idea. She had climbed plenty of trees as a child, much to the dismay of her nanny, but it couldn't be that much harder now. She was older, but not old. She could still manage. She had to.

Securing a foothold, she clawed a few feet up the trunk, her gaze fixed on a low branch. She lifted her arm and stretched for it. Curling her fingers around the solid width, she scrambled higher and hefted her body over it, belly down. From there she rose until she was standing, both hands gripping the tree to keep her balance, and stared down, relieved to see she wasn't that high up yet. She had a good view of the area below. Which also meant she was visible, too. At least for anyone at a distance. She frowned. Too visible.

Gritting her teeth, she reached for a branch to start working her way higher and it snapped in her hand, shattering into twigs and fluttering down to the ground.

"Ah. Rosie. There you are. Come down, love, and take your punishment like a good girl."

She gasped and peered through the latticework of branches at Horley. His face was cast in shadows, but his eyes glittered brightly, like a predator looking out from the dark.

"Not coming down? You don't want me to come up after you, believe me."

She flexed her grip around another branch, clinging to it and holding herself utterly still. She couldn't speak, much less move. She definitely wasn't going to climb down and deliver herself into his hands.

"Very well. Here I come."

She watched in shock as he started to climb. Then her shock turned to dread as she realized he was actually making progress. If she remained frozen where she was, he'd be on her in moments. So she climbed as well, telling herself that this wouldn't end as badly as she was beginning to fear.

Chapter 25

When Dec described Rosalie to a serving maid at the fourth inn they reached, an odd expression came across her face. They'd ridden hard, stopping at every inn along the north road until reaching this one.

"She might sound like someone I've seen." Her gaze shifted cagily, looking around the room.

He slid a glance at Will and Max and then stepped closer to the girl. Rosalie wasn't exactly inconspicuous with her hair. "You have no idea how determined I am to find her. You really don't want to play games with me. If you've seen her, you need to tell me. I'll tear this place apart, beam by beam."

She paled and called out, "Papa!"

Dec winced as she bellowed three more times for her father. A heavyset man lumbered down the stairs, clutching the railing. "Shut that cater-wauling, Frannie."

When his gaze landed on Dec, Will, and Max, he hesitated, assessing and scanning them before descending the final steps.

"Gentlemen, in need of a room? Food?" He smoothed his hands over his ill-used and soiled jacket.

"Papa . . . they're looking for her! That red-headed girl who ran away!"

The innkeeper's gaze shot to his daughter before returning to them, his eyes wide with alarm. "You're after the daft girl who—" His voice ended with a yelp as Dec stepped forward and grabbed fistfuls of his jacket in his hands.

"What do you mean daft?"

"Th-They told us she wasn't right in the head. That she's daft . . . sickly and—"

"Where is she?" He punctuated his words with two fierce shakes. "Where did she go?"

The innkeeper's mouth worked like a fish

before he managed to say, "She ran away. The gentleman went after her."

Sudden steps sounded on the floor above. Melisande appeared at the top of the stairs, knotting the belt of her cloak as though she were on her way out.

When she spotted Dec, her hand flew to her throat. "Declan!"

He released the innkeeper and turned for the stairs, his hand gripping the railing. "Where are they, Melisande?"

Cold resignation crept over her face. "You really want her. You *love* her." She shook her head, her expression twisting into something ugly in its bitterness. "What is so special about her? Peter wants her, too." She snorted. "Oh, he made it seem like marrying her was our only option, for the money . . . but he's salivated around her ever since she arrived."

In the blink of an eye Dec ascended the stairs two at a time at her words and took hold of her face, his fingers pressing into her cheeks. "If anything happens to her, I shall hold you accountable."

Her eyes widened.

"Where are they?" he demanded.

"Rosalie fled into the woods. Stupid girl. Peter

went after her. Wolves or brigands will probably find her first—"

He didn't wait to hear the rest of her words. He flung her from him and in two stretches of his legs, jumped back down the steps. Grabbing a lantern from one of the tables, he shoved past the innkeeper. He charged out the door, barely registering Will and Max following.

In the yard, he stopped at the tree line that marked the boundary into the forest and called out for her, unsure which way to begin searching.

Max appeared beside him, lantern in hand as well. "We'll fan out." He motioned Dec to the far left. He and Will moved farther to his right.

Nodding, Dec tore into the brush, bellowing her name. He raced several feet before forcing himself to stop and listen, turning with the lantern, letting it cast its light. His eyes strained through the long shadows, his heart beating like a wild drum against his chest. To his right he could hear his friends, tromping through the woods and calling for Rosalie. If she or Horley were near, it was difficult to distinguish them with the noise his friends made.

He threw back his head and shouted her name, silently begging . . . to God, himself, anyone who would listen, that she would answer him. He stilled, forcing himself to wait for a moment. Then he called her name again.

And then he heard his name. The pitch shrill. "Dec! Declan!" There was no mistake. It was Rosalie. He tore off in the direction of her voice. His name grew louder.

"Rosalie!"

"Dec!" She sounded close. So close. Like he was right on top of him. "Here! Here!"

He looked around—and finally looked up.

There, up in the trees, moonlight filtered through branches and he detected the faint yellow fabric of a dress.

He edged closer. "Rosalie?"

Max came up beside him, panting. "Is that her? What is she doing up there?"

"Declan!"

His heart seized in his chest at the tremble in her voice.

"Look!" Max pointed below her at the tree, and Dec made out another, darker figure. A man. Horley, working his way toward her.

"Bastard," he growled, setting down his lantern and starting for the tree. Max pulled him back, clamping a hand on his arm.

"Wait," he cautioned. "It looks like he's coming back down."

Dec could barely contain himself, but he waited. Once Horley's feet hit the ground, he was on him, grabbing him by the front of his shirt and whirling him around and slamming him on the ground.

Horley held up his hands on either side of his head. "Stop! I didn't touch her!"

The words relieved him. For her more than himself. He knew the wounds such a thing would inflict. The years she would spend pretending she was recovered from such a violation . . . the lie she would live. He knew because he had lived with it, too.

He dragged in a deep breath, filling his lungs. He would spare her anything if he could. Take any pain from her. He knew that with intensity, with an awareness so total and complete. He had never felt so certain about anything before.

"But you wanted to," he snarled, and slammed his fist into Horley's face. Once, twice. The sound of his knuckles connecting with bone filled him with satisfaction. Horley's neck snapped back from the force of each blow. He gave him a small shake, forcing his gaze back up. "Should I ever see your face again, should Rosalie suffer even a glimpse of you, I will *break* you. Understand?"

Horley nodded, blood flowing a steady stream

from his nose. Dec flung him away as though he couldn't bear to contaminate his hands with him. "Go nowhere. I'm not finished with you."

He launched back to his feet, his gaze fixing on Rosalie in the tree. "Everything is fine, Carrots. You can come down now." He held up his hands and waved her down, gratified that his voice rang out calm and clear, reflecting none of his alarm. Such fear wouldn't be alleviated until she stood on solid ground again. Until he felt her in his arms.

"I can't. I'm stuck." She paused as if the words she'd spoken might have somehow jeopardized her precarious position. "I—I'm afraid the branches are going to break under me. I've climbed too high and—"

She didn't finish her sentence.

He was up the tree, climbing, hand over hand, moving like he used to when he was a boy climbing trees. A flash of memory seized him of when he climbed up after Rosalie when she had gotten herself stuck.

"Dec!" she cried. "Stop! The branches aren't strong enough!" Her voice choked. "I went too high. They're brittle."

As if to prove her words, he grabbed a branch and it broke in his hand. He flailed, wobbling where he hovered, very nearly losing his balance. Rosalie screamed, the sound reverberating through the night.

He straightened, resettling his weight, and took hold of another, steadier branch.

He was just below her now. So close. It killed him, but he forced himself to hold still and assess when everything in him wanted to keep going and reach her.

"Don't come any higher. You can't," she ordered, her voice no less firm for all that it trembled. "I—I broke the branch directly under me. I don't have a safe way back d— Dec, no! What are you doing? Stop!"

He shook his head as he inched a little higher, finding her gaze through the branches. Her eyes were wide and terrified, glowing with moisture. "I'll inch back down when you start down."

"I'm scared."

"I know, Carrots," he said in a soothing voice. "But you can't stay up in a tree forever. Remember? I think I told you that once before. The last time I helped you get down."

She laughed weakly.

He continued, "And we've got things to do. Like get married so I don't have to sneak into your bedchamber again. Will's servants will talk."

She made a strangled sound. "You're making jests. At a time like this."

"No jests. It's been bloody hard as hell keeping my hands off you . . . it's the simple truth."

"Is that why you've been staying away from me?"

"No, I've been a bloody jackass. Too scared with how much I crave you every second of the day," he admitted, adjusting his position closer to the trunk. If the branch gave out beneath him, he could hopefully grab it for purchase. He eyed the distance between Rosalie and himself, debating grabbing for her while he had her distracted. With a shake of his head, he decided he needed to be just a bit closer.

"Dec," she admonished. "We're not alone."

"They can be trusted, Carrots. They're our friends. Besides." He rotated a foot, readying himself as he eyed his targeted branch. "They know I'm mad in love with you."

She gasped. He chose that moment to lunge for another limb, hauling himself higher.

"Dec! What are you doing?"

"Coming to get you, Carrots." He grunted, hefting himself up.

The branch under him dipped with a loud crack but held. For how much longer, he wasn't certain.

"Stop!"

"Calm yourself," he chided. Staying as close to the tree trunk as possible, one hand gripping it with clenched fingers. He was close enough to graze her boots with her fingertips. "I'm right here."

She made a sound that was half sob, half laugh. "I . . . you came for me—" The words so soft, he wasn't certain she meant for him to hear them.

"You think I wouldn't?" he asked in a low voice. "We're getting married, remember?"

She nodded. Her vibrant red hair spilled down her shoulders, limned in moonlight, dangling toward him like ribbons. "And you love me?" she whispered.

"Heard that, did you?"

She nodded again. "Anyone within a stone's throw heard you."

"You saved me, Rosalie. Being with you has made me a better man. I'm ready to wake up next to you every morning." His chest expanded. "I want those mornings. I want *you*."

He heard her faint sob. "Yes. I want that, too."

He deliberately hardened his voice, hoping that would spur her to action. "So start climbing down, Carrots. Trust me. I won't let you fall."

"What if I make us both fall?"

"Trust me, Carrots. Just start inching down. Remember you used to do this all the time."

She laughed nervously as she unwrapped her arm from the branch she clung to. "And the last time, you saved me, too."

"See. You're an expert—"

"At getting stuck," she cut in wryly.

"And I'm an expert at getting you down. We have this well in hand." Even as he said the words, his heart pounded almost violently as he watched her begin to sink down. They were higher up in the tree than the last one she got stuck in.

He tried to predict her movements before she made them . . . a branch that might not hold. He held out a hand, ready to grab her.

"That's it," he murmured, his fingers stretched, ready to grab for her.

Her slim fingers grasped air, stretching for his hand. Their fingertips brushed, and it was all the contact he needed. He lunged, seizing her entire hand in his, his fingers locking on her wrist. "I have you. Let go now, Carrots."

She released her grip on the limb she clung to and tumbled toward him.

Her warm body met his and he folded her close,

cradling her and allowing himself half a moment to bury his nose in her hair and inhale her scent.

He released a shuddery breath and then moved as quickly as he could, eager to get her down the tree. Together they descended, working as a team, taking turns stepping from limb to limb. He didn't make a move until he was certain she was stable.

As they neared the bottom, Max and Will stood there waiting, arms out to assist her down. Horley stood with his arms crossed a few feet beyond them, watching with a sulking expression.

Dec hopped to the ground, and she was there, in his arms. His breath fluttered her hair against his mouth as her hands locked into fists at his back like she would never let go. Which was fine with him.

Because he was never letting her go either.

Chapter 26

$\mathcal{D}$ec practically carried her back to the inn despite her insistence that she could walk. Will and Max followed, Horley between them like a captive. She didn't look back. She didn't want to see Horley ever again. She wanted him and her mother behind her. Other than Dec's confession of love, she wanted today behind her and buried. Forgotten.

After a few words with the innkeeper, Dec took her to the room she had shared with her mother and Horley before she escaped. Her mother was still there. Waiting. She rose from where she sat on the edge of the bed.

"You've found her!"

"Downstairs with you," Dec commanded as he set Rosalie on the bed. His hand brushed her face. "Are you injured? Do I need—"

"I don't need anything." *Only you.*

She touched his face. Mostly because she couldn't stop herself. She had to touch him. Feel him. She had to assure herself he was here. They were together. *He had said he loved her.*

"I'm going to take your mother downstairs to speak with her and Horley alone. For the last time." Rising, he glanced over at Melisande briefly before looking back at her again. "I realize she's your mother, but this can't . . ." He sucked in a breath and she noted the tense brackets edging his mouth. "No more. This can't happen again . . ."

Rosalie nodded, understanding without him having to say the words. Her mother had hurt them both. Too much. Especially him. They couldn't give her another chance to hurt them. She had used up all her chances.

"Mother." She looked across the room. "Goodbye," she uttered with finality.

She felt nothing as these words fell between

them. No pang of loss or conscience. Nothing. There was no remorse. Not after everything. The years. What she had done to Dec. And not after tonight. It was the only thing left to do. The only thing that made any sense.

Melisande glanced desperately between Rosalie and Dec. "You cannot mean . . . Rosalie, I'm your mother. You need me."

"No. I don't."

Dec's hand folded around her, his fingers strong and warm. His gaze fixed on her as he added, "She doesn't need you anymore. We have each other now."

Her mother left then, although Rosalie scarcely noticed. She covered their joined hands with her free hand, looking at Dec. Only him. He could have said: *Rosalie needs me.* But he didn't. He'd said they needed each other.

With his free hand, he cupped her face, his thumb grazing her mouth. As though he read her mind, he whispered, "I need you. I never thought I needed anyone before but I do. I need you."

"I need you, too," Rosalie returned.

He smiled slowly, his white teeth blinding in his handsome face. "So we're stuck with each other."

"I suppose so," she murmured.

He kissed her then, and it was the kiss of forever. The promise of all their tomorrows. When she looked up and glanced across the room, her mother was gone.

"I'll be back soon," he said.

"I'll stay awake for you."

"You don't need to. Rest." He pressed a lingering kiss to her mouth.

When he left her, she removed her boots and climbed into the bed. Curling on her side, she fixed her gaze at a spot on the wall, smiling as she thought of Declan. He needed her. He loved her.

They were her last thoughts as she drifted to sleep.

Dec watched her sleep, long after the morning light filtered through the curtains. He knew he should rouse her so they could both be on their way. He knew Will and Max must be ready to return to Town. They'd stood at his side as he delivered his ultimatums to Melisande and Horley and then sent them on their way. Horley and Melisande deserved no less than a prison sentence for what they had done, but he didn't want to drag Rosalie through that scandal and place a whiff of disgrace on her. He'd exacted a promise from Horley to return to Cornwall. If Peter Horley ever set foot in Town again, he would ruin him. He had the power to do it, but most important, he had the resolve.

His stepmother would return to Town, gather her belongings, and depart for Spain. He and Rosalie deserved a fresh start without the cloud of Melisande hanging over them. If she ever set foot on English soil again, he would cut her off. She had nodded, uncommonly mute, understanding at once that her best opportunity for happiness lay in a life abroad because he would make her days a misery if she stayed.

Even as dawn lightened the room, he didn't have the heart to stir Rosalie yet. It had been a long night for her. Shadows marred the skin beneath her eyes, resembling faint bruises. He never wanted her to look tired or haggard again. He supposed that was love. Wanting to shield and protect. Caring more for someone else than even yourself.

Rosalie slept with one hand tucked beneath her cheek on the pillow and the other palm down on his chest, and she looked so sweet, so fresh and untouched.

He'd stripped off his clothes upon returning to the room last night and climbed into bed beside her. She had slept so soundly he actually had to move her so he could squeeze his bigger body in beside her. Even now she occupied over half the bed.

Good thing his bed was enormous. However, he rather approved of her sprawled against him, her thigh tucked between his legs. He wanted to be able to feel her every moment like this when they shared a bed together. Every time he closed his eyes. Every time he opened them. He wanted to feel her against him.

He had never thought to have this. *Her*. Had never thought to find another person that made life more . . .

That made life more.

She opened her eyes and smiled, deep and lethargic. She stretched both arms above her head with a groan. "I fell asleep. Why did you not wake me?"

He came over her then, brushing the vibrant hair from her forehead. "You looked too content. So at peace. I didn't want to ruin that."

She smiled and looped her arms around his neck. "You can't ever ruin that. You're the reason I can even look that way."

He lowered his head and kissed her. He meant for it to be a simple kiss, sweet and undemanding, but with her body under him . . .

It had been too long.

She was eager for him, too. Her palms ran over his body. She arched and wiggled under him, parting her thighs, welcoming him to her. His fingers sought her, touching her wet folds, easing a finger into her tight channel. She cried out.

She was wet and ready, and he'd never been so glad in his life for the fact that he was undressed and she wore only a nightgown. He yanked it up and over her head and tossed it aside so they were both smooth, warm flesh gliding together. He entered her in one thrust, relishing her tightness.

She clenched around him, milking his cock, demanding more, demanding it harder.

It was fast, raw and fierce. He positioned her hips in just the right cant for his driving hips. His hand slid between them, his thumb finding and pushing on that sensitive spot at the apex of her cove. She cried out, flying apart beneath him. Ripples eddied through her, vibrating through him. She leaned up and pressed an open-mouth kiss to his chest, her tongue flicking out to lick his nipple. He came apart then, poured himself into her, collapsing over her.

He folded her into his arms and rolled to his side, taking her with him, their bodies slick from the coupling.

"That," he breathed, "shall be how we begin every day."

She sighed against his chest. "When we're married, at least."

"About that." He looked down at her, his fingers playing in her hair. "We've already begun the trip to Scotland. We could just . . . keep going." It was an impulsive suggestion, made from the desperate hunger to have her with him every night, every morning from now. He didn't want to wait months. He did not expect her to agree, of course. Every girl wanted her fairy-tale wedding. He understood that.

"Yes."

He blinked. "What?"

"If that means starting our life together sooner . . . waking in your arms every morning, having this every day, then yes."

He smiled slowly. "Carrots, you amaze me."

She snuggled against him, pressing her lips to his throat. "Now . . . we don't have to leave right away, do we?"

"Did you have something in mind?"

She came up over him, kissing him again, her mouth playing about the corners of his lips. "I might have an idea or two . . ."

Epilogue

Six months later . . .

*T*he orchestra played as couples waltzed in a kaleidoscope of colors around the Duke and Duchess of Banbury's ballroom. A ballroom that had not seen such use in over a dozen years. All of the *ton* was here tonight, emerging from their country homes for this most anticipated event. A ball honoring the duke and duchess's nuptials that had taken place several months prior.

"Remind me why we are doing this?" Rosalie

asked close to her husband's ear as he swept her around the room, his hand warm and familiar on her waist.

"I promised Aunt Peregrine. It was the only way to appease her anger at our elopement and, er . . . extended honeymoon."

Rosalie giggled. They had gone nowhere grand—no splendid sojourn to the Continent. She hadn't needed that. She hadn't wanted that.

No, they had lingered in Scotland for a month before moving on to one of his properties in the Cotswolds. They had laughed and loved, spending longs hours walking the countryside, barefoot like children. They swam naked together in his private lake and made love under the sun. She could have been quite content to stay there forever, but with winter approaching and their aunt's countless letters, they had to surface eventually.

"Laugh all you like, you heartless minx. Aunt Peregrine missed out on a grand wedding. This was the least we could do for her."

Lady Peregrine beamed across the room, chatting with a group of ladies as her satisfied gaze followed them.

"And," Dec continued, brushing his lips against her cheek as he spoke, "I wanted to show off my bride to everyone."

She smiled up at him. "Most of these people have seen me before."

His eyes gleamed down at her. "I assure you, these people have not seen *you*, the Duchess of Banbury, in love and well loved by that scoundrel rake, the Duke of Banbury."

She grinned coyly. "Scoundrel rake no more."

He cocked his head. "Untrue. I am still very much a scoundrel rake. Only I'm your scoundrel rake, wife."

He kissed her then, solidly on the lips, with no care that they were in a room full of people. "Careful," Rosalie chided when he lifted his head. "You shall send your aunt into fits again."

"Not me." He nodded his head in the direction of Aurelia. Rosalie followed his gaze and gasped as her friend tossed her glass of punch into Lord Camden's face. "My cousin will do that well enough on her own."

"Oh, no," she giggled, watching as Aurelia stormed off, leaving Lord Camden standing there, punch dripping from his face and his eyes spitting an unholy fire.

"They're going to kill each other one day," Dec muttered.

Rosalie tsked. "Perhaps I should go after her."

Dec placed a finger under her chin and turned

her face back to his. He kissed her again until a familiar simmer started in her blood, murmuring against her mouth, "Just hurry back to me, Rosalie. I have plans for us that involve leaving this ball early tonight."

Rosalie sank against him. "I'll meet you upstairs. Why don't you save us some time and get undressed?"

He gave her that smile that made her toes curl and belly flip. It was full of promise, hinting of pleasure to come. A pleasure she well knew, and yet it never ceased to amaze her and fill her with wonder. Every time was something new. Something beautiful in its own unique way. "I'll be waiting."

With a small secret smile of her own, Rosalie stepped from the circle of his arms and turned into the crowd in search of her friend, her steps quick, eager, knowing that he would be waiting for her. Always.

*G*ive in to your Impulses!

These unforgettable stories only take a second to buy and give you hours of reading pleasure!

Go to *www.AvonImpulse.com* and see what we have to offer.

Available wherever e-books are sold.

AVONIMPULSE